TAKA

A BIO-TERROR THRILLER

BOOK ONE

BY

TERRY FRITTS

THRILLOGY
PRESS

Books by Terry Fritts

BIO-TERROR SERIES

TAKA
KONA SNOW
KAPU ʻĀINA
(Forbidden land)

The Kevin Bridges Spiritual Warfare Series

BROTHERHOOD OF THE DIVINE
SEVEN OF THE CROSS
CONSUMING FIRE

This book is a work of fiction. Any similarity between characters in the book and real people is coincidental. *Taka* is the first book in a bio-terror series featuring the Hawaiian Islands.

Fourth Edition by THRILLOGY PRESS 2019
ISBN:978-1-950376-08-7

Third Edition Published by Echo Park Press LLC 2009
Second Echo Park Press printing March 2007
First Echo Park Press printing November 2006
ISBN-13: 978-0-9791514-0-8
Library of Congress Control Number: 2009940289

Cover photo: Spatter Burst © G. Brad Lewis / volcanoman.com.

Cover design by Katy Beirne

As I prepared the new Thrillogy Press edition I was taken-aback by how far my writing style has developed. TAKA is written mostly as a narrative and I rush to fill the reader in with an overwhelming amount of background facts. Not the most grabbing style of writing. I considered rewriting TAKA and possibly writing a prequel but thought my time would be better spent writing a fourth book in this series. Leaving it with just a few edits also gives the reader a chance to see how I developed as a writer. By the end of the book I believe it does leave you wanting more. I hope you agree.

ACKNOWLEDGEMENTS

Again, I want to acknowledge everyone who helped me with my first novel *Taka*. It was great to see the final product in print but I have to admit it was the process of researching and writing I really found most enjoyable. The fact that most of the research took place on the Big Island of Hawaii added a lot to that enjoyment. Since 2004, my wife Pauline and I have spent several weeks on the Hawaiian Islands researching this and the second and third books in my bio-terror series *Kona Snow and Kapu ʻāina*. We had seriously contemplated moving there but plans changed. We have made many acquaintances and several friends while visiting and researching my books on each of the islands. It is Pauline who I must thank the most for listening to my stories, putting up with all my hours spent at the computer and for helping me with editing. She was very understanding when I told her, only three weeks after having visited the Big Island, I was at a critical action sequence in *Taka* and really needed to go back to the Hilton Waikoloa Village to pace out the scene. Two days later we were back in Hawaii. Many of our favorite resorts, bars, and restaurants are written about in Taka. I hope you get the chance to enjoy them as much as we have.

Taka was written in 2004 and unfortunately my memory is not what it should be so I have forgotten the names of many of the chefs at of the fabulous restaurants around the island. Not only did they answer my many questions but fixed exquisite fish dishes my wife and I still talk about to this day. The Kamuela Provisional Company is still one of our favorite restaurants in the entire world. As you read Taka you will discover red meat plays an important part in the story. During my research and writing I quit eating meat. Two years later I am just now starting to enjoy it on rare occasion.

The Hilton Waikoloa Village is a location often talked about in Taka. It is a wonderful place and the workers have gone out of their way to help in my research and writing. In particular I want to thank the girls and guys at the Kimo Bean Coffee Shop who would have coffee for me sometimes as early as 5:00 a.m. when I was doing my early morning writing by the canal. I also want to thank the clerk at the Dancing Dolphin Sundry Shop who gave me his own personal catalog of the art work at the hotel. I would be remiss if I failed to thank the bartenders in the Malolo Lounge for their contribution to my research.

One of my characters in *Taka* is Dusty the ranch manager at the Parker Ranch. This character, and to a certain extent the main character Jim Rikey, is based on Corky Bryant who is the livestock manager at the Parker Ranch. Corky spent one morning answering dozens of my questions about the Parker Ranch operations, paniolos and the cattle industry in general. I owe him a big debt of gratitude for his help.

I want to thank my daughter Katy and my daughter-in-law Jennifer who were the first two to read and edit the early drafts. I want to thank my assistant Ms. Castillo who helps keep things under control at work. There are several teachers at school who helped me with the Japanese names and scenes, Roger Hull, Gail Matsuura, Linda Yoshioka, and Doreen Saito. I thank my good friend Paulino Fontes who was a great encouragement in starting my writing career as well as being my main ride from the train to work everyday. Everyone speaks about having a muse who keeps them writing and inspired. Since I first started writing, my friend Mike Corwin has been my muse. He has given me great ideas and feedback on my writing, as well as being an unbelievable help with research for this book and the two I have written since *Taka*. I cannot thank him enough for all he has done.

I want to give a special thanks to G. Brad Lewis for allowing me to use one of his photos for the cover of *Taka*. He is truly a gifted artist. Be sure to check out his website, volcanoman.com.

I also need to thank Gary Corwin and my wife who helped edit the second printing.

TAKA

BOOK ONE

TAKA

Chapter One

Takaishi Matsuura hated the opulence. It was an irresponsibly gross misuse of his hard-earned money. Not that he couldn't afford spending his money. He had inherited quite a princely sum when his 'ojiisan', or grandfather, passed away several years earlier. Since his ojiisan's death, Takaishi had turned that inheritance into a venerable fortune. Hard work and shrewd business skills had made Takaishi one of the 1000 richest men in Japan, but just barely. According to Fortune magazine Takaishi was ranked the 998th richest businessman in Japan. He was known as the largest cattle baron in Japan, which may sound silly coming from the country that brought the world sushi. Large sixteen-ounce mesquite grilled steaks along with Elvis and Rock and Roll were American traditions the Japanese people now craved and seemingly could not get enough of. Not only did this craze increase Takaishi's fortune but it was beginning to increase the waistlines and the rate of heart disease of the wealthier Japanese businessmen. Takaishi's grandfather predicted this trend toward American tastes and culture and prepared for it three decades past. He knew someday his preparation would make his progeny wealthy which in turn made him a content man. He like many traditional Japanese men found their happiness in planning for and assuring that their children and their children's children would live rich full lives. Unfortunately, many of today's Japanese men had lost sight of this part of their cultural heritage. Takaishi understood his ojiisan's vision and promised to continue to fulfill his grandfather's wishes. He knew this forward planning would someday too make him a content man.

Besides his cattle empire, Takaishi now owned the Far East's largest chain of high-end steak houses, 'Aioka's', named after his brother. Aioka's Steakhouses were world renown for their superb culinary masterpieces created from Takaishi's own recipes. 'Aioka's' was very successful, but not as profitable as another of Takaishi's enterprises. Most of Takaishi's new wealth came from 'Hurley's', Japan's fourth largest chain of fast food hamburger stands.

It had now become time for Takaishi to create his own progeny in order to continue his grandfather's dream. That is what brought him aboard the *Grand Maui*, Hawaiian Island Cruise Line's grandest and most luxurious ship. The *Grand Maui* was a connoisseur's ship. It was not designed for the upper-middle class tourist yearning to take a leisurely cruise of the Hawaiian Islands and see the sites. It was designed to cater to the whims of the exorbitantly rich or famous discerning traveler. Takaishi did indeed fit this description. Takaishi was on his honeymoon with his new bride, Nishiki Yoshi. It was Nishiki who now insisted Takaishi go by the name Taka instead of Takaishi. She preferred the nickname and Taka did not mind the change. In fact, his brother had always called him Taka as had many of his elementary school friends. When Taka went away to high school his ojiisan insisted he be referred to by his proper name, Takaishi. He was now pleased to be once again called Taka. Nishiki also preferred to be called by her nickname, Niki, even though many journalists continued to refer to her as Nishiki in the stories they wrote in the tabloids and fashion magazines. It was Niki's idea to cruise the Hawaiian Islands as part of her and Taka's honeymoon. Niki had spent several days posing for the *Sports Illustrated Swimsuit Edition* photo shoot on the *Grand Maui* last year and decided there and then, when she married, she would honeymoon on the ship. She just didn't expect it to be quite so soon. Niki was one of the highest paid fashion models in all of Japan. Actually, she was one of the highest paid fashion models in the whole world. Niki became famous as the first Japanese *Victoria's Secrets'* model. Her stunning good looks and tall undulating figure made her the idol of almost every Japanese schoolgirl and the desire of every young Japanese schoolboy. That was up until last Saturday when she married Taka. Their marriage broke the hearts and shattered the fantasies of thousands of young admirers. It was no secret Taka wanted her to end her modeling career and start her new career as mother and wife. The public couldn't believe Niki was willing to give up her jet-set life style for that of a traditional Japanese wife and mother.

Taka had been touted as one of Japan's most eligible bachelors. When he and Niki were first seen together the tabloids began to speculate about an eventual marriage. Taka was known as a very quiet and serious businessman who believed in Japanese traditions, even though he made his fortune mimicking the glamorous surrealism of 1950's Americana. Niki was anything but a traditional Japanese woman. As a young child, she was much taller than other girls her age and was constantly teased because of it. When she was in middle school her beauty began to radiate, separating her even further from her peers. It was at that age the boys and men also began to take notice. Niki grew up in a typical Japanese middle-class family from Tokyo, sharing a small apartment with her mother, father, brother and an uncle. Her father was a minor executive for Nissan Motors. He was caught in a job with very little chance of promotion and very little chance of making much of his life. He was trapped in a society that was designed to keep him entrapped. He lived with the anger this helplessness caused. It was an anger many other Japanese men of his generation shared and had bottled up inside. It was an anger he and the others blamed on the women in their lives. Women who were no longer the subservient beings these men grew up expecting their wives would be. He was so angry he refused to allow Niki to continue her formal schooling. School was teaching her the wrong values and he was sure she was associating with radicals. He constantly verbally abused her until one day she could take it no more and yelled back at her father. This was too much for him to stand so he sent her to Kyoto to live with her aunt while she trained as a Geisha. Niki vowed to never return to the apartment to see her father again.

At first Niki was glad to be away from her father and the verbal abuse she had suffered for so many years. She worked hard and did well with her Geisha training. However, it wasn't long before she realized she didn't need the Geisha training to please men. She found that her incredible beauty and the skills she had learned as a Geisha and as a lover, allowed her to demand much more from the men than a typical Geisha could ask. She established a very select and wealthy regular clientele. Within a few months, one of her clients convinced her to go with him to Germany and work for his modeling agency. It was an offer Niki could not refuse. When she left Japan, Niki seemed to just drop out of sight for about seven months. Although no one but her mother had tried to find her during that time. She reappeared in Hamburg with a new found focus and drive. Before a year transpired, her new friend had helped Niki to become a world-class model prominently featured on the covers of several major fashion magazines. She realized her fame and her income would be greater if she returned to Japan, so Niki returned to a hero's welcome. For the next two years Niki graced the front pages of most of the Japanese tabloids with her jet-setting escapades. When she started dating Taka last summer, the paparazzi lost interest in photographing her. At least to the extent to which she had become accustomed. It seemed she and Taka's quiet conservative life no longer warranted front-page interest to the tabloid editors.

"What a waste of food." Taka said in dismay as he watched the busboys throwing away several pounds of lobster tail and crab legs. "They could at least use that to make some cioppino."

"Can't you think about anything but food and money?" Niki replied harshly.

"Thinking about food and money is how I made my fortune. It is what pays for this overpriced opulence," responded Taka as he waived his arms at the lavish surroundings. He could tell his comment had saddened Niki. "But I would pay ten times more to please you and be with you." That seemed to soften his previous statement. "I am always concerned about food being wasted. Especially when I see those great pieces of beef being thrown out."

The busboys smiled at Taka's comments as they removed the prime rib from the table.

"Why are you getting rid of the prime rib?" Taka asked in a demanding voice.

The sharpness in Taka's tone startled the busboys. They all stopped bagging the food and looked at each other. Finally, one of them responded in broken English, "thees food eas too old. We must geet reed of eet."

"Nonsense," bellowed Taka. "If you had cooked it right it would have all been eaten."

What separates the *Grand Maui* from other luxury cruise ships is the remarkable level of service. That is evidenced by the throngs of crew entertainers available to assist the guests for any possible needs they may have. These so-called entertainers are crewmembers whose job it is to entertain any desire or request you may have. Hence, the name entertainer. It was only a matter of seconds before the head maitre de had arrived to see what the problem was and possibly entertain a solution for Taka.

"I'm sorry sir, was the prime rib not cooked to your pleasure? I would be happy to send for the chef if you wish to speak to him."

"That won't be necessary," responded Taka. "I just have a hard time seeing all this good meat go to waste." Taka was in a conversation he really did not want to be having.

"We try to keep the buffet as fresh as possible sir," replied the maitre de. "We really don't consider it a waste if our guests are pleased with the freshness of our buffet offerings." The maitre de continued to smile as he ran down the list of the elite first-class passengers in his head. Even though the cruise had just gotten under way, he prided himself on knowing all the prominent guests. "Excuse me for being so bold, but aren't you Takaishi Matsuura the famous restaurateur? This lovely lady must be your new bride, Nishiki. I would like to congratulate you on your marriage. Please allow me to get you a bottle of one of our finest champagnes." The wine steward was listening in and had already predicted the maitre de's request. He had uncorked a bottle of 1968 Roederer. Not the finest the ship had to offer but no doubt an exquisite vintage. "As I recall you have quite a reputation as a chef yourself, do you not?" continued the maitre de.

"Maybe at one time," replied Taka. "These days I just run the business."

"Sir, you mustn't be so modest. I have dined in your steak house in Tokyo and found your steaks and sauces to be some of the finest I have ever tasted. I am sure our chef would be honored to meet you."

Before Taka could refuse, the head chef was coming into the room. The ship's head chef to Taka's surprise was also Japanese.

"I am honored to meet you sensei." The chef bowed low as he greeted Taka. "I am Hiroshi Kurosawa."

"It is a pleasure to meet you, also," Taka responded as he bowed.

"I and my staff would be honored if you came to our kitchen and displayed your mastery at cooking steak and preparing your world-famous sauce," offered the chef.

Taka felt embarrassed. Had he not made such a big deal out of the food being thrown out he wouldn't be in this predicament.

"Oh Taka," whined Niki, "I love your sauces. You should treat them all to your recipe. It's not a secret recipe, is it? It was published in *'The World's Famous Chef's Cookbook'* last year."

Now Taka had no choice. Even his new bride insisted he show them how to cook.

"I would be honored to show you my recipe if you would be so kind to allow me to share your kitchen," Taka proudly responded and bowed.

"The honor is totally ours," replied the chef. He and the maitre de now bowed.

This could go on forever thought Taka.

Arrangements were made for Taka to join the chef and his staff in the main kitchen the following day. With a sigh Taka plopped down into an overstuffed leather chair and took a long swig of the Louis Roederer champagne. It could have been a better vintage Taka thought.

Niki had excused herself and left for a scheduled facial at the exclusive first-class spa. That left Taka alone to think about how he got stuck doing a cooking demonstration on his honeymoon. Next time Taka swore to keep his opinions to himself.

Taka was a master chef. At least at one time he was. His grandfather had sent him to Paris to learn the culinary arts when he was in his mid twenties. That was right after his brother, Aioka, was killed. Taka preferred to think his brother had just disappeared. His grandfather thought going to Paris would help Taka get over his brother's death. Taka's culinary studies in Paris seemed to please his grandfather and in fact did help Taka cope with the loss. Taka and Aioka never really got along well after their mother died.

Their mother was diagnosed with cancer when they were both young children. Their father was unable to deal with his wife's illness and left her to marry another woman. He never again contacted his former wife or his two sons. Their mother tried to hide the pain of her cancer for years from her sons and her own father, but eventually was unable to deal with the burden alone. Taka, Aioka, and their mother moved in with their ojiisan who took care of the boys and sought out the best medical help available for their mother.

Unfortunately, all the money in the world would not have been enough to prolong her cancer ridden body's life any longer than the year she managed to survive. When their mother finally succumbed to the ravenous cancer, arrangements were made for Taka and Aioka to continue to live with their ojiisan. Taka was sixteen at the time. Aioka was two years younger than Taka. Aioka accused Taka of being Grandfather's favorite and it caused quite a strain on their relationship. Taka continued to work hard in school and on his ojiisan's cattle ranch. Aioka tended to shun his chores on the ranch and seemed to always be in trouble. While Taka studied hard and learned his grandfather's cattle and feedlot business, Aioka spent his time protesting the current outrage of the Japanese youth in Tokyo. Aioka resented having to work at the feedlot and soon ran away to join a violent extremist group known as the Red Summit. The Red Summit is probably best known for the bombing and derailment of the Bullet Train in 1992 which killed over a hundred people. Up until that attack Aioka had been questioned about activities of the Red Summit but was never arrested or charged in connection with any of the violent acts credited to the terrorist group. After the train bombing Aioka was directly linked to the attack and credited as being the mastermind of the violence perpetrated by the Red Summit over the previous two years. With the entire National Police Agency of Japan searching for him, Aioka seemed to just disappear. He did once contact Taka to ask for money after he had gone into hiding. Taka sent him a little money, but when his grandfather found out he forbade Taka from further contact. This angered Aioka tremendously. He swore to make his ojiisan and Taka pay for what Aioka called their foolishness. Aioka was last seen in 1993 at an Al Qaeda training camp in Southern Lebanon. He purportedly met

Osama Bin Laden while being trained there. At that time, it was common for Osama to visit his terrorists in training at the various camps throughout the third world countries. Osama was even still receiving American financial support to finance his campaign against what the United States referred to as our mutual enemies. Aioka was so successful and skilled in terrorist techniques Osama asked him to stay on as an instructor at one of the camps. Several Palestinian terrorists learned their deadly techniques with explosives from Aioka. While teaching these terrorist skills to generations of new fundamentalists and idealists, Aioka also spent much of his time sharing Japanese philosophy with his Islamic friends. He tried to teach them that they must be patient in achieving their goals. He assured them that change would come but it would come for their children's children. Unfortunately, many of the Islam faith felt they had been waiting long enough and demanded immediate change and chose immediate terror as their vehicle to achieve their religious beliefs. Osama proved wiser than most and seemed to understand Aioka's vision.

Political philosophies towards terrorism began to change throughout the world as did the leadership of several third world nations. Not all of these leadership changes occurred by a free election process nor did the philosophies of these new governments necessarily align with the thinking of the United States and its allies. It was some of these leadership changes that led to an attack by Israeli jets on Aioka's Lebanon terrorist training facility in 1994. The media reported Aioka was killed in the missile attack by the Israeli jets. Israeli authorities confirmed Aioka's death though no remains were ever released to the family or even positively identified.

Taka became despondent with the news of Aioka's death. His grandfather sent him to Paris to help him get over his brother's death even though Taka never really believed Aioka was killed in the Israeli raid. Taka enjoyed Paris and approached his chef training with pugnacity for learning unequalled by his fellow trainees. Taka proved highly skilled at the culinary arts and received several offers to be a head chef upon his graduation. However, his grandfather had other plans for Taka. When he returned to Japan his grandfather financed and helped Taka open his first steakhouse. It proved to be a major success mostly due to Taka's superb culinary skills. In record time, several more steakhouses opened throughout the Far East with expert chefs from the Paris Culinary Academy, with special training exclusively provided by Taka, overseeing the kitchens. The steaks and sauces created by Taka and his Aioka Steakhouse chefs became world famous.

Taka was greatly saddened when his ojiisan died during the second year of the expansion of the business. Before his death, Taka's ojiisan created a detailed business plan he had prepared to take Taka through the next two decades. Taka had learned well from his grandfather and was very skilled at running the businesses. He followed his ojiisan's plan and expanded upon it. In one year, Taka created and opened the Hurley's' chain of hamburger stands modeled after the drive-ins and malt shops of the 1950's in the USA. The waitresses who worked at Hurley's wore roller skates to bring you your order. Taka also envisioned and designed a malt shop to be built inside each Hurley's that was based on the malt shop set on the old 'Happy Days' TV show. There was always a smiling jovial waiter behind the counter named Pops who not only served the malts but served as the master of ceremonies for the nightly karaoke.

Niki returned later that afternoon to their stateroom suite aboard the ship. Her cheeks were rosy and Taka figured the facial from the spa added the color to her face. They spent the afternoon gambling in the casino, dined on fresh seared Ahi tuna, and spent the evening sipping champagne on the deck while viewing the lava flowing from the crater of Kilauea Caldera. What made the view of the lava so spectacular was not that it flowed freely from the caldera, but that it flowed from a vent further down the mountain from which dozens of little interlaced fissure streams create a glowing matrix over the entire southeast side of the big island. The lava would be cool on the surface, but as it continued to flow underground, portions of the cooling surface lava would collapse forming skylights to the flaming underground lava. It was a spectacular sight that was best seen from the deck of a cruise ship at night or by helicopter during the day.

Niki made passionate love to Taka that night. Taka did not see she was crying as she did so. When they had finished, Taka fell soundly asleep while holding Niki lovingly in his arms. Niki continued to cry for almost an hour before she too fell asleep.

The next morning Niki would not stop talking about her desire to take a helicopter ride to view the volcano and lava flows. Taka complained it was too dangerous. He explained to Niki that every year several helicopters crash on the Hawaiian Islands and the travel industry somehow managed to keep it out of the news in both Japan and the United States. They did not want such news to impact their number one industry. Niki continued to insist, saying how she had already scheduled a tour for just the two of them. Taka tried several other excuses but Niki countered each one. Taka knew he had lost so he finally acquiesced to stop Niki's whining and agreed to the flight.

The *Grand Maui* was moored in Kona Harbor for the day. Kona is located on the dry west side of the big island. From Kona north is a very bleak landscape of black lava that stretches from Highway 19 all the way up to the top of the surrounding mountains. The blackness is only broken by the many graffiti messages that have been written on the lava using the white coral rocks that can be found along the beaches. From the highway, down to the Pacific it is a completely different landscape. Some of the most lavish and expensive resorts in all of Hawaii lie on the west side of the highway. Millions of dollars in landscaping has created a multitude of tropical oasis, jungle lagoons, incredible lakes, and a plethora of world-class golf courses for the rich and famous as well as the not so rich and famous. All of these golf courses are built around state-of-the-art hotels, houses, and condominiums. It is often referred to as the Gold Coast of Hawaii. On the opposite side of the island is Hilo. Hilo is on the wet east side of the island. It too is covered with the black lava but the numerous drenching warm rains quickly allow the tropical jungle to overtake the bleakness. The volcano and the vent that produce the current lava flow are on the southeast side of the island. The lava has been flowing continuously since 1983 and slowly is, and has been, destroying streets, homes, and businesses that still dotted the hillside. As an area was abandoned in preparation for the impending flow of lava, the jungle would overtake the roads and yards of the vacated towns. Before the jungle could completely retake the area, the lava would burn it away leaving only the bleak blackness of the fresh lava behind. South of Kona are the coffee fields. Many of the passengers leaving the boat that morning were headed for tours of the coffee plantations and a chance to buy some of the finest coffee beans grown in the world. The excellent quality of Kona coffee is attributed to the volcanic lava that predominates the soil.

While Niki showered, Taka called the chef to confirm his cooking demonstration that afternoon as well as inform the chef as to what preparations to make and ingredients to supply. The chef assured him all would be prepared as Taka requested and again told him what an honor it will be to have Taka work in his kitchen. As Taka and Niki prepared to leave their cabin, Niki surprised Taka with a very beautiful, distinctive, and expensive Hawaiian Aloha Shirt. It had an unusual configuration of geckos in an almost Escher like pattern. Niki had also purchased a matching day dress in the same pattern. She insisted they wear the new outfits for their helicopter excursion. Taka thought it rather trite and touristy but wanted to make his bride happy. As Taka and Niki were leaving the ship, Niki had one of the many photographers take their picture in their new matching clothes. They boarded a shore boat that ferried them to a waiting shuttle provided by the helicopter tour service parked on the Kona Harbor pier. The shuttle drove north along Highway 19 towards the Muana Lani heliport in the heart of the Gold Coast. They passed several bicyclists and runners on the way up the highway. These cyclists and runners were training for the Ironman Triathlon which would be held the following week. Highway 19 was a major part of the Ironman racecourse.

There were several heliports around the island. Niki had chosen the Muana Lani heliport due to its proximity to the King's Shops and the Hilton Waikoloa Village. The Hilton Waikoloa Village was one of the most luxurious resorts on the big island and had one of the finest jewelry stores in all of

Hawaii. She had heard other women at the ship spa talking about the elegant jewelry they had previously purchased there and she decided she had to see the shop herself. At least that is how she explained it to Taka. In reality Muana Lani was chosen because it had less traffic flying in and out than most other local heliports.

When they arrived at the heliport their pilot, John Greer, was there to meet them. John, like many of the other helicopter tour pilots in Hawaii, was an ex-Vietnam veteran who had flown a few too many missions during the Vietnam Conflict. John went over the safety requirements with Taka and Niki, got them strapped in, and headed for Kilauea Caldera. They flew over the main caldera at the top of the volcano. It was a dormant caldera and was now a series of walking trails and buildings that served as the Volcano National Park headquarters, restaurant and entrance. They then flew to the active vent and followed several skylights down to the water's edge where the molten lava emptied into the ocean, hardening as it met the ocean water to form the world's newest land. The pilot then flew them over some of the recent houses that had been abandoned that lay in the lava's path as well as some buildings presently burning as the lava flowed into them. To conclude the tour the pilot took them down just above the river to show them the falls on the Homakuah Coast. Up until that time Taka had no problem with airsickness but as the pilot skirted along the top of the river at an exceedingly high speed, following the turns in the river and the ups and downs of the waterfalls, Taka began to feel a little queasy. He wondered if the pilot was having some sort of Vietnam flashback as he dipped the nose of the helicopter to make the sudden changes in direction. The pilot noticed Taka's discomfort and gave him a pill he said would ease the airsickness. Taka hesitated but took the pill. Niki had already taken a Dramamine tablet before they left the ship as preparation for the helicopter ride. It was not the turbulent flight causing Niki her discomfort.

Taka looked at Niki and saw she was crying. He immediately told the pilot they had had enough and wished to return to Muana Lani. Taka tried to comfort Niki but she continued to cry. As the pilot started back across the lava fields the helicopter began to sputter. The pilot told them not to be concerned but he was going to have to land the copter for safety reasons. He assured them the lava was safe to land on and that he had already called for another helicopter to come pick them up. Taka was worried about Niki, as she still was crying, but she seemed not to be afraid of the helicopter's troubles. The pilot brought the helicopter safely to the ground about thirty feet from a lava skylight. He told Taka and Niki to get out of the helicopter but not to get too close to the skylight. They had barely stepped out of the helicopter when in the distance they heard and saw another helicopter approaching.

Taka tried to comfort Niki but she walked away from him towards the lava skylight shunning his supportive caresses. He yelled at her to come back but the rotor noise of the approaching helicopter as it prepared to land drowned his voice out. He started towards Niki to lead her away from the lava vent and towards the arriving helicopter but was suddenly dumbstruck by what he saw as the rescue helicopter landed. Stepping out from the passenger door of the rescue copter was Taka's brother Aioka.

"Brother, you look like you have seen a ghost. Or is it you see yourself as a ghost?" Aioka laughed as he walked towards his brother. Taka was shocked but had always felt he would some day see his brother again.

"People said you were killed in Lebanon. I always knew in my heart you were still alive. Why have you not come to me before this?" Taka asked as confused thoughts filled his brain.

"Me, come back to you? For what? So you could have me arrested. So you could turn me in to the police? I think not!" replied Aioka sternly.

"I would never have betrayed you Aioka," Taka replied

"Of course you would have. You are Taka Matsuura, one of the most important men in Japan. You would have had to turn me in. I would have been an embarrassment and would have ruined your career had you not turned me in. No, my brother, I know you. I have been watching you for many years. If my enemies knew I was alive I would soon be dead. You are not the only one who believes I was not killed in the bombing in Lebanon. Several counter-terrorist groups are constantly searching for news of me. They know the Red Summit is still a force to be reckoned with. I have plans Taka. I made plans long ago when I worked with Osama. He taught me it is the American government that must pay for their oppression of the rest of the world. He taught me it is up to every freedom fighter to give his own life in fighting American Imperialism. And I in turn taught Osama a valuable lesson I learned from our ojiisan. A lesson that embodies the essence of Japanese culture. A lesson lost in the Americanization of Japan. That lesson is time. Time is on the side of us freedom fighters. Victory will be ours in time, but sometimes it will take much time for a battle to be won. That is what I taught Osama. Together, Osama and I have devised a plan that will bring America to its knees. It just takes time. A lot of time. Our plan is already in motion." Aioka seemed possessed as he spoke of his plan.

"Aioka, this is foolishness. You must come back to Japan and turn yourself in. I will help you…" Taka was cut off in mid sentence.

"Turn myself in. You help me. Help me what? Help me live the rest of my life in prison instead of dieing a martyr. Brother, for the past several years you have helped me. You just don't realize how much. You have amassed a fortune. You have earned respect. You have married my girlfriend." Aioka smirked as Taka looked around frantically for Niki. She had returned to the helicopter and was looking away.

"That is right my brother. Niki and I have been lovers since we were young anarchists together in Tokyo. Her father tried to send her away but it was I who took her to Lebanon to be trained with my Al Qaeda warrior brothers. She has proved herself a worthy terrorist," Aioka paused. Taka was visibly shaken. "It was Osama's money that made her a world class model and it was Osama who sent her back to Japan to eventually marry you. You see, brother, it is all part of our plan."

Taka felt faint. His knees were weak and his head was spinning. He didn't know what to believe.

"You are looking a little ill, brother," said Aioka. "Is it too much seeing me after all these years? Or is it finding out your new bride is my lover and only married you because I told her to do so? Or is it the poison pulsating through your veins that is starting to take its affect?" Aioka looked smug as he waited for his brother to reply.

Taka was stunned. It was poison he had taken during the helicopter flight. The pilot had poisoned him.

"Are you not surprised by how much we now look alike? People say we always looked alike as children. Just to make sure I spent several thousand dollars with the best surgeons in Sweden to insure we would look identical. I think they did a fairly good job. Don't you?" Aioka asked as he grinned at his dazed brother.

"So… you plan to…to kill me and take over my…my businesses?" stammered Taka.

"But of course. Why else would I go through all of this trouble? I have spent years preparing for this. I know your business. I know your friends. I even learned to cook," responded Aioka. "But it is much more than that. Much, much, more."

Taka's knees buckled and he fell onto the rough lava. He didn't hear what Aioka had last said. Taka was dead. Which was fortunate for what was about to occur next. The pilots from both the helicopters picked up Taka's limp body and carefully removed his shirt. Aioka in turn removed his shirt and put on Taka's new aloha shirt the pilot handed to him. The pilots carried Taka's body the thirty feet to the lava skylight and threw him in the opening and onto the molten lava. Taka's body sizzled when it hit the glowing crimson lava. His shoes and remaining clothing instantly burst into flames. In a matter of minutes there was no sign Taka's body ever existed. Aioka joined Niki in John Greer's helicopter. Niki was still crying as she grabbed Aioka and held him tightly.

Little was said on the flight back to Muana Lani. Nor did Niki and the new Taka converse as the shuttle returned them to the Kona Harbor Pier. One of the ship's photographers was taking pictures of the guests as they arrived back at the pier. Niki did not notice the photographer as he once again took their picture as they exited the shuttle. Usually the photographer asked permission before he took a picture. However, this photographer also had a side business of selling snapshots of the rich and famous to several of the tabloids around the world. The photographer knew Niki and

Taka still generated a little interest to some of the Japanese tabloids.

As they boarded the shore boat that would return them to the *Grand Maui* one of the seamen remarked that he had called ahead to the ship's galley to inform them Taka was returning. He advised Taka that the head chef informed him all was ready for the demonstration. The new Taka shot a quick glance at Niki. What did the seaman mean by the demonstration? Niki suddenly remembered the conversation in the dining hall the previous day. She had not paid as close of attention as she should have and was trained to have done.

"I'm afraid my husband will be unable to continue with the planned demonstration," Niki spoke. "You see, he became extremely airsick on our helicopter tour. I must get him back to our stateroom immediately. Could you please call the ship again and advise them of this?" Niki asked the seamen. "I am sure when he is better, we can reschedule the demonstration."

"Certainly Mrs. Matsuura," responded the seaman. "I am sorry Mr. Matsuura feels so ill. Would you like me to call for the ships surgeon to meet you at your stateroom?"

The new Taka spoke up. "That won't be necessary."

"As you wish," the seaman continued. "I'm sure the chef and his staff will look forward to your cooking demonstration at a later date"

At least Taka and Niki knew what the demonstration was about. They now had time to decide if the new Taka should or would follow through with his dead brother's previous plans. Maybe it would be the test they needed to see if the new Taka could convince everyone he was the old Taka.

When the shore boat arrived back at the ship there was a golf cart waiting to take the supposedly ill Taka along with Niki back to their stateroom. Once in the stateroom the new Taka was swift to reprimand Niki for not having informed him about the dead Taka's planned cooking demonstration. She had been trained to pay attention to such details. He queried her for nearly an hour to find out how the cooking demonstration came about and what Taka was planning. Unfortunately, Niki knew little of the plan. She reminded Aioka that she had left Taka in the dining hall so she could meet and make love with Aioka instead of getting her facial in the spa as she had told Taka she was doing. That seemed to calm Aioka down. He still needed more information about what was expected of Taka in the cooking demonstration so he sent Niki to talk to the chef and the maitre de to see what she could learn.

An hour later Niki returned to the stateroom. This time she had used her training to illicit all the necessary information regarding the planned cooking demonstration from the chef and his staff. It was an easy task for Niki. She knew how to use her physical beauty to get just about anything she wanted. She explained to the new Taka the plan was for him to make the famous Taka Steak Sauce and to marinate and grill some steaks using this famous sauce.

"Is that all?" laughed the new Taka. "That is too easy." I know the recipe for that sauce. We made it in my culinary training. It tasted just like the bottled version of the sauce."

"But you have never tasted the sauce when Taka made it," whispered Niki. Thinking about the dead Taka made her sad. "It tastes much different than the bottled version."

"It is no matter," responded the new Taka. "No one will know the difference. I will easily fool these ignorant slaves of aristocracy."

"You must remember you are now the aristocracy. You are Taka Matsuura. You must act and speak as though you belong here," Niki scolded.

"I will act and speak as I choose. I will act as is necessary to fulfill my and Osama's plan. I am Taka Matsuura!" he said decisively. "Tell them I wish to reschedule the demonstration for tomorrow." Niki bowed and left the stateroom to fulfill her task. She knew better than to question Aioka.

The next day Hiroshi had his staff prepare the main kitchen as Taka had instructed. The ingredients were in place and the steaks were cut as Taka had requested. As Taka entered the kitchen Hiroshi bowed and his staff of chefs bowed as he did. Taka bowed in return and smiled at his audience.

For the next hour Taka entertained his audience as he prepared his sauce and grilled the steaks to perfection. His performance and the product of his cooking demonstration awed everyone. They all agreed how the steaks were the best they had ever tasted and the sauce was the finest in the world. That is, everyone but Hiroshi. To him the sauce tasted very pedestrian and common. He did not understand why Taka followed the published recipe for his sauce. He knew that was not how the sauce was truly made, but he could not and would not challenge Taka to explain why he fooled the staff. When Hiroshi was in culinary school, Taka had visited his class and prepared the sauce for the chefs in training. It tasted much better than this sauce. At the school Taka had been much more serious about preparing the sauce and had shared the real recipe with the chefs. Not this bottled recipe he prepared today. Hiroshi was extremely disappointed but did not show it. Later he would scold his assistant chefs for being so easily fooled. He would then show them how the sauce was truly made. Hiroshi bowed, but not quite as low as before, when Taka left the kitchen.

Chapter Two

Jim was beginning to wonder what the hell he was doing lying in a ditch in the middle of the night in a cotton field in Haskell, Texas. His only comfort was his two Colt 45 six-shooters and his Winchester Model 97 shotgun. However, he knew they would be no match for the four men holding the AK-47's fifty yards up and to his right in the field. These men were known as 'burros'. They were paid handsomely to smuggle 'illegals' into the United States.

Jimmy Bob Rikey was a Farm Service Field Agent for Haskell County Texas. It was his job to help the local farmers get the best crop yield possible out of their land and the most profit possible. These days in Haskell County that meant helping with fertilizer and weed abatement mixtures for the various farms, planting suggestions, and feeder cattle concerns. It seemed more and more farmers were supplementing their income with feeder cattle. This was probably due to the high price beef was getting on the market. The farmers in the area would take the young calves from the northern ranches when they reached a weight of around 400 pounds. They would then allow these calves to graze on the winter wheat the farmers planted between cotton crops. When the cattle reached around 700 to 800 pounds, they would ship them off to the feedlots where the cattle would have another 300-400 pounds quickly added to their weight from high protein feed and supplements. Next the cattle would be butchered and the meat sold.

In past years, being the Farm Service Field agent meant helping the farmers deal with the boll weevil infestations. Most all of the planted acreage in Haskell County was cotton, some of it on irrigated land but most was dry farmed. That meant Mother Nature had a whole lot to do with who could make their payments to the Federal Land Bank after harvest. It also used to mean how bad the infestation of weevils would be. The good thing was that most of the Boll Weevils in the Rolling Plains Central area were history thanks to the Texas Boll Weevil Eradication Foundation. Jim had been instrumental in pushing for that program, although, he tried not to let any of the local farmers know. They were all still pretty upset about the $10.00 per acre annual assessment they had to pay. Especially, since no boll weevils had been reported in the Rolling Plains Central Region for the past two years. That is until last week. That was when a half a truckload of baled cotton showed up infested with Boll Weevils on the Pierson Farm. Jim was called in when Gordon, who sharecropped the Pierson farm, found a pile of baled cotton scattered all over one of the service roads on the farm. Jim knew this type of Boll Weevil was found almost exclusively in Mexico. After investigating the area around the cotton, he knew why and how the cotton got there. It appeared a group of smugglers were bringing in 'illegals' from Mexico inside a truck carrying a hollowed shell of cotton bales. They would unload the 'illegals' into other vehicles and push the cotton bale shell off the bed of the truck.

Jim doused the bales with gasoline and burned them hoping to kill all the weevils. He told Gordon to keep an eye out for trucks carrying baled cotton and told him to ask the other local farmers to watch for anything suspicious. It was still several weeks till most of the local cotton bolls would be ready to pick. They could not afford an infestation at this stage of the crop.

Jim called the border patrol and advised them of what he had found. He also notified the Texas State Police. They all told Jim to call them if he heard anything and not to handle it himself. They all put a lot of emphasis on the not.

Jim had a reputation as a cowboy. Both figuratively and literally. Jim and his older brother Billy were raised on a ranch in Waco, Texas. Jim was the high school quarterback and Billy was the running back. They both were always looking for a good fight. Jim was the brightest student in his class at Midway High School. Billy struggled in school. When Billy graduated, he enlisted in the Marines. He figures that was someplace he could always find a good fight. Jim went to Texas A & M on a football scholarship. However, he dropped out of football his sophomore year so he could concentrate on his double major of microbiology and animal husbandry. By the time Jim graduated Billy had re-enlisted in the Marines. Jim started working on a PhD in Biology and worked part time as a research assistant for the United States Department of Agriculture. He was about to complete his PhD when Billy was killed while training for Desert Storm. Jim was so distraught he dropped out of school and moved back to the ranch. After getting in several bar fights with the locals, the district attorney advised him it might be in his best interest to enlist in the Marines himself. That is exactly what Jim did. He excelled in the military and became part of an elite team that performed special tasks for the CIA. Jim decided not to re-enlist and was offered a clandestine position with the FBI to perform the same type of tasks he performed for the CIA. This Jim refused. He went to work for the Farm Service Agency, one of the sub-divisions of the USDA. It seemed Jim was always getting in situations that required him to use those special skills he learned in the military for the CIA. That was how the local authorities knew him figuratively as a cowboy.

He was literally known as a cowboy with his friends in the Single Action Shooting Society. His SASS friends knew Jim as 'One Bad Hombre'. All members of the society go by an alias, wear authentic cowboy outfits, and compete in western style shooting competitions. They are required to wear two single-action six-shooters and carry either a Model 1897 Winchester pump shotgun or a double-barreled coach gun, along with their lever action rifle. Jim preferred his Marlin Cowboy to the Winchester Repeating Rifle. Jim carried two second generation blued 10" barreled Colt 45 Army model pistols. Most people found that length of barrel much too cumbersome. Jim's 6'5" frame had no trouble handling the long-barreled pistols. He wore them constantly. At least constantly when he was in Texas. Several times he had used them to kill a rattler that didn't particularly like Jim walking by. Seems there were a lot more rattlers in Haskell County these days but Jim was working on that. He also had used those Colts several times for more serious purposes. He had bison horn pistol grips he had won in last year's SASS Regional Shootout. They were custom fit to make his Colts feel like extensions of his hands. He actually had two Winchester Model 97 pump shotguns. He loved them both and would have been hard pressed to pick one over the other as his favorite. One was original with an unmodified 31" barrel. It was extremely accurate up to at least a hundred yards. The one he tended to use the most had been sawed off to make it easier to use quickly. It also made it easier to conceal.

The fact he could conceal the shotgun really made no difference right now. Jim had gotten a call about midnight from Gordon. Gordon and a couple of friends were on their way back from the county line where they went to pick up a case of Lone Star. Haskell was a dry county, so if you wanted to buy some beer, like most people, you headed down Highway 277 towards Abilene to the county line. There were several stores as soon as you crossed the line more than willing to take care of the liquor needs of the Haskell County residents. It seems Gordon and his buddies passed a couple of trucks hauling baled cotton headed west out of town in the direction of the Pierson farm. They actually could be headed to one of a hundred farms out that way. Gordon said he would have followed them but he and his buddies had already had a little too much to drink. Jim assured him he was smart not to follow the truck and thanked Gordon for calling. Jim thought about calling the Texas Ranger's office in Abilene but didn't know what he would tell them. He had no idea where the trucks were headed or even if these trucks were legitimate or smuggling 'illegals', even though he knew there was no good reason for trucks to be hauling bales of cotton in these parts at this time of night.

Jim had been watching an old John Wayne movie and hadn't yet undressed from his workday. He put on his holster and made sure his Colts were loaded with high velocity shells and not the low powder competition cowboy loads. He grabbed his sawed-off Winchester Model 97 and jumped in his pickup. He really had no idea where he was going. On a hunch decided to head back to the Pierson farm. He was hoping the 'burros' were stupid enough to return to the same place as before. When he turned right off the main road, he turned off his lights. It was still a couple of miles to the Pierson farm, but out there the land was so flat you could see the back of your head and he didn't want anyone to know he was coming. That is, if anyone was even out there. It was a moonless night but he had driven this road hundreds of times so he knew where to go. He parked his truck in a mesquite pasture on the northwest side of the Pierson farm and started walking down the streambed that ran the length of the pasture. On both sides of him were fields of cotton bolls almost ready to pick. As he neared the area where the infested cotton had been dumped the previous week, he could hear voices yelling out commands in Spanish. He crawled along a ditch next to a dirt access road and stopped about fifty yards from the trucks. He counted four 'burros'. Each was holding an AK-47. They were guarding about twenty 'illegals' who were being forced to unload what appeared to be kilos of marijuana into a black Chevy Suburban. The Chevy's headlights were on to help the workers see what to do. Jim couldn't see where the driver to the suburban was. The windows were tinted and he was unable to see inside. That's when he heard a young girl scream in the cotton field directly to his right. He looked over and saw what appeared to be a man in his twenties beating and dragging one of the young 'illegals' who couldn't have been more than twelve years old into the cotton field. There was no doubt what this man intended to do to the young girl. The 'burros' also heard the screams but just looked over and laughed. They ordered everyone to keep working and not look towards the cotton field. By this time nobody was able to see anything any way because the man had the young girl down on the ground and the plants obscured everyone's view.

In an instant Jim was out of the ditch and crawling on his stomach towards the field. The moonless night made it easy for him to cross the road unseen. The girl was struggling with the man so he never heard Jim sneaking up behind him in the cotton. In one quick movement Jim grabbed the man and broke his neck. He had no feelings for anyone who would rape a little girl. He then clasped his hand over the young girl's mouth telling her in Spanish to keep quiet and to get dressed.

Jim was trying to figure out the best way to take down the four 'burros' when headlights appeared coming down the access road towards them weaving noticeably. It was Gordon's truck. Gordon and his buddies had continued their drinking binge. In their drunkenness, they convinced each other they needed to stop these outlaws from ruining their crops, so they got their rifles and headed out to the Pierson farm.

Two of the 'burros' opened fire with their AK-47's. The truck immediately veered into the mesquite and ran into one of the ponds in the pasture. The farmers call these ponds 'tanks' because they have the sides built up around the edge of the pond forming somewhat of a tank to hold as much water as possible. Jim hoped Gordon was unhurt but now had to take quick action as he focused on two of the 'burros' who were running towards Gordon's truck. They continued firing as they ran but the bullets just buried in the dirt along the side of the tank. The two 'burros' made one big error as they ran. They stayed together. That allowed Jim to take them both out with one blast of his Winchester Model 97.

Jim had no sooner fired on the two 'burros' when a state trooper came racing down the access road. It seems the trooper started following Gordon's truck when he saw it weaving down the highway at high speed. He fell behind and lost the truck when Gordon turned off the main highway and onto the farm road. When he heard the automatic gunfire, he called for back-up and headed down the access road. Upon seeing the lights of the patrol car, the two remaining 'burros' dropped their AK-47s and ran into the cotton fields, as did all the 'illegals'.

Jim ran to the tank to check on Gordon and his buddies. The truck was sitting in only three feet of water. All three of them were still seated in the truck. None of them seemed hurt. At least none of them were shot. There were a few bullet holes in the front of the cab from the Ak-47s. The windshield had also been blown out, but that happened when Gordon's shotgun went off in the panic.

For the next twelve hours state troopers and the border patrol rounded up the 'illegals' who had run throughout the neighboring cotton fields and mesquite pastures. Three of the 'illegals' actually ran to the law officers after rattlesnakes bit them. They were smart enough to realize that if they wanted to live, they had better get to a hospital right away, and turning themselves in was the quickest way. One of the burros was captured, but the other seemed to disappear. That was until his body started smelling about a week later. It seems he had crawled into a pipe in a culvert by a tank about two miles west of the Pierson farm towards Rule, Texas. He didn't see the two rattlesnakes that both struck him several times. He was too afraid to run for help, so he just lay there and slowly died. He did manage to kill one of the snakes before he died. The other one was coiled next to his bloated body when the paramedics came to pull him out.

Like several times in the past, Jim's cowboy style in taking down the 'burros' had gotten him in trouble with his bosses and with the local law enforcement. Usually after these little misunderstandings, Jim found himself sitting at a desk in the Abilene USDA office making calls and writing reports. It was his 'penance to pay' before they would let him return to his Haskell County Farm Service duties. Last time this happened Jim had been assigned to work with the Rolling Plains area cattle feedlots. It was his job to convince and then advise the feedlots on how to install security systems. There was a fear that either, intentionally or unintentionally, someone would somehow infect the cattle herds with 'Hoof and Mouth' disease, or somehow taint the ruminant feed that was given to the cattle. This had become a major concern since there seemed to be a global panic over the outbreak of mad cow disease in England. "And rightfully so," thought Jim.

Jim had been on the cutting edge of Prion research at Texas A & M while working on his doctorate. Prions are those mutant proteins that attach themselves to the brain and cause mad cow disease. He and his colleagues had made very significant discoveries regarding the human form of mad cow, Creutzfeldt-Jakob disease. That was until Jim suddenly left the university for his ranch then joined the Marines. His knowledge about what could happen if the feedlots were infected had helped him easily convince the feedlot managers of the necessity of a security system. It was this knowledge that also determined his new assignment. Or as Jim viewed it, his new assigned punishment. Jim was told he would have to leave his beloved Texas and move to Washington, D.C. It seems the United States Department of Agriculture decided Jim could best serve them, and his country, by coming to Washington to teach at the USDA Graduate School. In the process, he was to finish his PhD and continue his research in mad cow disease. It wasn't exactly how Jim wanted to work his way back to Haskell, but he did want to finish his PhD, and he knew the world was in for some real trouble from mad cow disease. Maybe, just maybe, he could do something about what he saw as a major storm just over the horizon.

Chapter Three

"Man, don't go smokin' that shit in here. I can't afford to lose this job." Efram had only been working for Hamilton Security for two months. It was the latest in a rather lengthy succession of minimum wage jobs he had held since he dropped out of Long Beach Community College last spring. When the governor said the tuition had to be raised for all California schools, Efram was left with no choice but to drop out and find a job. He was hoping to save enough money to start back next spring, but jobs were hard to come by for a twenty-two-year-old black man in Los Angeles. That was why he was so pissed off that Jamal was getting high in the warehouse.

"Be cool my brother," said Jamal. "Ain't nobody coming by here. I've been working this place for six months and ain't never been no one by here. So just be cool."

Efram couldn't afford to be cool. He needed this job. "Well at least go out back if you have to smoke that shit." Efram was mad and Jamal could tell.

"It's cool, it's cool," said Jamal. "No problem. I'll just go out back and walk the fence. Make sure nobody trying to break in here." Jamal was laughing as he walked out the door.

"I'll be checking the monitors, so make sure the cameras don't see you smokin'." Efram yelled at Jamal as he was walking out the door.

Jamal and Efram were bonded security guards working at a USDA cold storage impound warehouse in San Pedro, California. Most of the goods stored in impound at this facility were bulk shipments of high-risk bovine tissues and tissue derived ingredients. This included meat or meat products as well as bulk animal byproducts to be used as the raw material in cosmetics and pet foods. Most of the products stored at this site had been impounded for testing. All of these products had come from countries and regions where BSE, Bovine Spongiform Encephalopathy, better known as mad cow disease, was known to exist.

Efram watched the monitor screen showing the loading dock as Jamal walked by and flashed the camera the peace sign. He smiled as he turned back to the television to finish watching a rerun of one of his favorite Fresh Prince episodes.

Jamal was sitting on a crate smoking his weed when a small man dressed entirely in black dropped from the roof directly in front of him. The man's face was covered, except for the dark piercing eyes fixed on Jamal.

"Who the hell are you? Some kind of San Pedro Ninja? Ain't nothing worth stealing here. Just get the hell out of here before I call the police." Jamal was worried the intruder would report him for smoking his weed. He didn't think something dire could happen. He was trying to hold the joint behind him as he spoke to the black dressed intruder. Jamal continued to speak, "Get the hell outta here I said. I don't want no trouble." As he spoke a second, then a third similarly dressed small man dropped from the roof next to the initial intruder. Jamal dropped the joint and started to reach for his radio. He was dead before his hand was half way to his belt. In a flash, the first ninja ran a ten-inch barbed pointed spike through Jamal's left eye and into the left frontal lobe of his brain. It was so quick he didn't even get any blood on the sleeve of his black 'gi'. As if in slow motion Jamal's lifeless body seemed to melt to the ground, with the spike still protruding from his eye socket.

During the next commercial Efram scanned the monitors but saw no sign of Jamal. He called him on the radio but received no answer. "Damn him," Efram said to himself. "He probably smoked too much shit and fell asleep." Efram turned from the monitors and began to rise out of his chair. Before his brain was even able to send the signals to his muscles to rise up from the chair, it was short-circuited by another ten-inch barbed spike plunged through his eye and into his brain. Efram no longer needed to worry about losing his job. Efram no longer was able to worry about anything.

No words were spoken. The lead ninja used hand signals as he gave instructions to his accomplices. They quickly opened the warehouse door and a small non-descript delivery truck entered the warehouse. The leader grabbed a clipboard off the wall and scanned the documents attached. On the third page he found what he was looking for. There were several crates that had come from Japan. Even though the crates were labeled as prime steaks, the USDA had labeled them as 53P—01 and 53P—02. This identified them as being cosmetic raw material derived from bovine amniotic fluid and collagen, cosmetic raw material. These were high-risk bovine tissue and tissue derived materials. The USDA had placed an import alert for this type of material coming from several countries. Japan was one of those countries.

Quietly and efficiently the intruders loaded the designated crates into the van and exited the warehouse. They made sure to close the door behind them. As they were leaving the warehouse, the original ninja flashed a peace sign at the same camera Jamal had flashed a peace sign to only minutes before. Only the ninja's eyes were visible, but you could tell from his eyes, he was smiling.

It would be several hours until Jamal and Efram's bodies would be found. By that time the ninjas would be on a flight leaving the mainland and the stolen materials on its way to being processed.

Chapter Four

When the new Taka returned to Japan, he wasted no time in making major changes to the Matsuura business empire. His initial plan was to sell the 'Aioka' Steakhouses located throughout Japan and Asia. Narcissism, however, got the best of him. The new Taka had already once given up his real name when he killed his brother and assumed his name. He couldn't give it up a second time. His plans began to change. He sold the Hurley's hamburger chain of restaurants instead. This caused quite a stir in the Japanese business world, as well as with his employees. Since he had returned from his honeymoon he had become reclusive, often refusing to meet with his executives, and when he did speak with them it was only briefly and from across the room. Or worse yet, they had to meet with Taka's new assistant. This man sent shivers down their spines whenever they spoke with him. They all had concerns about Taka's new business decisions and direction, but in proper Japanese fashion kept their concerns to themselves and did not talk among each other. Taka had always treated them fairly and they had too much respect to question him on his decisions. With the money, he made from the sell of the Hurley's chain he increased his cattle and feedlot operations. He continued to supply the beef to the new owners of the Hurley's chain. He also negotiated a deal with Sizzle Burger restaurants to supply their Hawaii stores with beef from his Northern Japan packinghouse. He knew if things went well in Hawaii, the western United States Sizzle Burger restaurants would soon be using his hamburger as well. There were many questions as to how he could afford to sell the meat so cheaply to Sizzle Burger. There was much speculation that Taka was losing a considerable amount of money due to the Sizzle Burger deal. Fortunately, Taka had no shareholders to whom he needed to justify his dealings. His grandfather had kept himself as the sole owner of the business. He was beholden to no one. Now the new Taka was the sole owner. He was only beholden to his cause.

Sizzle Burger's importation of beef from Japan did not go over well with the ranchers and beef producers in the United States. They caused quite a stir in Congress with their letter writing campaigns and lobbying efforts. The various regional rancher associations organized protests at all the farm shows and increased their advertisements in the industry trade magazines. It did lead to stricter import restrictions and more stringent testing of imported bovine products. Greater restrictions probably would have been implemented had it not been for several others of the major fast food chains negotiating their own deals with beef producers from China, Korea, Australia, and Argentina. It seems they too had a fairly strong lobby force in Washington D.C.

Niki had extraordinary beauty and still generated a lot of public attention. Taka had plans to take advantage of this. Niki had been out of the tabloids for the past year or so, but it didn't take long for her face to start showing up on the tabloid covers. It was just a matter of being seen at the right places with the right people. Sometimes that included Taka, but often times not. The new Taka did not feel his image should be that public. He knew there were government agents who thought Aioka was still alive. It was best if he not press his luck. It was a well thought out and orchestrated manipulation of the media that made Niki once again one of

Japan's, and the world's, most watched celebrities. Taka had her resume her modeling career and waited for her fame to grow.

As the months went by, Niki's fame did grow and Taka's troubles grew as well. The packinghouse losses were greater than Taka had anticipated and the new import inspection requirements implemented by the United States on Japanese meat were costing him dearly. Both financially and with regards to his ultimate goals. Even though he was losing more money than he had planned, money was not an issue. He still had plenty of his own, as well as access to an almost unlimited amount through his terrorist network. More disconcerting, were the inspections and restrictions that had become a stumbling block to his plans. Japan had very strict meat inspection procedures. Of the 1.2 million cattle butchered last year in Japan, all 1.2 million were tested for diseases. They were primarily looking for mad cow disease. In the United States, of the 35 million cattle slaughtered, only 20,000 were tested for diseases. Taka realized he had to make a change in his business plans and his terror plans. It had become obvious Japan was no longer the best place to run his operations. His key executives were starting to ask questions about what direction Taka was taking his business. Stories were beginning to show up in the business journals questioning his judgment. One of the Japanese tabloids even ran a story claiming the real Taka, had been replaced by an imposter. They had side-by-side pictures of Taka on their cover taken of him and Niki on their honeymoon. One of them as they were leaving the boat in Kona, and one as they returned to the boat. It was ironic such a far-fetched fabricated tabloid story was so close to reality. Taka needed to move his operation, and move it soon.

What was working well for Taka was his new business deal manufacturing and marketing a line of cosmetics named after Niki. It had always been part of his plans to create a cosmetics line for Niki. He only needed to wait till her fame returned, which Taka knew wouldn't take long with Niki's personality and looks. For years the packinghouse had supplied cosmetic firms with bovine byproducts, which became the main ingredients in several types of cosmetics. Now the new Taka had rewritten his contracts with one of these firms allowing them to create and market a line of Niki cosmetics. The firm was elated with the prospect of such a deal, as was Taka. What the manufacturer failed to see was how Taka structured their contract in such a way that once the cosmetic firm marketed the Niki line into a major seller, a clause in the contract allowed Taka to separate the Niki line from the cosmetic firm and Taka and Niki would become the majority owners of a new separate company. The cosmetic firm understood the risk when they signed the contract, but thought the chances of it happening were slim. For the clause to take affect, it required Taka to sell most of his seemingly highly successful cattle, feedlot, and packinghouse business and leave Japan, which is precisely what Taka and Niki arranged to do, at least on paper. Taka took the entire Japanese business world by surprise when he did so. There was much speculation as to what his plans were, but he had kept them very secret. No one could believe he would give up all his companies, contracts, and restaurants in Japan just to gain control of the Niki line of cosmetics. Even though it was a lucrative business, it in no way compared to the cattle business and the spin-off companies Taka's grandfather had spent years developing. He did maintain a minority interest in all of the businesses he sold and took with him the Sizzle Burger contracts to supply the Hawaii restaurants with beef.

It was assumed his minority ownership of his old companies would allow him to fulfill the terms of his Sizzle Burger contracts by continuing to supply them with the beef they needed. The new majority owners would of course be happy with this deal because it was well known in the business world that Taka was sustaining a considerable loss on the Sizzle Burger deal. In actuality, the new owners were nothing more than a series of shell corporations Taka owned and controlled.

What wasn't known in Japanese business circles was that even before the original Taka was murdered in Hawaii, the new Taka had one of his most trusted men, Minoru Sakura, quietly buying ranch property on the big island of Hawaii. That proved to be a much more difficult task than Taka had predicted. Although the Japanese had little difficulty buying small parcels of resort property throughout the island, there was an unmistakable organized prejudice that kept them from buying large acreage of ranch land.

There are approximately eighty ranches in and around Waimea, which is located on the northern part of the island. This is known as the Kohala area. Waimea is one of the more populated towns on Hawaii. That is probably because of its mild Northern California type of climate. The size of the ranches varied from as few as 10 acres up to the mammoth 225,000-acre Parker Ranch with its 35,000 head of cattle. The cattle rancher's association on the big island had over 130 members. Several of the members had but one cow, but still wanted a say in what went on regarding Hawaii's ranching policies. One of those not so unspoken policies was to keep the ranch land belonging to the native Hawaiian families. When someone decided they needed or wanted to sell their ranch, the cattle ranchers association made sure they were part of the negotiating process. If necessary, there were several ranch owners with more than enough assets to make the purchase and eventually resell the ranch to a 'proper buyer'. That was the challenge Taka had to overcome. To most Japanese it would have been too costly and formidable of a task. For Taka, money was not a hindrance. No price was too high in the pursuance of his cause.

After several months of trying to buy property with no success, it was a not so chance meeting in the Waikoloa Hilton bar that proved fateful for Taka's plans. It was there Taka's agent, Minoru, met David Paleaka. David was a hard-drinking womanizer who liked to flash his money in hopes of getting into bed with some beautiful mainland tourist looking to party. David's family had owned the Paleaka ranch on Highway 250 between Hawi and Waimea for eighty years. Seven years ago, David's parents were killed in a head-on collision while visiting friends on Maui. They were driving back from Hana when a pickup truck with several locals sped past the slower tourist traffic and slammed into the Paleaka's compact rental car, killing them instantly. Four passengers in the bed of the pickup truck were killed as well when their bodies flew out of the back and over a cliff. The three passengers inside the truck survived the crash and received minimal punishment from the local court. Unlike most Hawaiian families, David was an only child. He did have several uncles and aunties on the various islands, and thus a lot of cousins, but no siblings. The ranch became his alone. David didn't know much about ranching, but he knew a lot about partying. His relatives on the big island all had their own ranches and offered to take over the Paleaka cattle. David was happy to let them go. His uncle also offered to buy the ranch from David as well, but not for nearly what it was worth. It was a large ranch of close to 14,000 acres. At one time it was the second largest active ranch operation on the island with over 15,000 cattle and its own feedlot and packinghouse. Both of those facilities closed down almost twenty years ago and now the buildings sat vacant and run down. Even Parker Ranch closed its feedlot and packinghouse almost twelve years ago. It was just not profitable to run a feedlot operation in Hawaii. Everything had to be shipped in and that had become too expensive. As far as the packinghouse was concerned, there just wasn't a large enough market or demand for beef on the island to justify the expense. David's parents had always kept him supplied with money. He had never moved away from home. He saw no point to moving away. He had his own small house away from the main house, and his parents left him alone. Although, for several years, they did pressure him to first learn the ranching business, and after that failed, they tried to get him to go to school or find a job. Neither of their choices worked. After years of trying, they finally gave up and just gave him the money he needed for his partying life style. After their death, it didn't take David long to burn through the family's cash savings. His cocaine habit was out of control as was his alcoholism and his desire to always party. That was what brought him to the Bank of Hawaii the first time. The Bank of Hawaii was more than happy to loan him the $500,000 he requested. They knew the farm was worth at least twenty times that amount. They also knew David would eventually default on the loan. It would only be a matter of time. In less than two years David was back at the bank requesting another loan. It was more difficult to get this time, but he still received another $300,000. David swore to himself to not waste the money this time, but of course the partying soon dwindled away most of the assets from his second loan.

David was beginning to get letters of concern from the bank regarding his ability to repay the money loaned to him.

The Paleaka ranch had been one of the choice properties Taka's agent had inquired about, although he was never able to see it except from a helicopter. When he asked about the local ranch properties to try to find the owner, the local government, the rancher's association, and the banks always put him off. Minoru never seemed to receive a straight answer from anybody. It should have been a simple matter of researching the public records, but somehow those records never seemed to be available to Minoru and nobody ever seemed able to help. That was until he got into a conversation with one of the locals at a small bar in Hawi. After buying the local resident several beers, he not only got David's name, description and where he liked to hang out, but he got the whole story on how David inherited the farm and was probably going to lose it because of his drinking and cocaine addiction. Minoru couldn't have been happier. Minoru was staying at the Waikoloa Hilton and had spent several evenings in the very same bar where David preferred to party. With the description he was given, he realized he had seen David on several occasions and felt disgusted by his actions. That attitude was about to change.

That night in the Hilton bar, Minoru waited for two hours hoping David would show. David never did. Nor did he show up the following night or the night after. This did give Minoru the opportunity to acquaint himself with what appeared to be several other of the local island bar patrons. He freely bought them drinks and was soon accepted as part of the group. Part of the group just as long as he continued to buy the drinks for everyone else. It was his fourth night in the bar when David finally made his entrance. David was edgy and made no bones about walking directly to the local sitting next to Minoru.

"I've been looking for you for two days. I need some shit, and I need it now. I went by your house yesterday and Julie said you had gone to Maui to score. When I went by tonight, she told me you were here. Man, I need some coke, right now." David was almost frantic as he spoke to the local.

"Cool it." the local told David as he nodded towards Minoru. "Let's go outside."

Minoru pretended not to hear, but he could tell the local got very agitated with David for speaking out like that in front of a stranger.

The local turned to Minoru, "Watch my drink and save my stool, will you? I'll be right back."

Minoru nodded and tried not to look at David. Less than ten minutes later they were both back and David's demeanor had completely changed. He was now calm and collected with a charming smile for all the women in the bar and a witty comment for all the men.

"Thanks for watching my drink," said the local as he sat back down. "Sorry about my friend. I sure hope you're not a cop."

"Far from it," Minoru said smiling, as he pulled from his fanny pack what appeared to be about an ounce of the pinkest Peruvian flake coke the local had ever seen. He made sure David noticed the cocaine as well.

In a flash, David was next to the two of them. "You might want to be a bit more discreet about flashing that around," David said. "Let me introduce myself. I'm David Paleaka."

"Minoru jumped off of his stool and bowed, "My name is Minoru Sakura. It is an honor to meet you David Paleaka."

This made David smile.

"Please honor me by joining us and allowing me to buy you a drink," continued Minoru.

"How could I turn down an offer like that," responded David as he eyed the cocaine Minoru placed back in his fanny pack.

At least four times that night, Minoru and David visited Minoru's room at the Hilton. They became good friends in those next few hours while doing almost half an ounce of cocaine. David was quite a talker and said much more than he should. The conversation allowed Minoru to devise a plan he was sure would eventually get Taka ownership of the Paleaka Ranch. He invited David back the next night telling him there would be plenty more of the Peruvian flake, as well as some of his female acquaintances who were sure to meet with David's approval. It was an offer David could and would not refuse, but Minoru already knew this.

It wasn't long before Minoru and David were best of friends. Minoru had a seemingly endless supply of cocaine and women, and David had an endless desire for both. David's life centered on his partying with Minoru and all else didn't matter. That was until the letters from the bank started coming from an attorney rather than the bank officer who had worked with David. He confided his concern with Minoru, and Minoru was quick with a solution.

"Why don't you and I go into business together," suggested Minoru. "I have been looking for a ranch like yours as a legitimate business investment for the money I have made off my drug dealings. I would start a small-scale cattle operation, take care of the bank and the bills, and put you on a salary that will keep you supplied in enough money so you can party like you always have. Plus, I guarantee you we will make money off the cattle. You will have plenty of cash to stash away in savings. Besides, I will pay you $3,000,000 up front for a fifty percent interest in the ranch. All you have to do is let me run it and stay out of the way."

David knew his 'ship had come in'. Keeping a fifty percent interest in the ranch would keep the Rancher's Association off his back, and the money would get the bank off his back. He didn't see how he could lose. "It's a deal," David responded.

Minoru cautioned, "Don't be so hasty. I know this is a big decision. Take some time to think about it."

"That won't be necessary." David reassured Minoru. "What you are offering me will save my ranch from foreclosure. It's a Godsend. This is more than I could ever have hoped for. Of course, I accept."

Minoru already knew he would. "Well in that case, I will have my attorney draw up the contract in the morning. You should have your attorney look it over and then get it back to me as soon as possible so we can sign and make it official."

"The only attorney I have is the bloodsucker who has gotten me out of my DUI's and drug busts. He wouldn't know the first thing about a contract like that." David replied.

"Well if you like, I can recommend an attorney who can go over the contract with you. He is excellent at making legal mumble jumble sound almost normal," Minoru reassured David.

"That would be great," David replied as he eyed the baggie of cocaine on the table.

Minoru noticed David's attention was drawn to the coke. "Well then, let's celebrate and start the party. You make us some lines, and I'll call the girls. But first, let's toast to our new partnership."

David and Minoru clicked together their drink glasses and David immediately headed for the coke. Minoru smiled as David walked to the table and began chopping the cocaine. It had been much easier than he expected. He already had the contract drawn up and he had made arrangements with another attorney to explain the contract to David. An attorney who also had quite a little appetite for Peruvian flake cocaine. The attorney understood if he wanted to continue getting the cocaine, he needed to explain the contract to David, or at least parts of the contract. Several paragraphs were to be left out of the explanation. David would never know, and most likely would never remember what the attorney told him. That is if he was around to remember.

The following day, Minoru gave the contract to David to take to the attorney. He also gave David an ounce of the Peruvian flake to hold him over for a couple of days. He told David he had some business on the mainland, which would only take him two or three days to complete. He assured David that he would quickly return to move forward on their plans for the ranch. In reality, Minoru already had several colleagues working on getting the ranch, feedlot, and packing house back in operation. The necessary building materials and operating equipment had cleared export custom inspections and were already awaiting transit in a bonded warehouse at a large Japanese port. Most of Taka's breeding stock was at the same port being tested for diseases prior to their exportation clearance as well. Within the next two month's the Paleaka Ranch would be back in business.

Chapter Five

Law enforcement would be so much more efficient if they all could get their computers to network together. It was getting better, but for the most part it was still chaos. Every since that incident with Charles Manson's gun after the Tate-La Bianca murders, politicians had been pushing for better communication among agencies. It was a great idea, but sometimes, great ideas take a lot of money to come to fruition. The money just wasn't there at the local levels. At least not yet. The federal government did see the need and had invested heavily in bringing the FBI, CIA, and NSA into the computer age. Information was now quickly available among those agencies. That is, information they chose to enter into the system. Many things were best left unsaid or un-entered outside the individual agency offices. Contrary to what the media and the politicians claimed, there was still much jealousy between the various federal law enforcement agencies.

What was much improved was the local police's ability to access the FBI databases. Investigators were able to type in key words or descriptions of crimes or crime scenes and within a few minutes get a list of similar crimes or clues discovered elsewhere. Such was the case for the double-murder of two security guards at a cold storage warehouse in San Pedro, California. Actually, the case belonged to the FBI since it occurred at a facility leased by the United States Department of Agriculture. Or possibly it belonged to the National Security Agency since it occurred at a bonded customs facility and the products stolen had not as of yet cleared customs. Although, in actuality, the stolen items never would have cleared customs. They had been sitting in the warehouse for several days, waiting for USDA testing. So far, no one had come in to claim the shipment and pay for testing, meaning that the shipment was soon to be destroyed. In any case, it was the Los Angeles County Sheriff's department who got the call and who started the investigation. Even they weren't sure who should handle the case. They did call both the FBI and the NSA, but both of these agencies were too busy and short handed to immediately send out agents. They did both request reports and asked the sheriff's investigator to contact them if they deemed it a matter of national security. It was their way of telling the sheriff's office they wanted nothing to do with the murder of two black men in San Pedro at a facility that held nothing of real value.

When the sheriff investigator did arrive on the scene, he knew there was more to what had occurred than the murder of two black men during the theft of some impounded bovine byproducts. The videos showed the three men dressed like ninjas entering the yard, then entering the warehouse, and eventually bringing in the truck and loading it. It also showed the lead ninja plunge the spike into Efram's eye. It was amazingly quick and heartless. What troubled the sheriff's investigator the most was the eyes of the ninja who stared at the camera and flashed a peace sign immediately after he killed the guard. The eyes burned a hole in your heart and made you cringe with fear. You knew when you viewed the video these men were professionals, and there was no doubt this was not a random or isolated incident.

The spikes left in the victim's eyes were also a very grisly clue as to the ninja's intentions. There was something written on the spikes, but it was unreadable unless the spikes were removed. That was something the coroner needed to do. The ninjas had left few clues. Besides the video and the spikes that were still lodged in the eyes of the security guards, there was very little to go on. The material stolen was obviously a clue, but a clue to what? It was nothing more than bovine byproducts destined to be used for who knows what. It had come from a wholesaler of such products in Japan and was being shipped to a warehouse in Los Angeles. When the investigators went to the address given for the warehouse, they found a donut shop. Obviously, someone had a bad sense of humor. The video also was of little help. The faces were covered and only the leader ever looked at the camera. When he did it sent shivers down your spine. That left the spikes as the most promising clues. The investigators went to the morgue for the coroner's autopsy. The coroner did not realize the spikes were heavily barbed on their ends. When he removed the spike from Jamal's eye, almost a quarter of his brain was attached to the spike and came out as the coroner pulled the spike back out through the eye socket. This made one of the investigators puke, and even made the coroner's assistant a little queasy. It took several minutes to remove the brains from the spike and clean it up before the investigator was able to look at it.

Unfortunately, that was all he was able to do. Look at it. There was something written on the spikes but it was written in what seemed to be two distinct languages. One appeared to be some form of Arabic, while the other looked like it was Japanese. The coroner's assistant was able to confirm one of the writings was in fact Japanese. He was able to translate the writing as well, though it made little sense to him.

"It says, 'The Red Summit'," the assistant said.

"That's it? That's all it says?" questioned the investigator.

"That's all it says in Japanese. There is this other writing, but I can't read it," responded the assistant.

"Well thanks for your help," said the investigator. By that time the coroner had removed the other spike and cleaned it off. It proved to be identical to the first spike. They would have to get the remaining writing translated when they reached the station.

Back at the station one of the investigators decided to check the FBI database for the words The Red Summit. His partner went looking for a sheriff deputy who could read Arabic. Immediately after typing in The Red Summit and pushing the query button on the keyboard, the screen started flashing information about The Red Summit terrorist organization. It gave a brief history of their known activities but very little else. It did say to contact the FBI at once if you came across information relating to activities of The Red Summit.

"I guess this would qualify as an activity relating to The Red Summit," the investigator said out loud to no one in particular. Just then his partner rushed into the room.

"You won't believe what this says," the partner said.

"And you won't believe what I just found out," responded the investigator. "But you go first," he continued.

"Well I had that new guy Jhallid, look at the spike. You know Chauncey's new partner." The investigator nodded. "He turned as white as toilet paper when he read it."

"Well what the hell did it say?" the investigator asked rather impatiently.

"He told me it translated as 'my gift to Osama, our glorious victory is near at hand," the partner stared at the investigator. "What the hell do you make of that?"

"A lot when you put it with what I just learned. The Red Summit is a Japanese terrorist organization. They are the ones who killed those hundreds of people on that bullet train suicide bombing a few years back," said the investigator.

"Yeah, I remember that one. Weren't they the ones who also poisoned all those people in the subway?" asked his partner.

"That along with many more, according to this FBI file," he responded.

The investigator knew he was out of his league with this investigation, and really wanted nothing to do with it. He picked up the phone and called the number on the computer screen.

Jotty Joplin had worked for the FBI for seven years. He came to them from the military where he had worked in special operations researching and tracking terrorist cells in the Middle East and Far East. He did do a little more than just research the terrorists. Once he had identified a certain cell that was responsible for some heinous crime against USA interests, he and his special ops unit would quietly make the cell disappear in their own special way. He was very good at what he did, but the military prefers younger men doing that sort of job. They felt Jotty had become too valuable to allow him to do the covert dirty work. Dirty work is how the military referred to the killing of the terrorists. Jotty disagreed and soon found himself no longer working for the military. The FBI was more than happy to put his expertise to good use even though Jotty still didn't get into the field as much as he would have liked.

Sitting behind a desk for so long had begun to take its toll on Jotty's previously superb physical condition. Jotty was a big-boned man who stood around six feet tall. He had wide shoulders and large defined muscles. At least he did at one time. Jotty was a little softer than he used to be when he worked for the military. As he began to age, it became more and more difficult for him to maintain his rock-hard physique. Jotty still remained relatively fit, but lacked the quickness and sharpness he once prided himself in. Lately he had no need or time for such a strict workout regiment his body would require to stay in top form.

Jotty had been assigned to researching The Red Summit for the past six months. British intelligence had asked for the FBI's help when what turned out to be The Red Summit terrorist cell broke into the British National Health Laboratory in Weybridge and stole the BSE contaminated meat being stored and tested there. That burglary happened in the middle of the night and cost three security guards their lives. Two had their necks broken while one died in a much more gruesome manner. He was stabbed in his right eye with a barbed spike with the words 'The Red Summit' engraved in Japanese on the spike. So far, Jotty had spent most of his time researching the history of The Red Summit. That task had taken him on several recent trips to Japan. It was there he met his Japanese National Police Agency counterpart, Haruko Ozawa. She had been the lead NPA investigator assigned to The Red Summit for five years. There had been several terrorist acts in Japan that The Red Summit took credit for. As of yet, they still remained an enigma to the National Police, and even though Haruko had quite a list of possible cell members, they all seemed to be dead or missing. With the crime in Britain, it became obvious The Red Summit had decided to move their terrorist act to the world stage. In the health laboratory burglary, they left no doubt as to who was responsible with their engraved spike in the eye of the guard. There was also a video of the burglary and murders, but so far, the video had proved to be of little value. Jotty was working on that. He was running an enlargement of the eyes

from what appears to be the leader of the terrorists through
the FBI data bank of known terrorists, searching for a match
of the eyes. It was a new system and not nearly as efficient as
the fingerprint matching system. Jotty never-the-less was still
hopeful something would turn up before the tainted meat
did. He also was hoping to gather some information to
impress Haruko. During his visits to Japan to meet with
Haruko, her work and dedication had impressed him. It was
his infatuation for her as a person that had really blossomed.
He hoped it was somewhat a mutual feeling, but that was just
a dream, and Jotty knew it. At least a dream for the time
being.

Jotty's computer screen notified him the Los Angeles
County Sheriff's office had accessed the Red Summit file. That
caught him by surprise. Up until now only British Intelligence,
Japan's National Police Agency and some unknown user who
tried to hack into the FBI computer system had ever
requested that file. Jotty's initial thought was some computer
hacker had gained access to a supposedly secured terminal
site. That was until his direct phone line rang and the sheriff
investigator was on the other end. Jotty listened to the story
and told the sheriff to keep it out of the papers and not do
anything until he arrived. The investigator said he understood
and told Jotty not to worry. If the investigator knew what was
about to happen, he would be the one who could not help
but worry. Within an hour Jotty was on an FBI jet headed
towards the Long Beach International Airport.

It always seems the more you know, the more afraid
you become. At least it was that way with Jotty. Once he
visited the USDA warehouse and read the manifest of what
had been stolen, he knew The Red Summit had more in mind
than poisoning a few people with tainted meat. There had
not been a lot of the tainted meat stolen in the British

burglary. At least not enough to do any serious damage to a large portion of the population. Now however, they had a serious quantity of possibly affected bovine amniotic fluid and other bovine byproducts. These could be manufactured into a large number of cosmetics that could be easily marketed and distributed in the United States. It was now a whole new ball game for Jotty. The Red Summit's terror campaign had moved to America. When he viewed the videotape, he immediately knew the eyes of the lead ninja were the same eyes he had been trying to identify for the past month. The barbed spikes were also more troubling. Besides the Red Summit being engraved on the spike, a reference to Osama and Al Qaeda was now also engraved on the spike. Could it have been a ruse to throw him off, or had there been a quantum leap in the escalation of the stakes? It was obvious to Jotty he needed some expert help in dealing with the Red Summit and understanding just what they may be planning. He had a good idea where to get the help he needed. He just needed to convince his bosses, as well as Haruko.

Chapter Six

Haruko Ozawa had no time for men or for dating. She was all business. That was why she had advanced so quickly in the ranks to Special Investigator, Counter-Terrorism Unit of the Japanese National Police Agency. When she first received the appointment to the terrorist unit, many of her colleagues attributed the promotion to her beauty and the National Police Agency's desire to improve job equity for women. They soon learned differently. Haruko was not only extremely smart and wise, with what seemed like an ability to see into a person's brain and know what that person was thinking, but she had a highly toned lithe body skilled in the martial art of Kung Fu. Many of her male colleagues found out she was all business the hard way, when they mistakenly made too physical of a pass at her. They soon found themselves lying on their backs looking up at an angry Haruko. Fortunately for them, her anger ended there and the action was never reported to supervisors, just as long as the offender never repeated the action. Even when it was the occasional supervisor who ended up on the floor, she never complained as long as it never again occurred. Privately, many of her colleagues thought she might even be a lesbian since she never seemed to date or talk about dating. That was something never talked about among her coworkers. She had become too respected for people to gossip about her personal life. Haruko's life was her job. She was married to it. At least she had been since the murder of her parents. Their murder was just a random act of violence. They were in the wrong place at the wrong time. They had become lost one night while heading to the subway station after leaving a movie theater in an unfamiliar part of Tokyo. According to the police investigator's report, they turned down an alley where a drug deal was taking place, or more accurately falling apart. The alleged killer had just shot and killed a drug dealer for having previously sold him some heroin with too much cut in it. Haruko's parents unintentionally witnessed this murder and were summarily executed for having seen what occurred. What troubled Haruko the most was that the National Police Agency had the dealer under surveillance but did not respond as quickly as they should have to stop the dealer or her parents from being murdered. At the inquest that followed the murders, there were rumors the police on surveillance purposely chose not to intervene in the dealer's death. Their intentions were to allow the drug dealers to kill each other. A poor choice this time, but as in all police agencies there is a 'code of silence' when it comes to protecting your own. No officer was ever charged or even reprimanded. That may in part be why Haruko never befriended her colleagues. It also may have played in her eventual promotion to the Special Investigations unit.

When she was assigned to the counter-terrorist division of the special investigation unit, she inherited the task of a retiring agent whose assignment had been tracking down the terrorist cell known as the Red Summit. It was a militant homegrown terrorist group that had been around since Haruko was a young girl. They were best known for the suicide bombing of a bullet train several years ago. The bombing killed 162 people counting the suicide bomber. That was the case the retiring agent had supposedly been working on when he retired. In actuality, he had mentally retired even before the bombing occurred. The Red Summit had been considered a deactivated cell for several years prior to the bombing. There had been several minor events such as the subway poisoning, which killed five people and injured thirty others two years ago, as well as a few murders that an anonymous caller claimed were the actions of The Red Summit. The subway poisoning was very similar to the poisoning that first brought The Red Summit to national attention. That was the first Sarin poisoning recorded in Japan. It took the lives of twenty-seven Japanese and two French tourists. It also brought the name Aioka Matsuura to the attention of the National Police Agency.

Aioka was the grandson of a very prominent and wealthy Japanese businessman. Aioka, unlike his older brother Taka Matsuura, chose not to follow in his grandfather's business enterprises. Instead, Aioka spent his time in Tokyo leading student demonstrations. That was when he founded The Red Summit, or as he initially claimed, joined the political arm of The Red Summit. The National Police were never able to connect Aioka to any of the original violence associated with the so-called 'military arm' of The Red Summit. On several occasions, he was brought in for questioning, but always released for lack of evidence. At least that was until the bullet train bombing. There were several witnesses who connected Aioka to the suicide bomber just minutes before the bomber boarded the train. There were also several video cameras that not only showed Aioka with the bomber, but many other suspected individuals who the National Police had also been trying to connect with the Red Summit for years. Before the police could arrest him, Aioka managed to slip out of Japan. He later surfaced in Lebanon and was seen at an Al Qaeda terrorist training facility. Several other members of the Red Summit also managed to disappear before the National Police were able to track them down. A few were reported to have gone to Lebanon with

Aioka. Many of the other terrorists were unable to be identified from the videos. Several younger students associated with political activities of the Red Summit were taken into custody, but only two were held as being involved with the terrorist attack. That was based on resemblance that the students showed to terrorists on the videos. They were initially convicted of terrorist activities to appease an angry nation and show the police were doing their job. Both convictions were overturned on appeals when the national uproar over the bullet train attack had died down. That was just about the time Haruko took over as Special Investigator in charge of the Red Summit terrorist cell. She was avid and relentless in her search for members of the Red Summit terrorist cell, but mostly she wanted Aioka. She pressured Aioka's grandfather and his brother Taka for information. That is how she found out Aioka had initially gone to Lebanon. He had contacted Taka requesting money and Taka foolishly sent him some. That happened only once according to Taka, for the grandfather found out about Taka helping Aioka and forbade him from future contact with his brother.

Haruko followed Aioka's movements in Lebanon as closely as possible. She was able to identify three of the Red Summit cell members still active in Japan with the help of Israeli intelligence. They supplied her with photographs of the cell members near the Al Qaeda training camp. She was able to cross reference the photographs with those in her own files and identify the members. She then crosschecked their visas to determine when they left Japan and when they returned. She had them arrested and learned much about Aioka's work with Osama and the terrorist camps during the interrogation of the three cell members. She shared her information with the Israelis, which in turn led to the attack on the terrorist training camp in 1994. Aioka was reported killed in that raid along with several other Japanese and Islamic terrorists. Unfortunately, no bodies were ever produced, so there was never any definitive proof Aioka died during the raid. Israeli intelligence said they had no doubt Aioka was killed, but Haruko was unconvinced. For the next several years she continued to search out other Red Summit cell members with moderate success. She also, quietly but constantly, kept track of Aioka's brother Taka. Taka had as difficult a time believing his brother was dead, as Haruko seemed to have. He seemed to believe that one day his brother would again be part of his life. The grandfather recognized Taka's difficulty dealing with Aioka's death and allowed Taka to name the steak house restaurant they were planning on opening after his brother. Taka built such a restaurant empire he had to expand his cattle and feedlot enterprises in order to keep up with the demand for beef all the restaurants generated. This brought much pain to Haruko. Haruko was haunted by the name Aioka and found it unbelievable the public made a success of a business named after one of Japan's most deadly terrorist assassins. That was what prompted her to become a Vegan. She swore she never again would eat any meat or animal product. She became a fanatic about her avoidance of any business associated with the Matsuura family. When Taka Matsuura married Nishiki Yoshi, Haruko was so upset she stopped wearing Victoria Secret's panties or bras.

Haruko was at her desk researching old terrorist photos from the Red Summit Data base. It was a secured data base file only accessible through a limited number of computer terminals located throughout the National Police Agency headquarters and on a limited basis in some of the district offices, as well as select international police and government facilities. Every time the file was accessed, her computer screen would display the terminal used to acquire information from the database along with what specific files were being accessed. This particular instance, an Investigations Supervisor's computer terminal at a suburban Tokyo Police Agency Office had logged on to the data base and was seeking photos of Aioka and Taka Matsuura. Haruko found this odd since rarely did anyone in the National Police Agency find it necessary to access the Red Summit files. If they did, they usually would contact her first. The information on her screen also included a contact phone number of the terminal accessing the files. She called the number, but received no answer. Moments later the terminal accessing her files logged out. This puzzled her. Again, she tried the phone number listed on her computer screen. There was still no answer. She decided to take a trip to the suburban facility to see who and why someone was seeking information on the Red Summit.

When she arrived at the suburban satellite police station, she discovered the computer terminal used to access her database belonged to the investigations supervisor. That she already knew. What she didn't know was he was out ill that day. She started asking questions about who had access to his office and who had the security codes to access secured databases. Remarkably, no one seemed to know anything about anything at the police station. The 'code of silence' once again reared its ugly head. Haruko was furious. This was why she struggled to remain a member of the National Police Agency. She left the station in a rage and returned to her office at the headquarters. As she stewed in her anger, she finally lost control of her calm demeanor and stormed into her supervisor's office. Her boss was taken aback but managed to calm Haruko's fury as she ranted through her angered story over what had occurred. Her boss promised to investigate and contacted the satellite station's supervisor who was at home ill. He agreed to investigate at his office when he returned and told them he would send a list of officers with access to his office as well as those with the security codes that would allow them access. Haruko also demanded to see a copy of the security video that monitored the comings and goings of personnel in and out of the various floors in the station along with the video that monitored the entrances to the station. As days passed no list was received. Nor did the supervisor send copies of the security videos that monitored the station. When Haruko contacted her supervisor seeking information, he too seemed somewhat evasive. Finally, she confronted her boss in the weekly briefing, challenging him in front of her fellow officers to do something about the breach of security. This angered her boss tremendously. He had a difficult time trying to disguise his fury. He had no choice but to agree to follow up on her concerns immediately, but left no doubt in anyone's mind Haruko had overstepped her bounds. You could almost see Haruko's fellow officers move away from her in the meeting room. They all knew it would not be advantageous to their careers if they were perceived to be too friendly with Haruko.

The next day Haruko's boss gave her a list of officers at the satellite station that may have had access to the supervisor's office. In actuality, it was just a copy of the roster containing the names of all the officers and investigators at that station. He also gave her a copy of the video that monitored the entrance to the police station, but not the station's interior videos. When Haruko questioned her supervisor about where the interior videos were, he told her he was informed by the satellite station's investigations supervisor that those videos were errantly erased and recorded over. Haruko was angry but became angrier when her boss told her in so many words that she needed not to concern herself with this investigation any longer and needed to get back to more important concerns. Haruko bit her tongue, turned, and swiftly walked back to her office. At that moment, she knew her tenure at the National Police Agency of Japan, would soon be coming to an end. She was very frustrated, but she did have the entrance video to monitor, and in reality, just how important was the fact there was an unauthorized visitor to the Red Summit database?

Chapter Seven

Spencer was on the edge. Again, he quickly turned around hoping to get a glimpse of the man he was sure had been following him. No one was there.

"Where are you, you little son-of-a-bitch?" Spencer muttered to himself. "Come on asshole, show yourself."

No one out of the ordinary was there. Yet Spencer knew he was being followed, and had been followed for the past two days. Most people would think Spencer was just being paranoid. At least that is what his parole officer thought. He told Spencer there was no reason for anyone to be following him. Not the Texas State Troopers, the Dallas Police nor the FBI was watching him. The parole officer checked with them all. Spencer's story was no longer of any interest to the media, and if indeed a reporter were following him, they wouldn't stalk him like this. Still, Spencer knew. It's a third sense you develop when you've been in prison. You are always watching your back. You learn to just know when that person is stalking you. If you don't learn that skill, you won't be around long. Especially, in a federal penitentiary like Leavenworth. That was where Spencer Tyler had spent the past four years of his life.

Spencer continued down the street looking at the glass storefronts hoping to catch a reflection of the man he knew was pursuing him. "What the hell could this guy want?" Spencer said to no one. Suddenly he caught a glimpse of the small Asian man who he was sure was the one following him. He quickly ducked into a doorway and entered what turned out to be a Thai restaurant. He asked for a table that faced

the door and allowed him a clear view of the street out the
front window. The Thai restaurant turned out to be a poor
choice. It was almost lunchtime when Spencer entered the
restaurant. Now several patrons were entering, many of
them Asian. Spencer broke out in a sweat. Now he was
turning his head frantically in a panic staring at the several
Asian men who were now seated throughout the restaurant.
He had no idea which of these men might be the one.
Abruptly, he leaped from his chair knocking it over backwards
and ran out the door. Everyone was staring at Spencer as he
ran, including the small Asian man who had indeed been
following him, and waiting.

Spencer Tyler had once been one of the most
respected research scientists at Texas A & M. He joined the
Prion research team when Jimmy Rikey dropped out. Up until
then, he was one of the leading authorities on animal
diseases with a specialty in anthrax research. He was a
brilliant scientist with a very promising future. That was, if he
could somehow learn to control his gambling problem.
Spencer had spent much of his free time, and work time, at a
computer terminal logged into some Internet gaming site. He
loved to play poker. 'Texas Hold 'Em' was his game.
Unfortunately, he wasn't any good at it. He always seemed to
lose. He had amassed a substantial debt that was getting very
difficult to conceal from his family and co-workers. Shortly
after he joined the Prion research team his gambling
addiction was about to cost him his job and his marriage. He
wasn't making his house payments, and had been siphoning
off funds from his research to help pay his bills and gambling
losses. Texas A & M announced they were sending in an audit
team to see where all the research funds were being spent.
That was when Spencer made his big decision. A decision

which turned out to be his big mistake. Spencer stole some active anthrax spores, cultured the spores to produce considerably more, and then sold the anthrax to several individuals. He was not interested in what they intended to use the anthrax for. He only cared that they had the cash to pay him for it. He just assumed, or at least he convinced himself that all the buyers planned to use it in their research. It wasn't long before one of his buyers was an undercover FBI agent. Spencer was arrested, tried, and convicted of crimes against the United States government. He lost his wife, his job, his reputation, and five years of his life. One year in a state prison while he worked with the FBI, and four in a federal penitentiary serving hard time. He was very fortunate it was only five years. He could have been charged with treason, but Spencer was very cooperative in supplying the names of everyone to whom he sold the anthrax. His Prion research had also proved to be very beneficial, so the government was very lenient, though his research was not completed. However, now Spencer wasn't allowed to go near a university or a research facility. Since he had been released to the halfway house in Dallas, Spencer had been working as a law researcher for a free law clinic at a local mall. He had spent a lot of his time in prison studying law, and now was helping out the attorney who used to come to the prison and give the prisoners advice. Spencer was very smart and the attorney recognized his value.

Spencer was still sweating when he got back to the small storefront law office located in a strip mall on the south side of Dallas. It wasn't a very good area, but it was all the attorney could afford. It also happened to be in an area where a lot of people needed law services, but couldn't really afford to pay much for the service. As he walked to the office his paranoia seemed to grow as he continually turned and looked around for someone, or anyone who might be following him. He saw no one. When he reached the office, the door was locked, which wasn't unusual. The attorney had been in court that morning and had told Spencer he probably wouldn't return until lunchtime, or shortly after. Spencer wasn't concerned. He entered and relocked the door. He always kept the door locked if he was there by himself. As he shut and locked the door, he noticed it seemed darker than normal in the office. Someone had closed the curtains. Spencer became rigid as his body tensed. Something was not right in the office and he knew he was in for some kind of trouble.

"Please turn around slowly and be seated Mr. Tyler." A voice with an Asian accent demanded. "And please make no sudden moves. I would not like to kill you. My name is Minoru."

Spencer slowly turned and sat on the couch usually reserved for waiting clients. When he turned, he saw the small framed Asian man who he knew had been following him. Sprawled across the desk was the attorney. His neck was twisted in a peculiar manner that reminded Spencer of a chicken with a wringed neck. There was no blood, only a lifeless body.

"I'm sorry to say your friend here was not very cooperative," Minoru continued.

Spencer then noticed the body bag on the floor next to the desk. There was undoubtedly a body in the bag. Just then, the door to the inner office opened and another man walked in with what appeared to be several canisters of gasoline and explosives.

"Mr. Tyler, I have a proposition for you. I hope you accept, but if you don't..." Minoru stopped in mid sentence and gestured towards the body collapsed across the desk.

"What is it you want from me?" Spencer asked.

"I offer you the opportunity to go back to the career you know best. We would like you to continue your infectious disease research for us," Minoru calmly explained.

"I see," replied Spencer. "You want me to develop contagious cultures so you can kill off a rival gang or over throw some government by infecting them with bio-germs. Is that it? You expect me to help you do that?"

"That is exactly what we expect, Mr. Tyler," replied Minoru. "Do you have a problem with that," he said as he pointed to the attorney's lifeless body.

"Not at all," Spencer snapped back. "Just wanted to make sure I knew what to expect."

"Indeed, a very wise choice Mr. Tyler," Minoru smiled as he responded.

Spencer knew if he didn't cooperate, he too would end up as dead as the attorney.

"Look," said Spencer. "I'm on parole. If I don't check in daily with my parole officer, the police will be out looking for me. Hell, when they find Bob's body here on the desk they will be all over me. There will be no place I can hide where they won't find me."

"Do not be concerned with that Mr. Tyler," replied Minoru. "I already have a new identity for you. Spencer Tyler is about to cease to exist." The second man opened the body bag that had been lying on the floor next to the desk. "We thought you would agree to work for us, so we have spent considerable time finding someone similar to your build in whose mouth our dentist was able to recreate your dental work. A considerable task to say the least," explained Minoru.

"Do you plan to burn down this office with both bodies inside?" Spencer asked.

"But of course." Minoru responded. "That is why we have gone to so much trouble. Your death, as the death of your attorney friend, will be blamed on one of your anthrax buyers, who you so eagerly gave up to the FBI. We will leave just enough clues to ensure the blame falls their way. We are taking a chance just burning the bodies, but we feel you are not deemed to be of enough value to the FBI to warrant a DNA check on the remains. We are sure the dental identification will be sufficient."

"How do I know you won't kill me when you get what you need from me? Spencer asked.

"You don't know," replied Minoru. "But what choice do you have. I assure you that as long as you cooperate and help our cause, you will be allowed to live a luxurious life. We will have to do some minor facial surgery to help conceal your identity, but that is little to ask for what we'll offer you."

Spencer had to agree. Besides, he always thought his nose needed to be smaller, and he needed a manlier squared jaw line.

"Now we must give you a sedative so you will sleep. When you wake up, your surgery will be complete and you will be living in a tropical paradise."

The second man injected the compliant Spencer with a strong sedative. Within seconds Spencer was unconscious. The two men removed his clothes and placed them on the body they had brought. They placed Spencer in the body bag and carried it out the back door and into the open van, which was pulled close to the doorway to avoid curious eyes. They spray painted a note on the back door that read 'this is the payback you deserve for ruining my life.' They soaked both the bodies with a highly volatile flammable gel, and set the timer for one minute. When the van was two blocks away Minoru heard the muffled explosion. Minoru looked at his partner and smiled as he spoke. "Righteousness will soon be ours my comrade. We are on the path to glory."

His partner only grunted in response. In the distance, they heard the first siren begin to wail.

Chapter Eight

As he did everyday, at least everyday he was in town, Jim spent his lunch either, sitting and staring in amazement at, or walking around the Mall in Washington D.C. Jim found great pleasure in basking in the splendor of the buildings and architecture that was abundant in D.C. Jim had been to several capitols around the world, but to him, none of them compared to the good old USA capitol here in Washington. Paris came close to being as grand, and in reality, probably would have been grander if Paris had been built initially to be the capitol of France. Paris was more of a city that became a capitol. Washington D.C. was built specifically to be a capitol and to impress all those foreign dignitaries with its grandeur. It was purposely designed with long avenues, which had small parks every few blocks. These parks were constructed to serve as staging areas to defend the city from attacking adversaries. These parks now contained monuments to great Americans and foreigners who played important roles in the growth of America. Many of the most important intersections in the city are marked by key buildings, or by major monuments. The city's design, like much of the public art, monuments, and the building construction itself, is symbolic of the power of Washington D.C. radiating from a central source. That is what makes the Mall so incredible. And we owe this incredible visionary design to a Frenchman. When Congress decided it was time for our country to build a capitol, there just weren't a lot of Americans with that kind of architectural and engineering expertise around to do it. George Washington was smart enough to hire Pierre L'Enfant to design the capitol.

L'Enfant was hired to design the capitol out of a large hundred square mile plot of mostly marshland. The land for building Washington D.C. was donated by Virginia and Maryland. L'Enfant was doing a great job fulfilling his vision, when his ego suddenly got the best of him. Construction of the capitol Mall had only just begun, when a prominent businessman's house proved to be in the way of a major avenue in L'Enfant's designed plan. The businessman wouldn't sell the house, and L'Enfant refused to alter his design, so one morning L'Enfant and several workers tore the house down when the businessman was at work. As much as he hated to do so, because L'Enfant was a good friend of his, George Washington had to fire L'Enfant as the architect for the capitol. Needless to say, L'Enfant was devastated at his firing. He asked to be paid for his work but the government only offered him a pittance. At least he felt it was a pittance. So like any disgruntled employee, he took all his plans with him and destroyed them. This was a problem since construction had just begun and there was no other copy of L'Enfant's plans. His two American assistants who had done most of the architectural renderings of L'Enfant's design tried to recreate his plan as best as they could from memory. What they could remember is basically what constitutes the capitol today. Except there have been way too many museums built around the outskirts of the Mall. At least Jim thought that to be the case.

Jim was sitting by the Korean War Veteran's Memorial next to the Lincoln Memorial at the west end of the Mall. It was his favorite monument to the soldiers who fought our wars. It has a group of nineteen larger than life ground soldiers dressed for battle in their rain gear, spread out in a defensive formation crossing a rice paddy, moving towards an American flag. He loved to visit it on rainy dark days. The statues almost came to life under those conditions. It made Jim proud and sad when he visited it.

Jim was watching the tourists taking their pictures when he noticed a man rapidly approaching. The man was large and muscular, though a little out of shape, and walked with a purposeful hurried stride. It was the man's gait that Jim recognized.

"Jimbo, how the hell are you?" Jotty said in greeting.

"The last person to call me that got their ass kicked," replied Jim.

"I kind of remember it as being a draw," Jotty laughed as he responded.

"I guess you're right," said Jim. "I was pretty drunk that night."

"Don't try to blame it on alcohol," said Jotty. "The fact is, I kicked your butt."

They both laughed.

"It's good to see you again Jotty. It's been a long time."

"Too long," replied Jotty rather hesitantly.

"I'm guessing you weren't just passing by and ran into me by chance," said Jim.

"You're right about that," replied Jotty. And I'm not here as an old buddy just making a social call either. I stopped by your office. Your secretary told me you always spend your lunch hour at the Mall. Next time tell her what end of the Mall you plan to visit."

"I tend to move around a lot to keep it fresh and exciting. I think this is one of the most beautiful places in the whole world." Jim became silent as he looked around reverently. "What is it you came to see me about Jotty?"

"It's about an old friend of yours. Spencer Tyler,"

"More like an old acquaintance than a friend. An old dead acquaintance if I'm not mistaken. Didn't I read he was killed by one of the anthrax buyers he turned in to lighten his prison sentence?" questioned Jim.

"That's what the papers said," replied Jotty.

"By your response, I'm guessing that's not what happened. What…, did the FBI fake his death so they could use him as a covert agent? Did you lose him? Did he bail out on you guys, or something?"

"Fake death, yes. By the FBI, no. Someone went to a lot of trouble to make us believe Spencer was killed along with the attorney he worked for. It was the body of the attorney, but the other body wasn't Spencer's." Jotty continued, "Two bodies were found severely burned in the ashes of the fire. The dental records for Spencer matched one of the bodies exactly. Only after we became suspicious did our forensics people notice all the dental work in the burned body was recent."

"What made you suspicious?" asked Jim.

"Nothing at first. It was cut and dry. From those dental records, we were sure it was Spencer. No one claimed his remains, so they were sent here to Washington. The remains were used in the graduate school forensics lab at Georgetown for the students to practice obtaining DNA readings from charred remains. None of the results the students came up with matched the ones on file for Spencer Tyler. That's when we got suspicious and looked into things a little deeper."

"And…?" Jim prodded Jotty to continue.

"And that's when we discovered the dental work was recent and the whole thing was a setup. We fell for it, hook, line, and sinker." Jotty said.

"And…?" Jim kept pushing for more information.

"And then we started putting two and two together and realized there was a lot more going on than we knew…, and decided we needed your expertise and help." Jotty humbly replied.

"By help, does that mean I get to go back into the field?" Jim asked excitedly.

"Regretfully, yes," Jotty smiled as he said it. "You will be on loan from the USDA and working for the FBI, with me."

Jim was thrilled to be going back into the field. Especially working with the FBI. He had worked for the FBI on several occasions, but usually just in an advisory capacity. That was until he met Jotty. Jotty was as gung-ho as Jim was. He also loved a good fight as much as Jim did. They first met in a bar in Texas where Jotty was working undercover trying to get close to some members of a paramilitary white supremacist group. Somehow Jotty's cover was blown and he was trying to fend off five of the extremists who meant to do him some serious harm, if not kill him. Jim, always up for a good fight, jumped in just to make it a fairer fight. All he managed to do was piss off Jotty, who was holding his own against the five extremists. After the two of them pounded the extremists into the floor, they went after each other. They had both been drinking more than any human should. It was quite a show for the rest of the bar patrons. After about ten minutes they decided to call it a draw. They ended up sleeping it off in jail that night in Stamford, Texas. They were pulled over on their way up Highway 277 heading to Jim's house. Fortunately for both of them, the trooper who pulled them over was a friend of Jim's who knew they just needed a safe place to sleep it off. The extremists all ended up in a hospital in Abilene.

That next day Jotty told Jim about the white supremacist group and their plans to build bombs to blow up several churches throughout Texas. Jotty told him of a conversation he overheard about the extremist's plans to steal farm chemicals to make the bombs. All Jotty knew, was they were planning on stealing the chemicals somewhere in the Rolling Plains area. That is why he had followed them to that bar in Abilene.

"Well one thing for sure," said Jim, "they sure were in no condition to steal anything last night."

Jotty laughed as he responded, "It's a good thing too, 'cause we were in no condition to try to stop them."

"Yeah, but we did manage to delay them. Now we can get some more help and really put to an end to their plans." Jim added.

"What do you mean we? This is FBI business." Jotty said seriously.

"What…, you have five hundred FBI agents to stake out the hundreds of farms in the six counties within a hundred miles of here? And then you might catch them only if you get lucky. Or, do you plan to try to follow them. Hell. It's so flat out here they could see anyone following them for ten miles. You can't use aircraft. They could see that from twenty miles away. No, you need me. You need me because I know where they will try to steal the chemicals." Jim said smugly.

"Is that so," responded Jotty. "Just how do you know that?"

"I know, because it is my job to know where those chemicals are. I am the one who helps these farmers figure out just how much fertilizer they will need each season. I know how much they have used, and I know how much they have on hand. Besides I also know those strangers were asking around at the co-op as to which farms just made major fertilizer purchases. It seems your agents need to be a bit more effective in their research." Jim smiled at Jotty.

"You son of a bitch," Jotty responded. "How many farms do we need to stake out?"

"How many men do you have?" Jim countered.

"Seven including me," answered Jotty.

"Then we can only watch four farms, using two men at each farm," replied Jim.

"I said there were only seven of us," Jotty was smiling.

"You mean eight of us, partner." Jim smiled as he pulled on the brim of his Stetson.

"Actually partner, we know more than you think. We have a satellite positioned over this area that gives us real time information about what our extremists are up to." Jotty said in a cocky voice.

"Remember what I said, though. They will see you coming from miles away. We are going to have to be waiting at the farm to catch them in the act. Sure, your satellite may help you track them after the fact, if you can recognize which one of those thousand trucks is carrying your chemicals. No, we need to catch them in the act," Jim concluded.

Jotty knew Jim was right. They did need to be lying in wait for the extremists. That was the only way they could be guaranteed to catch them in the act. Jotty listened as Jim pointed out the most likely locations for the theft. Jotty contacted his agents and gave them their instructions. They would work in pairs staking out the most likely targets. They all knew to come running when given the signal that the extremists were about to be taken down. It was risky, just having two agents at each farm, but you work with what you got, and they had only eight men to cover a lot of area. Jim would be partnered with Jotty. They also took the farm that was most likely to be hit.

It all went down just as Jim expected it would. Around midnight, Jotty and Jim watched as the two vans drove down the dirt road through the freshly planted fields to the fertilizer storage tanks located in the center of the fields. Three men jumped out of each van. One carried a portable pump to siphon fertilizer from the liquid tanks while two others carried containers for the liquid. The three others were grabbing the bags of Ammonium Nitrate pellets. Five of the six were still bandaged from their previous encounter with Jotty and Jim.

When all of the extremists had partially loaded the vans Jotty and Jim confronted them. Jotty was pointing a shotgun while Jim had his hands resting on the pearl inlaid bison horn grips of his pistols. It was as though he was taunting the extremists to draw their guns on him. The five who had met the two lawmen before were quick to put up their hands. The sixth one however, grabbed a sawed-off shotgun from the van, and prepared to fire.

"GUN," yelled Jotty.

At that, the rest of the extremists dove to the ground and pulled out their own guns. Jotty could swear he heard a 'Yeehah' come from Jim as he drew his matching six shooters from his holster. Jotty's first blast of his shotgun took out the sixth man holding the shotgun, causing the man's initial shot to go wide to the left of them. Jim's face lit up. He loved a good gunfight. He would have been a 'shootist' had he lived a hundred years ago. To him, it looked as if the bad guys were moving in slow motion. As the five were pulling their guns and diving for cover, Jim managed to shoot the guns out of the hands of three of them. The first two he shot using the pistol in his left hand. The bullets shattered the right hand of

the first and the right wrist of the second extremist. The third
he shot using the gun in his right hand. The bullet from his
pistol seemed to cause the third extremists' gun to explode in
his hand. Pieces of the gun flew in all directions. The fourth
man managed to get off a shot in Jim's general direction. Jim
returned fire with both pistols. The bullet from the gun in his
left hand hit just right of center in the unlucky victim's
forehead, blowing off about one fourth of the man's skull as
it exited. The bullet from the gun in his right hand shattered
the man's upper spine as it exited the center of the man's
neck. Jim didn't take kindly to being shot at! The fifth
extremist threw his gun down and started crying along with
the three others whose hands had been shot. By the time
Jotty turned his shotgun towards the five other men, the gun
battle was over.

"Damn you're fast," Jotty said in amazement. "I've
never seen shooting like that."

Jim just smiled and re-holstered his pistols.

That was how Jotty and Jim had first met. Since that
time Jim had occasionally worked on an advisory basis with
the FBI, but was not given the opportunity to do anymore
field work for them. Up until now.

Jotty had been working on learning as much as
possible about the Red Summit terrorist group. He convinced
his bosses he needed to put together a task force to work on
finding out what the Red Summit was really up to. Especially
after the theft from the USDA warehouse and murders of the
two guards in Los Angeles. He had always wanted to get Jim
on board, but after Jim's shoot-em up performance in Texas,
Jotty's bosses had been reluctant to allow that. They told
Jotty to just use him in an advisory capacity for information
related to stolen BSE contaminants, as well as the possibly

contaminated byproducts stolen in Los Angeles. Jotty wasn't happy, but was about to agree with his boss's wishes, when the Spencer Tyler fiasco came to light. It was just too coincidental that an expert in Prions and other mutated proteins, BSE contamination and infectious contagions, suddenly disappeared in a rather elaborate hoax designed to fool the FBI. Jotty knew he needed an expert like Jim on his team. The FBI's reluctance to use Jim as a field operative was no longer valid. Now it was up to Jim to decide.

"If I come to work for you, I won't be stuck behind some desk or in some research library, will I?" Jim asked Jotty.

"I can't guarantee there won't be some of that," responded Jotty, "but this is a field operation, and I need you with me to try to chase down some very bad people."

"Well hell, let's saddle up and get the hell out of Dodge City," Jim replied.

"You sound like such a hick when you talk with those stupid ass clichés," Jotty scolded with a smile, "but I guess that means you're joining me."

"I guess it does." Jim replied. "I can't wait to get back to Texas."

"Who said anything about Texas, my friend," Jotty was grinning.

"I thought that's where we were heading to look for Spencer. Isn't that what we need to do first?

"We'll get to that in time. That trail has long gone cold, so a couple of weeks won't make a lot of difference." Jotty explained.

"Well just where in tarnation are we going?" Jim prodded.

"We're going to go get the third member of our team," Jotty told Jim. "That is if I can talk her into it."

"Am I mistaken or did I hear you say 'talk HER into it?'" Jim asked.

"You heard right my friend. Now let's get out of here. I've already made arrangements with your boss. He knows the FBI will be borrowing you for a while, so you need to go home right now and pack your saddlebags. It's time for us to mosey on out of here and take a little ride." Jotty was shaking his head in disbelief. "I can't believe I said that. Twenty minutes with you and now I'm talking like a hick."

Jim just smiled as he started thinking about what he might need to pack for the trip and just who exactly was this 'her' Jotty had mentioned.

Chapter Nine

Hiroshi Kurosawa was still troubled by what had occurred the previous year in his kitchen aboard the *Grand Maui*. The famous chef Taka Matsuura was nothing more than a fraud, a fakir, a mediocre chef at best. How could this be? He had trained some of the greatest chefs in the world. He had many of the finest Japanese chefs working in the kitchens of his Aioka Steakhouses through the Far East. Surely, they would have seen Taka was at best an amateur chef. It just didn't make any sense to Hiroshi. He had called his cousin who was a pastry chef at one of the Aioka Steakhouse's in a suburb outside of Tokyo. He explained to his cousin how Taka had made precise and specific requests as to what ingredients and meats he wanted and how these were to be laid in preparation for the cooking demonstration. Hiroshi had already prepared most of the ingredients based on the published recipes of Taka's sauces and specialty dishes. He was not surprised when Taka asked for cinnamon oil and the Dr. Pepper syrup to be included in specific amounts with the ingredients Hiroshi had already prepared. These two ingredients were on none of the recipes Hiroshi had ever seen, but remembered Taka using them when he demonstrated the preparation of the sauce at the culinary academy where Hiroshi had trained. He had to send one of his kitchen helpers to shore to obtain the Dr. Pepper syrup, for none was available on the ship. He prepared them, as Taka requested and placed them precisely as Taka had instructed him to do. When Taka prepared his famous sauce at the demonstration in the ship's main kitchen, he seemed confused as to why the syrup and cinnamon oil were included with the ingredients. Taka just set the two ingredients aside not including them in the sauce. Taka's finished sauce was good, but it was no better than the Taka Sauce one of Hiroshi's assistant chefs was assigned to make on a regular basis. In fact, it was made exactly the same as Taka had made it, and as the recipe said to make it. Hiroshi was confused by Taka's demonstration but was too polite to say anything or question Taka. Nor did he mention it to his assistants. The next day, Hiroshi himself, made the Taka sauce, but included the cinnamon oil and Dr. Pepper syrup in the amounts Taka had specified prior to the demonstration. Hiroshi was astounded by the taste. The two ingredients turned a good steak sauce into an exquisitely fabulous tasting sauce. Why had Taka not included the two ingredients in his demonstration? Was he trying to keep them a secret? Was Taka angry he had to put on the demonstration? Hiroshi needed to find out why Taka had deceived them. That is what prompted Hiroshi to eventually call his cousin.

Hiroshi explained what had transpired aboard the *Grand Maui*. He told him of his initial meeting with Taka, the scheduled demonstration, the conversation regarding preparation for the demonstration, and finally the demonstration itself. He also went into detail of how it seemed like two different Takas. The eloquent but subdued Taka he met at first, and the more aggressive self-centered Taka who performed the demonstration. When Hiroshi read off the list of ingredients Taka had requested for the demonstration, his cousin assured him the cinnamon oil and Dr. Pepper syrup were indeed key ingredients. Hiroshi questioned his cousin as to why they were not listed on the published recipes. His cousin told him, while they were not necessarily secret ingredients, he had been told they were left out of the published version of the sauce recipes to insure the Aioka Steakhouse experience would always delight the patron with the brilliance of the sauce. A taste that could only be experienced when one dined at an 'Aioka's.'

Hiroshi could only assume he for some reason must have offended Taka. That could be the only reason Taka chose not to share with Hiroshi's staff the two ingredients left out of the sauce. Still, Hiroshi didn't understand Taka's reluctance. Before he ended his conversation with his cousin, the cousin commented on something Hiroshi had mentioned. He told Hiroshi that it is funny Hiroshi should say he felt like there had been two different Takas on the ship. One of the tabloid newspapers in Japan was asserting that very same thing. They had been running articles on a monthly basis making all sorts of claims about Taka being different since he had returned from his honeymoon aboard the ship. Taka and Niki were big news these days in Japan. The cousin promised to send Hiroshi a copy of the tabloid right away. Hiroshi thanked his cousin for the information and headed to the ship's library to see if the ship carried the Japanese tabloids.

Chapter Ten

Haruko had watched, and re-watched, and then watched again the video from the police station. She was able to recognize many of the station officers coming and going from the station. She was also able to identify many of the other individuals in the video by comparing them to the visitor sign in log at the front desk. However, there were dozens more that she had no idea who they might be, and no way of ever finding out. She really needed the interior videos, but those had been erased. Haruko had no choice but to give up trying to find out who had accessed her database and this displeased her greatly. Haruko hated to give up on anything.

Haruko had received copies of the surveillance video cameras from both the burglary of the tainted beef in Britain, as well as the theft of the animal byproducts in San Pedro, California. Jotty Joplin had sent her copies of both, along with an invitation to go to dinner the next time they were in the same city. Just as long as it was a Vegan restaurant, thought Haruko. "Whoa!" Haruko said to herself. "What was I just thinking? Did I actually mentally agree to go on a dinner date?" Haruko was surprised by her reaction. It wasn't as if she was asked out to dinner in person and had accepted. It was only a suggestion on a note with the videos from an American FBI agent. Jotty made it no secret he was interested in getting to know Haruko on a personal level. On several previous occasions, when they had met to share information concerning terrorist activities, Jotty had invited her to join him for dinner or for a drink. She had of course always politely refused his invitations. Haruko always refused dinner invitations, or movie invitations, or any invitation as far as that goes. Now for some reason she was questioning herself on why she stayed so aloof and avoided making personal, let alone intimate, friendships with anyone. Her only physical contact with a male in the past year was when she threw her sensei to the ground at her weekly Kung Fu class. Maybe it was time she started dating someone. It was obvious her job was no longer giving her the pleasure she had expected. In fact, it was beginning to suck the life right out of her. She was spending her entire existence sitting in a tiny cubicle, in a tiny room, watching video after video on her tiny computer screen. Or sitting for hours in the Police Agency archives reviewing file after file remotely related to activities possibly attributable to the Red Summit. At least, Haruko thought, the Red Summit is once again attempting to make a name for itself, and giving me something to do.

Haruko's computer notified her she had a new email. It was from Jotty. He was coming to Tokyo with his new partner to share some recent information with Haruko. He wanted to go over the two burglary videos, and show her one of the barbed spikes left as the Red Summit's calling card in the eye of the security guard. Haruko was excited to get to look at the spike, as well as hear the new information Jotty referred to in the email. What bothered her, and that surprised her, was Jotty said in the email he was bringing his new partner. Was Haruko actually feeling a pang of jealousy? She couldn't believe her state of mind could shift so remarkably in such a short time. Did Jotty mean his new work partner, or his new significant other partner? He had invited her out for dinner on the note that came with the videos. Haruko opened the drawer to her desk and began searching for the note. She found it and read it over several times. She tried to figure out when Jotty had written it, and just exactly what he meant by it. She used all of her analytical skills trying to derive some sort of significant meaning from Jotty's note, which in reality, just wasn't there. She finally gave up in frustration. She carefully formulated a response to his email that was rather matter of fact, saying she would pick them up from the airport, or have a driver meet them there to take them to their hotel. Before she sent the response, she added a well-constructed veiled reference that alluded to the dinner invitation. The way it was written would lead you to believe she was accepting the invitation..., maybe. It was really hard to tell what she actually meant by the response. Haruko didn't really know what she meant by her response either. She had not had these feelings before. After much mental debate, she finally pressed send and her response headed to Jotty.

As expected Jotty couldn't figure out either what the hell Haruko meant by her response. He finally decided she was accepting the dinner invitation. He came to that conclusion because Haruko said she would either pick them up, or have someone pick the two of them up at the airport. On every one of Jotty's other visits to Japan, he had to get to his hotel on his own. Things were indeed looking up.

As Jotty was reading Haruko's email response, so was Minoru. Minoru was back in his room at the Hilton Waikoloa Village. For the past two years he had been monitoring all of Haruko's computer activity. One of his ninja team members had placed a program on Haruko's computer that allowed Minoru to view any and all information that was on the computer monitor. He had implanted the software when he came one day to check to see if the phone lines or the computer terminals in the National Police Agency offices were tapped. He had the correct credentials, so no one questioned his actions. Haruko's supervisor in fact had been very helpful in pointing out the various officers' computer terminals. Taka's terrorist cell was now able to monitor most all of the computers and phone lines in the headquarters of the Counter-terrorism Division of the National Police Agency.

Minoru was becoming more and more concerned about Jotty and Haruko. He knew it was only a matter of time until either Haruko or Jotty identified his eyes as the ones of the lead ninja on both of the videotapes. He needed to slow down their investigation. The easiest way to do that would be to kill them. However, before he could take any action he needed to confer with Taka. After all, Taka was in charge, and he made the final decisions when it came to the activities of the Red Summit. Although, it seemed Niki was becoming quite a leader in her own right. She had shared in designing the master plan the Red Summit was now working towards. History would one-day show, she too was one of the primary visionaries responsible for altering world power.

Minoru did speak with Taka and it was decided two or three local Tokyo Red Summit activists should kill Jotty and his partner. Haruko was to be spared at this time. There was still much information Taka and the Red Summit stood to learn by continuing to monitor Haruko's computer. They were not yet willing to jeopardize that source of information. Minoru at first requested he be allowed to go to Japan to insure Jotty was properly removed, but Taka said the need for Minoru to stay in Hawaii at this time was far greater. Minoru of course agreed with Taka's decision. From Jotty's email to Haruko, Minoru had the arrival time of Jotty's flight and the name of the hotel. He and Taka devised their plan and contacted the Tokyo terrorist cell to relay their instructions.

Haruko decided she would pick up Jotty and his partner at the airport herself. She took the subway back to her house during lunch and changed out of her daily generic drab business suit, and replaced it with a conservative but charming blouse and long skirt. She drove her own car back to the office. When she returned to work from her lunch break, her new attire turned the heads of all her coworkers. None of them could ever recall seeing Haruko in anything but her drab business suits. Several of her fellow officers were taken aback by her stunning figure, which the business suits had hidden so effectively. Haruko's embarrassment was evident as she strode quickly through the office failing to make eye contact with anyone. As she sat back down at her desk the red flush on her cheeks began to diminish. She calmly began viewing the videotapes of the two break-ins and murders Jotty had sent her. As hard as she tried, she could not seem to concentrate on what she was supposed to be looking at on the videos.

Haruko was not accustomed to driving her car in and around the Tokyo area. She like most of the population relied on the subway system. She typed the name of a mapping website onto her computer and printed out driving directions from her office to the airport and then to the hotel. Just for fun she also had the computer print out directions to a Vegan restaurant close to Jotty's hotel. She still had a couple of hours until she needed to leave to pick them up, so once again she tried to view and analyze the videos.

Minoru had been hoping to find out if Haruko would be the one picking up Jotty and his partner at the airport or if she would assign someone the task. It seemed she had decided to do the driving when she requested the directions from the mapping web site. Minoru called the cell members in Tokyo to let them know Haruko would be going to the airport and advised them on how to handle her. Haruko was not to be harmed. They assured Minoru she would never make it to the airport and no harm would befall her. Minoru hoped they were correct.

When it was time to leave to pick up Jotty, Haruko notified her bosses via email of her plans. She didn't wait for a response, for she expected no response. She was just in the habit of letting them know where she was when she left the station during the day. When she went into the garage to get into her car, she discovered her front tire was flat. It would take at least an hour for a service truck to come change it, and she was by no means dressed to change it herself. She called the motor pool to request an agency car, but none were available. When she told the dispatcher about her car, he said he would send one the motor pool mechanics right over and change the tire for her. He told her he would have her up and running in less than fifteen minutes. Haruko was pleased and thanked him for his help. She would be late picking up Jotty, but not too late.

When Jotty and Jim arrived in Tokyo it took a few minutes for them to go through customs. Both Jotty and Jim received special government clearance and were allowed to bring their guns into the country, but they had to be checked by the customs authorities first. Jim had left his six-shooters locked in his safe with his other guns back in Washington D.C. He brought with him a Walther PPK. It was just like the gun James Bond always carried. Jim liked to think of himself as a kind of secret agent now that he was working for the FBI. The Walther PPK helped him with that fantasy.

As Jotty and Jim left the customs office, two National Police Agency officers met them. The officers were rather taken aback when they saw Jim's six-foot five-inch frame come walking out the door behind Jotty.

"Welcome to Tokyo Mr. Joplin." The shorter of the two officers said in greeting as he bowed. "We were sent by

Investigator Ozawa to take you and your friend to your hotel."

Jotty had hoped Haruko herself would be picking up him and Jim. He figured he had just read too much into her email.

"This is Mr. Rikey my associate," Jotty responded.

"Nice to meet you boys," said Jim as he shook both their hands. He noticed both men had sweaty palms and seemed a little nervous. But then a lot of short men got a little nervous when they stood next to Jim.

"I see you already have your luggage, so if you would kindly follow us, the car is this way." Both police officers turned and headed out the door.

"Not the friendliest guys in the world," Jim said to Jotty before they went out the door behind the two officers.

Jotty nodded in agreement.

When they got outside, the officers took Jim and Jotty's luggage and placed it in the trunk of their car. The bags were not necessarily large, but they still had difficulty making the bags fit in the car's small trunk. The two officers both jumped in the front seat of the tiny Toyota, leaving the back seat for the two Americans to try to fold their large bodies into. Needless to say, it was not a very comfortable ride to the hotel.

When they reached the hotel, which the officers said was fortunately just a short twenty-minute drive away, Jim and Jotty were both beginning to have muscle cramps from the awkward positions they were forced to sit in while riding in the backseat. This time the two officers grabbed the luggage and said they would be happy to carry it to the hotel room for them. Jim and Jotty were in no condition to disagree with that offer. As they entered the hotel room someone slammed the door shut behind them. When Jim and Jotty turned to see what was going on, the two officers who had carried in their luggage now stood behind them smiling as they locked the hotel room door. In front of them was a man dressed in a dark suit holding a small semi-automatic pistol.

"Don't move or you are both dead men," said the man in the suit. "Please allow my colleagues to remove your weapons."

Both the Americans turned around and saw the two National Police Agency officers were now also holding guns on them. They had no choice but to allow the Japanese Police officers to take their guns.

"Let me guess," said Jotty. "Somehow, I offended Haruko, and she sent you guys to teach me a lesson."

This brought a smile to the face of the man in the suit.

"No Mr. Joplin," the man spoke, "You know that of course we are not members of the National Police Agency. We are here to kill you and your friend."

Jim now spoke, "I don't think I like the sound of that Jotty. Just what kind of friends do you have here in Japan? Or actually, what kind of enemies?"

Jotty saw Jim was positioning himself to try and take out the two officers standing behind them. Before he could make a move, the door to the room opened and a cleaning maid entered.

The two officers behind Jim and Jotty stepped in close and shoved the barrels of their guns into the backs of the two Americans. The man in the suit tried to conceal his gun in the pocket of his suit coat.

"Not now woman," the man in the suit scolded. "Leave this room immediately."

"I'm so sorry sir, I should have knocked first. They told me the room was empty and needed to be cleaned," the maid responded.

"Well it doesn't. Please leave now!" The suited man insisted.

As the maid turned to leave, she made eye contact with Jotty. It was Haruko dressed in a maid's uniform. Jotty in turn looked at Jim. In a flash, the maid struck the suited man hard in the throat while at the same time dislodging his hand from the gun. When she made her move, Jotty and Jim made theirs. The two officers had made their first huge mistake when they moved up close to Jim and Jotty. Their second mistake was being distracted by the maid coming into the room. As Haruko collapsed the suited man's larynx, Jim and Jotty broke the arms of the two fake police officers causing their guns to fall harmlessly to the floor. Instantly, real National Police Agency officers flooded into the hotel room taking the two men into custody. They would prove to be nothing more than hired assassins, and knew nothing of the suited man who had hired them. They were members of a local gang who were paid to just do a job and nothing more. Unfortunately, the suited man died before he could be questioned.

Jotty wanted to grab Haruko and give her a hug for saving their lives, but Haruko was all business. She had taken charge of the crime scene and was barking out orders to the swarm of officers.

Jim was staring at Haruko, as she took control of the situation. Jotty didn't care for the way Jim seemed to be leering at Haruko.

"I've always had this great fantasy about hotel maids...," Jim was starting to say to Jotty when Jotty quickly cut in.

"You're talking about my future wife," Jotty responded.

"In your dreams maybe," Jim replied, and they both laughed. Still, Jotty felt a little uneasy at the way Jim was checking out Haruko.

Jotty turned to Haruko and asked, "How did you know we needed help?"

"When I was leaving police headquarters to pick you up, someone had flattened one of my tires. Normally it would have taken at least an hour to get it changed or repaired, but luckily the motor pool had a mechanic immediately available, so I was out of there in less than fifteen minutes. I saw you in a car driving away from the airport terminal as I was driving up. I didn't recognize the car as an agency car, nor did the two men in the Police Agency uniforms look familiar. I made some calls as I followed you to the hotel. The car was stolen and some uniforms had also been reported stolen earlier this week. It didn't take too much to figure out something was going on. I called for backup and quickly decided how to proceed," Haruko responded.

Jim spoke up, "Had nothing been going on in here, you would have sure as hell made a good impression on me, coming through that door unannounced, and dressed like that."

Haruko began to blush and turned away. Jotty was glaring at Jim.

Jotty and Jim were moved to a suite on another floor of the hotel while the investigation continued in their original room. Haruko told Jotty she would send a car for the two of them in the morning. They were to meet at her office at 8:00 a.m. She then excused herself to return to the crime scene. Jotty wanted to speak with her more but felt awkward in front of Jim. Haruko did not seem to notice this as she quickly exited the suite.

Haruko had completely forgotten about the jealous feelings she was having imagining who Jotty's new partner was. She had also completely forgotten about going out to dinner. She did pick up on the fact Jotty did not like the look Jim was giving her. Actually, she thought Jim was rather handsome.

Haruko was looking forward to their meeting in the morning. She also was very troubled. Somehow, someone was aware Jotty and Jim had come to see her about the Red Summit, and was concerned enough about their visit to try and kill them. She spent the evening trying to find out who the man in the suit was. It turned out he was a known terrorist who was believed to be operating a terrorist cell in Indonesia. There was nothing that previously connected him to any of the Red Summit suspected crimes or activities. When she received his file, she did read that it was rumored he and Aioka may have been together in a training camp in Lebanon, but there was no solid evidence to prove that fact.

When Haruko finally left work that night, she stopped by a market near the police headquarters to pick up some tofu. As she was waiting in line to pay for it, she noticed the pictures and headline of one of the Japanese tabloids. It showed a recent picture of Taka Matsuura next to an older picture of him. The headline was said, "Is this the real Taka?" She bought the paper and sat in her car to read the article. The article went on to question if the Taka in the photo was the same Taka who built a Japanese culinary industry. It also questioned why he was selling off his businesses and holdings and moving out of Japan with his wife Niki. The article speculated Taka was moving to Hawaii where he had a contract to continue to supply the Hawaiian island Sizzle Burger restaurants with ground beef. It was also rumored Taka was building a new Aioka's in Hawaii and opening other unspecified businesses on the big island of Hawaii. The article fascinated Haruko. The author was speculating on some of the very same beliefs Haruko held. That was when it suddenly dawned on her. The old photo of Taka on the cover of the tabloid was a photo only available from her Red Summit database file. It had been taken by an undercover police officer posing as a tourist. Haruko had assigned him the task when she thought Aioka was still alive and hiding out at Taka's cattle ranch in Northern Japan. The only way the author could have obtained a copy of that photograph, was by accessing her personal database. Haruko was ecstatic. She believed she had solved a baffling mystery that had been haunting her. She would go find the author first thing in the morning. Then she remembered she was to meet Jotty and Jim at 8:00 a.m. The tabloid writer would have to wait till the afternoon she decided. There was much she wanted to learn from Jotty and Jim as well.

Haruko was once again all business. The romantic thoughts she had experienced the previous days had been pushed to the back of her mind. Her social life would have to wait.

Chapter Eleven

s Taka had planned, the cattle ranch, feedlot, and slaughterhouse were all up and running in a matter of months. Taka had transferred many of the calves from his Japan ranch to his new Paleaka Ranch facility. There were stringent import inspections, but the calves all passed with no trouble. He had a little more difficulty getting some of his older breeding cattle shipped over, but they too, eventually cleared custom inspections. Preparing for his new venture, Taka had purchased his own cattle transport ship and used it to ship over all the building materials needed for refurbishing the Paleaka facilities as well as the necessary equipment to operate the businesses. Taka had a 'state of the art' laboratory built into the side of a hill near the middle of the ranch. It was in an area that was hidden from the view of any neighboring ranches, roads, or hillsides. It was cut deep into the ancient lava. Several floors of the laboratory were built hidden underground and required special authorization to gain access. In the process of cutting away the lava to build the lab, several lava tubes were discovered that led to underwater entrances far out in the Maui channel between the big island and the island of Maui to the north. It was only a few miles between the two islands, but no boats ferried passengers between them. Few pleasure boats dared to cruise the channel as well. An extremely powerful and swift current required even the most powerful boats to strain their engines and waste their fuel supply while attempting the channel crossing. Consequently, it was more economical to fly from one island to the other. It was this strong current that kept scuba divers out of the area and allowed these lava tube tunnels to go undiscovered. The tunnels into the water were of little use to Taka. He did however, have a house built for him in an area adjacent to the ranch, upwind and far from the laboratory and feedlot operation. It was built over one of the ancient lava tubes, and allowed Taka access, via a hidden entrance, to the secured section of the laboratory.

The construction workers hired to build the laboratory and refurbish the other ranch buildings were all brought in from Japan to do the work. They were housed on the ranch and worked around the clock until the construction was completed. As soon as they finished their part of the construction project, they were immediately shipped back to Japan. Taka managed to keep the lava tubes a secret along with the lower floors of the laboratory. Only Taka, Minoru, and a few Japanese laborers who built the secret entrances into the tunnel knew of its existence. Minoru made sure the few laborers who did know of the secret entrances were not around long enough in Japan to tell anyone about them. Taka only allowed the local building inspector access to the ranch after portions of the construction were completed and then carefully camouflaged.

The ranch hands, as well as the feedlot and slaughterhouse workers, were also Japanese. No local Hawaiian residents were hired to work at the Paleaka Ranch. This did not please the local rancher's association. They were very upset David Paleaka went behind their backs and allowed a Japanese company to get control of such a large amount of acreage. The fact no local paniolos, or Hawaiian cowboys, were hired to work on the ranch didn't sit well with the other ranch owners and or other local workers as well. The locals tried various means to keep the number of Japanese workers allowed to come to the island and work at the ranch to a minimum by pressing the local government for stringent work visa regulations. They also pressured the local inspectors to nit-pick when they were making the building inspections and later the same was true during the USDA and health inspections of the ranch feedlot and packinghouse. Even with all their effort, it failed to slow down Taka's progress of rebuilding and running the Paleaka Ranch. There already seemed to be fewer workers at the ranch than needed to operate the ranch efficiently. At least that was the feeling among the other big ranch owners. The other owners also didn't know how the Paleaka Ranch was going to survive. It was much too expensive to run a feedlot operation. All the feed for the cattle had to be shipped in. That just made no sense. And where were they going to graze all those feeder cattle? The ranch was large enough to allow several thousand feeder cattle to graze, but were they then going to be shipping some of those feeder cattle away to a feedlot on the mainland? Shipping cattle of that size and weight just made no economic sense whatsoever. As far as the slaughterhouse went, there was just not enough demand for beef on the islands to support a packing house of that size. Sure, Taka did have a contract with Sizzle Burger to supply them with ground beef, but what about the rest of the cow? Taka would be hard pressed to get the local resorts to buy his steaks. Even with his great reputation as a culinary master chef. The resorts could buy it and have it shipped in from packinghouses in the Midwest and still get it cheaper than Taka could afford to sell it. At least that was the general thinking among the local ranchers.

Despite all of the animosity towards what was happening at the Paleaka Ranch, David Paleaka was not ostracized by the community. Many of the ranch owners were pretty upset with David when he sold part of the ranch to the Japanese, but they realized they were partially to blame. They all knew of David's financial troubles. They also knew about his drug and alcohol problems. Many of them had taken advantage of David in the past, because of these problems. Now that David seemed to be in the money, many of them still took advantage of him by drinking his liquor and doing his cocaine.

The locals also spent a lot of time asking David questions about just exactly what was going on up at the ranch. David still lived in the main house on the ranch. Minoru saw to it David was kept away from the construction of the laboratory and any other happenings Taka wanted kept secret. Minoru would arrange for a room at the Hilton or the Marriott in Waikoloa Village for David to stay in when the ranch was off limits. David never seemed to mind because Minoru made sure he always had company to keep him happy. Both female company and chemical company.

David knew very little of what was going on at the ranch. He really didn't care, just as long as they kept him supplied in drugs and money. Some of his buddies suggested they were importing or making drugs at the ranch. David told his friends not to be so stupid in thinking along those lines, but it did get him thinking maybe that just was what was happening at the ranch. David decided he needed to check things out a little closer.

That night he went back to the ranch with a couple of buddies. Minoru didn't like it when David brought friends to the ranch, but he couldn't forbid him from bringing them. He did instruct David that several of the buildings were off limits to visitors because of health and safety regulations. The laboratory was even off limits to David. Minoru told him it was because of the sensitive research that took place inside. David was allowed to inspect the building during and after construction, but even he did not know about the underground levels to the lab or the lava tube tunnels.

That night David's buddies talked him into taking them on a tour of the ranch. He knew Minoru forbade such things, but he was too high to really think clearly. Which was how David was most of the time these days. He and his buddies jumped into David's jeep and drove around the feedlot and the packinghouse. When they headed towards the laboratory, another jeep approached and ran David's jeep off the road and into the ditch. Four Japanese men dressed in black and carrying assault rifles jumped from the other jeep and pulled David and his friends from their jeep. They held the three of them at gunpoint until Minoru was summoned and arrived a few minutes later. David and his buddies were very scared. David started to get angry but Minoru calmed him down by explaining to him in a very paternal tone of voice that he should have known better than to drive around the ranch at night. He told David because of threats from competitors and terrorists, they needed to be vigilant in protecting the ranch businesses. That was why the armed guards were necessary. After Minoru's scolding, David and his two companions seemed to better understand what had happened and that it was just a big misunderstanding. At least that was what they were supposed to believe. Minoru drove David and his friends back to the main house. He came inside with them and brought out a large bag of the Peruvian flake cocaine. Within a few minutes several women arrived to take David's and his friend's minds off of what had just occurred. As usual, the women and the drugs did the trick.

One non-Japanese worker who was allowed on the ranch was Spencer Tyler, or as he was now known, Karl Spencer. Spencer arrived on the big island by private jet and was taken directly to the laboratory at the ranch. There were medical facilities in the laboratory as well as isolation and recovery rooms. Spencer recovered from his plastic surgery in one of those rooms. He spent his first six weeks on Hawaii inside the laboratory healing from his surgeries and memorizing facts about his fictitious new persona. He believed he was still in a facility in the Dallas area up until the day he was first allowed to leave the laboratory. Spencer was brought to Hawaii by Taka because of his expertise in bovine diseases, as well as for his Prion research at Texas A & M. Prions are believed to be the primary cause of mad cow disease and several related human versions of the disease such as Creutzfeldt-Jakob disease. It was originally thought such diseases were bacteria based or the result of a virus. Prions are proteins, which for a number of reasons mutate and begin to replicate in the brain, causing the brain to be overwhelmed by these mutant proteins. This disease is not a virus or bacteria and does not metabolize or grow as would a germ. Therefore, these Prions do not infect the brain but affect the brain of any animal that ingests a mutant Prion. These Prions replicate not reproduce. These Prions can also be transmitted from cow to cow or cow to human, if Prion affected tissue is consumed by another animal or human. These Prions are only found in the brain, spinal cord, and other nervous-system tissue. This meant most fleshy parts of the cow were safe for humans to eat. It was only when the potentially affected tissues were possibly mixed as filler in ground beef that humans needed to be concerned. Or the remote chance affected tissues may have been nicked by the knife when the fleshy meat was cut from the cow. Cooking the meat cannot destroy Prions. The scary part is the symptoms will not appear in humans for seven to ten years, and when they do, there is no cure. The proliferation of mad cow disease that was now becoming more prevalent throughout the world could be directly attributed to the feedlots and slaughterhouses. Until recently the brains and other possibly affected tissues of cattle were ground up, mixed with an array of vitamins and other protein-based products, and fed to other feedlot cattle as part of their ruminant feed mixtures. Ruminant just means the feed is meant to be chewed by a cud-chewing mammal. Which in turn means it goes into one stomach and is regurgitated back into the mouth for re-chewing. Cattle now starting to show symptoms of the disease were affected several years ago before the feedlots started changing their feed mixtures. Cattle do not show symptoms of the disease for at least four years after initially affected, and they become affected as soon as they ingest the tainted ruminant feed mixture or a protein randomly mutates in their brain.

Spencer theorized these bovine-based diseases, specifically mad cow, could also be transmitted by absorption through the skin from products contaminated by Prion affected tissue. This was the theory he was attempting to prove when his research was interrupted and he was arrested and sent to federal prison. Now Taka was offering him the opportunity to continue his research. Actually, Taka was offering Spencer the chance to live. If he refused to cooperate, he would be killed. Taka had other scientists with similar expertise who he could call upon, but none with a background in the absorption theory. In Taka's grand scheme, Spencer's absorption research would play but a minor part in the Red Summit terrorist plans.

However, that was not the only reason Taka needed Spencer. It was Spencer's expertise in developing the equipment for the weaponization of anthrax Taka valued the most, but its importance, he tended to downplay for now. The anthrax would play a key part in Taka's terrorist plans at a future time. Presently, he had another plan in motion he needed to follow through.

Chapter Twelve

Byron Downing had worked as a reporter for the British Broadcasting Corporation for ten years. He was their on-camera reporter stationed in Japan. What wasn't known about Byron at that time, was he was also writing articles for one of the sleaziest tabloids in all of Britain.

One day his double life caught up to him. Prince Charles had come to Japan on official British business. He was there to sign some environmental pledge of cooperation. Not a real newsworthy visit. Byron borrowed some of the photos taken by the BBC photographer, doctored them up a little, and submitted to the tabloid editor a rather provocative article on the Prince concerning his sexual preferences, with accompanying photos, that of course were faked. The tabloid published the article, and it caused quite a scandal in Britain. The Royal Family pushed the legal system to its limits in order to "ferret out whoever was responsible for such damning fallacious accusations," as the Royal spokesman stated to the media. As much as the tabloid tried to keep the author of the article secret, public pressure forced them to reveal Byron as the author. Investigators were close to discovering his identity anyway, so the tabloid felt it could weather the storm better by giving him up before the government investigators discovered Byron on their own. Needless to say, Byron lost his job as a writer for the tabloid, as well as losing his career with the BBC.

After the scandal, Byron thought it best if he remained in Japan. There were rumors his health might fail if he returned to Britain. Byron had lived for several years in Japan.

He knew the country well and spoke fluent Japanese. He could also write in Japanese as easily as he could write in English. During his stay in Japan he had made several good friends and business acquaintances. Through one of his acquaintances he was able to land a job as a writer for one of the larger Japanese tabloids whose offices were located in Tokyo. The only stipulation was he needed to write under a Japanese 'nom de plume'. The tabloid felt its readers would be more apt to respond to a Japanese writer rather than to a British one. Especially a British writer who was known to have fabricated many a story in the past.

Byron's identity was a well-kept secret at the tabloid. Only the publisher, his editor, and the lead editor knew the writer known as Ono Saito was in reality Byron Downing. This was very fortunate for Byron, because Taka had instructed Minoru to put an end to the writer of all the tabloid articles that were casting doubt over Taka's identity. Fortunately for Taka, although Byron somehow seemed to make remarkably accurate speculations about Taka not being whom he used to be, Byron also wrote wild fanciful articles about how aliens had abducted the real Taka and left an android in his place. Taka found many of the articles to be humorous, but too many of them were too insightful, and might lead to other people asking questions. That is why Taka had ordered Minoru to kill Ono. Fortunately for Byron, no one seemed to know who Ono was, or where to find him. His articles for the tabloid were emailed or mailed to the editor. Minoru had tried, but was so far unable to track where the emails originated. He tried to find out where Ono's checks were sent, but discovered Ono's paychecks were directly deposited into a numbered account at an offshore bank in the Bahamas. One of Minoru's agents had spent several weeks courting and dating a rather homely secretary in the tabloid office just to get that little bit of information. Minoru however, would not give up on trying to discover Ono's identity, and in fact, had one of his agents working on it constantly.

Hiroshi found several issues of the Japanese tabloid in the ship's library. Almost every issue contained an article about Taka Matsuura. Hiroshi found the articles to be both amusing and supportive of his own suspicions regarding Taka. One of the articles talked about how changed Taka was after marrying Niki. The author of the article, Ono Saito, speculated Niki had brainwashed Taka, by turning him into a kind of sex slave. This made Hiroshi smile. Several of the other articles explored a host of bizarre speculations, ranging from Taka and Niki being abducted by aliens, to Niki's plan to take over the Taka Matsuura business enterprises and donate all his cattle to the PETA organization. PETA is an acronym for the organization, People for the Ethical Treatment of Animals. Hiroshi read all of the articles concerning Taka. He also read several of the other stories in the tabloid. Then he saw an advertisement offering payment for information that could be used and published by the tabloid. Hiroshi decided he would contact this Ono and explain to him Taka's strange behavior at the cooking demonstration as well as Hiroshi's opinion that it was not the same Taka who started the cruise as the Taka who finished the cruise. Hiroshi took two of the pictures he had gotten from the ship's photographer and headed to one of the library computer terminals to compose his letter to this Ono person. Hiroshi knew the tabloid would pay him well for his information. Hiroshi sent the email to the address given in the tabloid advertisement. In the email, he briefly explained about the cooking demonstration and about the several photos that seemed to show two different Takas. He invited this Ono person to come view the photographs and to speak with him further about his belief. Hiroshi completed his email and pushed send. As he relaxed back into his chair, a smile came to his face as he dreamed of the large sum of money the tabloid would have to pay him for his story.

Minoru knew his luck was beginning to change. His Tokyo agent in charge of finding Ono Saito had good news. The secretary from the tabloid, who he had been dating to gain information, had come up with some important news. It seemed a chef on the ship the *Grand Maui*, had written to the tabloid requesting Ono Saito to contact him for some valuable information he had concerning Taka Matsuura. The chef claimed to have photographic proof there were indeed two different Takas. He also told how the fake Taka inadvertently revealed himself to Hiroshi during the cooking demonstration. The chef wanted to find out how much the tabloid was willing to pay for the photos and his story. The secretary had forwarded the email to the editor and he in turn had sent it to Ono. She was yet to hear what Ono's response to the offer would be, but she guessed Ono himself would be flying to Hawaii to meet with the chef. This was indeed good news for Minoru. Soon he would be able to take care of what were now two loose ends.

Chapter Thirteen

Niki was spending most of her time in Los Angeles modeling and promoting her new cosmetics line in the United States. The cosmetics business had been her idea. Taka thought it was brilliant and made it part of his master plan of conquering the American demon. It wasn't so much Niki wanted to overthrow America like Taka and his Islamic terrorist friends, but she felt she needed to get back at the Americans and the Europeans for exploiting her body in the 'geisha' house when she was so young. She had been no more than thirteen when her father sent her away to Kyoto to be a prostitute. At least that was how she was made to feel, and in fact, that was how it turned out. She hated her father for sending her away. I guess it was her father she saw in the faces of most all men, and that made her want to see them dead or punished. She would punish them. When her father sent her to Kyoto, she had been in love with Aioka. Aioka was a rebel and a leader. He had a vision for change in Japan. He wanted to stop what he considered the Americanization of Japan. That is why he helped found the Red Summit. It would be the organization that would once again make Japan the world leader it should be, and should have always been. Niki believed in Aioka and was a loyal supporter at his demonstrations and protests in those early days. It wasn't long before they were lovers. Her father found out about her affair with the older Aioka and forbade her from seeing him or attending the protest rallies. Several times she disobeyed her father and went to Aioka. Her father told her if she was going to act like a whore, he was going to send her to Kyoto to be trained as a whore. If

110

she refused to go, he threatened, he would have Aioka arrested and sent to jail for several years. Niki was devastated, but had no choice but to go to Kyoto. She never forgave her father. Aioka did manage to go to Kyoto several times to see Niki. He promised her one day soon he would get her out of Kyoto and they would be together. That was right before the bombing of the bullet train. When that occurred Aioka had to leave Japan. Aioka went to Lebanon where he trained terrorists for Islamic extremist organizations. One of his trainees was a German businessman who happened to own a modeling agency. He convinced the businessman to go to Japan and bring Niki to Lebanon via Germany. Aioka told him it was necessary to help fulfill a plan Aioka and Osama had devised. The German agreed and brought Niki to the terrorist camp where she too was trained in both the skills needed by a terrorist, as well as educated in the philosophy of terrorism. Niki was an excellent student and proved to be much more of an asset than Aioka could have imagined. Her beauty, though not approved of by the Islamic terrorists, was determined to be important in promoting her role as a terrorist courier. She began modeling for the German businessman's agency and was soon on her way to becoming a world class model. This allowed her the opportunity to move around the world serving as a courier, passing on instructions to various terrorist cells around the world undetected. It all almost ended when Aioka was reported killed in the Israeli air raid on the terrorist training camp. For days Niki was heartbroken over the death of Aioka. Then she learned from the German, Aioka was alive and the raid was a set up to make it appear Aioka was killed. There was just too much international pressure to capture or kill Aioka. His death was faked to allow him the freedom to move forward on his new plan. Aioka had some minor plastic surgery to disguise his appearance and he too moved to Germany where once again he and Niki were lovers. When Niki became a 'Victoria's Secrets' model her fame skyrocketed and it became more difficult for her to serve in her capacity as a courier. It also made it more difficult for Aioka to be with her. Niki had always had her share of admiring fans, but now when Niki went out in public, she was always followed by a contingent of paparazzi along with the hoards of fans. That was when Aioka devised a new plan that Niki would play an important role in.

During his time in the training camps, Aioka had much time to discuss political philosophy with many terrorist cell leaders, including Osama himself. Islam seemed to demand the infidel be dealt with immediately and harshly. The purpose of terrorism was to instill terror in the hearts of all men. To give your life in the battle, and become a martyr in the process, was the highest honor these terrorists could hope for. They wanted the world to change immediately. That was why there were so many Palestinian suicide bombers. They all chose martyrdom. Osama rewarded the families of these martyrs. Aioka never condemned this method of terrorism, and actually trained many of these men for their acts of martyrdom, but did spend much of his time preaching the Japanese philosophy of bringing about change for your progeny. Yes, he did want to stop the Americanization of the world, but he was a realist. He knew it would take time, and he thought he had a plan that would bring about this eventual change, and in the process, fulfill the ultimate goal of terrorism. He wanted all the people of the United States, for years to come, to feel the fear of his terror campaign.

Aioka's terrorist plan came about as a response to his hatred for his grandfather and his grandfather's legacy. His grandfather had started, and his brother Taka had continued his grandfather's legacy of the Americanization of Japan. The Hurley's fast food restaurants were atypical of the worst features of American society. Before long, Japan too would be full of overweight lethargic citizens addicted to fast food and spending all of their time in front of television sets. The women of Japan were now dressing like lowly whores or even worse dressing like men. The values and traditions of Japan were disappearing in the influx of American popular culture. Taka was the epitome of the men leading Japan down this sorry path. Aioka knew he could and would stop it from continuing. He also knew it would take more than the bombing or poisoning of an occasional commuter train to bring about this change. He needed to take his terror campaign to the United States, and with the financial support of Osama, knew he had a plan that would bring fear into the hearts of all Americans.

Niki smiled as the cameras flashed. She was doing a photo shoot for her new cosmetic line. It was about to be released in the United States. It was already highly popular among the young girls all over Japan. How ironic it was that now she chose to exploit her own body to get back at those who had exploited it when she was a child. It had been several days since she had been with Taka. She knew all of their plans were beginning to come together, but she was once again starting to really enjoy this jet setting star treatment life style. Sometimes it made her question her own values. She would soon be returning to Japan to be with Taka. She no longer anticipated her time with Taka as joyfully as she once had. She had heard about the blundered attack in Tokyo on the FBI agent and hoped it wasn't a sign of more difficulties ahead.

"Niki, show us more leg." One of the photographers yelled out.

Niki smiled as she hiked up her skirt. She wondered what her Islamic friends would say if they saw her now.

Chapter Fourteen

"**N**ow just why is it we came here to Japan?" asked Jim.

"Sure as hell not to get killed," responded Jotty. "Somebody knew we were coming and set us up."

"Do you think it was your friend Haruko who set us up?" Jim asked.

"Not a chance in hell," Jotty was quick to respond. "But I think it was somebody who works for the National Police Agency. Who exactly, is what I hope to find out this morning. If I know Haruko, she has been working on that same question all night."

"I sure hope so," Jim replied. "I don't want to have anymore close encounters while we are playing tourist."

"Do you think this has anything to do with the Red Summit?" Jim questioned.

"I think it's got everything to do with the Red Summit," Jotty told him. "Who else would go to all of that trouble to kill us?"

"You got any old jilted girlfriends in town?" Jim laughed.

"I was just about to ask you the same thing," Jotty said. "You got any old enemies living in this part of the world whose ass you might have kicked while working for the military."

"Hell, nobody even knew my name back then," Jim replied. "And if they had an idea who I was, I'm sure I did more than kick their ass. I probably killed them."

Jotty just shook his head in agreement. "Yeah, when I was working covert special ops, we didn't leave too many witnesses around either."

They both were quiet as they reflected on their respective pasts and got ready for bed.

The police car was waiting for Jotty and Jim in front of the hotel the next morning at 7:30. When they came out of the front door, the police officer sent to pick them up made it a point to show them his credentials. He was also driving a National Police Agency patrol car rather than an unmarked car.

"I guess they just want us to feel safe." Remarked Jim as he got in the back seat. Jotty sat up front with the officer.

It was a short drive to the police headquarters. When they arrived, they were immediately taken to Haruko's cubicle. Jim's six- foot five-inch frame forced him to have to duck around several hanging plants as he maneuvered the narrow passageways in the office.

Haruko was sitting behind her desk in her usual drab business suit. She did manage to smile when she saw Jotty and Jim come around the corner, but that was probably because Jim hit his head on a hanging plant he didn't notice until it was too late. As they approached, she closed the image on her computer screen. She had been reading several past articles in a Japanese tabloid written by Ono Saito. That was information she didn't want to share quite yet with Jotty.

Jotty and Jim both raced to be the first one to enter the doorway to her cubicle. They wedged themselves together in their haste to be the first to greet Haruko. Neither one wanted to back out. Finally, Jim was able to squeeze through first to shake Haruko's hand in greeting. After Jim shook her hand, Jotty politely bowed, and Haruko bowed in response.

"You need to learn the customs Jim," Jotty chided.

"Maybe," Jim responded, "but I got to touch her."

Haruko was laughing at their macho display. For an instant, she felt her emotions begin to stir and she liked it.

"What have you found out about our friends from yesterday," Jotty asked getting straight to the business at hand.

"Quite a lot, yet not very much," Haruko replied.

Jim shook his head. "You just can't seem to ever get a straight answer from a woman."

Jotty punched Jim in the leg. "Don't be such a chauvinist pig. I can never get a straight answer from you either, only your hick cowboy philosophy."

Jim started to respond, but Haruko interrupted.

"Mr. Rikey, if you are trying to offend me, you will fail. Several of my coworkers have done a much better job than you just did trying to get a rise out of me or get me upset. It will take a better man than you to do that."

Jotty began to laugh. "I guess she told you, Jimbo."

"Don't call me Jimbo." Jim replied in a serious voice.

Haruko continued, "The two gentlemen whose arms you broke were nothing more than local gang members who were hired as assassins by the man in the suit. He unfortunately was unable to give us any information. From his fingerprints, however, we determined he was a known terrorist supposedly in charge of an Al Qaeda affiliated cell in Indonesia."

"Did he have any ties to the Red Summit? Jotty asked.

"None we have been able to discover so far, but I will continue to work on it," Haruko said. "Now, if you would please show me the spike and tell me why you came all the way to Japan just to talk to me."

For the next half hour or so Jotty showed Haruko the spike and discussed its significance to the Red Summit. Haruko had seen similar spikes before in museums and at martial arts exhibitions. Certain traditional ninja groups used such weapons decades ago to create terror in the hearts of their enemies. Today such weapons were banned from sale or manufacture in Japan. Jotty then explained the details of the two burglaries and murders to Haruko. He didn't want to tell her everything he knew or what he thought the Red Summit was planning. Though it was certainly easy enough for Haruko to speculate based on the materials stolen in the two burglaries. As she listened, she suddenly realized Taka was in that very business. He was in a position to distribute tainted meat through his restaurant chains. Now she really wanted to speak with Ono Saito.

"Do you think the Red Summit is planning to make Japan the victim of a terror campaign?" Haruko asked Jotty.

"Maybe," he replied, "but with the strong government testing and supervision of your meat industry, I don't think Japan is the likely target."

Haruko knew it would not be long till Jotty started to focus his attention on Taka as well.

"The main reason we have come to see you, is to ask if you would be willing to join us in a multi-national task force to try to stop the Red Summit." Jotty told Haruko. "We could really use your knowledge and expertise."

"When you say multi-national, just what nations are you talking about, and just who is in your task force?" Haruko asked.

"Well...," Jotty started to respond. "There's me...and Jim...and hopefully you."

This made Haruko smile. "And just what nations are we talking about?"

"I can answer that one," said Jim. "That would include Japan, the United States, and Texas ma'am."

"I don't recall Texas breaking away from the union," Haruko was smiling.

"Well it sure the hell should." They all laughed at Jim's response.

"Our State Department has already spoken to your National Police Agency, and they are willing to loan you to us for a while if you are interested," Jotty continued.

Haruko was indeed interested. She did not care one bit for the way she was being treated in the National Police Agency. They would probably be glad to get rid of her not just for a while, but permanently. She also liked the idea of being able to travel around the world in search of the Red Summit without having to worry about justifying her expenses. The idea of being around two men who both obviously desired her was also intriguing to Haruko. Then she remembered the articles by Ono Saito.

"At this time, I think I must refuse your wonderful offer," Haruko said apologetically. "I have some things I really need to finish here in Japan before I could possibly accept such an offer."

It almost made Haruko cry to have to turn the offer down.

"Maybe in a few weeks if you still want me, I could manage to finish my business here," Haruko was hedging her bets and Jotty knew it. He could tell she wanted to join them, but something else had come up she wasn't telling them about. "Of course, you can have access to any of my files if they will be of assistance," Haruko added.

"Even the one you erased from your screen as we were walking in?" Jim asked.

"Haruko blushed. She had been caught by her own words. Before Jim could press her anymore, Jotty spoke up.

"Well, we hope you will soon change your mind, and we thank you for the access to your files." He stood and bowed to Haruko in preparation to leave. Jim just sat there staring at Jotty in disbelief. He started to say something to Jotty but before he could, Jotty had turned and was walking down the corridor.

"It's been a pleasure to see you ma'am, I hope you will reconsider joining up with us." Jim rose and bowed as Jotty had.

Haruko was too sad to respond. She couldn't decide if she was sad because she seemed to have feelings for both of the Americans or if she was sad because she couldn't leave the agency just yet and had to lie to Jotty and Jim.

Her sadness did not last long. The business side of Haruko took over before the men were out of sight. She was back on her computer reading the Ono Saito articles. She had to meet and talk to the author. He had information she needed. And if she didn't get his cooperation or that information then she would arrest him for breaking into her database and stealing that picture.

Haruko contacted the editor at the tabloid. She tried to schedule an appointment to meet with the editor. He told her he was just too busy. She told him it involved the national security of Japan and concerned one of the tabloid's reporters, Ono Saito. She could hear the editor sigh at the mention of the name. Reluctantly the editor agreed to meet with Haruko that afternoon.

Chapter Fifteen

or Karl Spencer, 'paradise' did not live up to the hype. It might have been different if he wasn't on such a tight leash. Spencer spent most of his time working in the lab at the Paleaka Ranch. For the first few months he worked, ate, and slept at the ranch. When his scars from plastic surgery were completely healed and he had totally immersed himself in the cover story Minoru had devised for him, Spencer was allowed to spend time at the lounges of the local resort bars. He was always accompanied by at least two of Minoru's men, and they in turn were always watched by at least one other. After a while, Minoru allowed Spencer to spend his weekends staying at the Hilton Waikoloa Village Resort. This seemed to improve Spencer's work habits at the ranch and make him a bit more tolerant of the big island.

When devising a cover story for Spencer, Minoru and Taka decided to allow Spencer to keep his old first name as his new last name. That way if someone happened to call his name, and he responded, he had a plausible explanation for the response. The plastic surgery, while not extreme, did alter his facial features enough to minimize any possibility of Spencer being recognized by someone from his past. If asked, Spencer was to say he was on the island working as a quality control inspector for the meat coming from the packinghouse at the Paleaka Ranch. Spencer didn't object to the charade, but wished Minoru would soon allow him to take a trip to Las Vegas so he could play a little poker. Spencer knew he would be accompanied by Minoru's men, but had no objection. For now, he at least had his computer and a generous limit on the credit cards Minoru had given him as part of his new identity. Spencer spent several hours each week logged on to his favorite on-line poker site, where for hours he would sit at the computer and play his favorite game, seven card Texas Hold 'Em. Spencer was an aggressive player, always staying in the game until the flop. That is when the first three common cards were dealt. That wasn't always a smart strategy for Spencer, or for anybody for that matter. Spencer lost a lot of money not folding when the two cards in his hand just weren't good enough to justify staying in the game. That was what had got him in so much trouble at Texas A & M in the first place. At least this time he had the money to waste. Or at least so he thought. Nobody had said anything to him about the credit card balance getting a little too high, so he thought it must be okay to continue his aggressive gambling. As long as he kept up on his absorption experiments, he figured he had nothing to worry about. He also had helped the laboratory's other scientists with the development and testing of several different cosmetic formulas. He worked with a team of fellow researchers in monitoring several cows that were infected with BSE, or mad cow disease, and then analyzing the results. These cows were kept in an area next to the lab, far from the rest of the herd. When one of these cows became a downer cow, which means it was unable to stand on its own any longer, the cow would be butchered and examined by Spencer. He would test the level of Prion affected cells in the different parts of the cow's nervous system. If the cow showed an abnormally high level of Prion contamination it was noted and then the affected parts, as was the rest of the cow, were removed from the lab for disposal. At least that was what Spencer was told. In actuality, much of the Prion affected portion of the cow was sent to the feedlot, while the portions showing the highest level of infection were sent to another level of the laboratory. Spencer had suspicions something like this was happening, but was smart enough to know not to say anything to anyone about it. The Prion affected part of the cow that went to the feedlot was mixed with several other ingredients and became part of the ruminant feed for the other cattle being kept at the pen by the laboratory. At least for now those were the only cattle receiving the tainted feed. The number of these cows kept for experimentation did seem to be increasing, Spencer had noted. Spencer had no idea what became of the tainted material sent to the other level of the laboratory. He did have a feeling that what ever it was, it probably wasn't good, and he was just as soon glad he didn't know. It was safer that way.

Spencer's credit card debt was not going without notice. One of Taka's accountants had brought it to Taka's attention one day, and Taka was not very pleased. He contacted Minoru and told him to instruct Spencer to cut back on his Internet gambling. Minoru told Taka that the gambling did keep Spencer occupied while not at the lab, and it kept him from wanting to spend too much time at the local bars. Taka understood, but still told Minoru to give him a strong warning to cut back on his gambling expenditures. Minoru told Taka he understood and would see to it immediately.

Spencer had a rather inflated belief as to how important he was to the operation of the laboratory at the Paleaka Ranch. He had the same ego problems as to his importance when he was at Texas A & M as well. He had been a graduate student at the same time Jim Rikey was working towards his PhD. When they were forming the Prion research team at Texas A & M, Jim was chosen over Spencer. Spencer was not happy and spent a lot of time politicking behind Jim's back trying to get Jim removed from the research team. He said some pretty ugly things about Jim, but was unable to have Jim removed. Fortunately for Spencer, Jim was unaware of most of the things Spencer was saying, or he would have surely kicked his ass. Spencer only was asked to join the Texas A & M research team when Jim left to return to his ranch following his brother's unfortunate death. Spencer was not the visionary of new approaches to problems like Jim was, but he was an accomplished and diligent researcher capable of designing, recording, analyzing and completing a research project. He proved his abilities when he was assigned to the anthrax research project. His success in completing that project not only earned Spencer his PhD, but also gave the military valuable information on the use of a deteriorating form of weapon grade anthrax. This success is what got Spencer the funding grant for his absorption research project. It proved very unfortunate for Spencer, that his addiction to gambling and his easy access to the weapon's grade anthrax interrupted his absorption research. Spencer's theory on absorption was indeed very promising with the possibility for many military applications. It just needed time to be proven. Spencer ran out of time when he went to prison. Taka had read in Time Magazine about Spencer's research and his fall from grace. He knew someday he would give Spencer the chance to continue his research, but this time, for Taka's application and use. What Taka didn't realize was the length of time it required to conduct the experiment trials to test Spencer's theory of absorption. Although the preliminary results were very promising, Taka was beginning to question whether Spencer's absorption experiments were worth the money and trouble it was starting to cost him. There was also always the risk of someone possibly recognizing Spencer, or Spencer inadvertently saying the wrong thing to the wrong person about the experiments at the laboratory. That was why Taka decided Spencer needed a little reminder to keep his gambling debt down and his mouth quiet about what was happening at the Paleaka Ranch.

Minoru had never cared for Spencer. That is why he decided to give the subtle reminder to Spencer as Taka had asked. Normally, Minoru would have had one of his men deliver Taka's message. Minoru's dislike for Spencer prompted him to want to deliver the message himself. He wanted to scare Spencer, more than hurt him, but he did want to hurt him at least a little. He had to be careful not to scare him too much so that Spencer would react by doing something stupid. That would be difficult for Spencer to do since he always had guards accompany him wherever he went away from the ranch. His computer had also been modified to not allow him to send emails, so inadvertent contact on-line was impossible as well. Still, if Spencer over reacted, Minoru would have to kill him. Minoru smiled when he thought about killing Spencer, but the smile turned to a frown when he realized he would then have to explain his actions to Taka. That he did not want to have to do.

That afternoon Minoru went to the laboratory to deliver Taka's message. He showed Spencer the credit card bills and told Spencer to cut back on his on-line gambling. Spencer was arrogant, as usual, and with a wave of his hand, brusquely told Minoru to leave his laboratory at once. In a flash, Minoru had Spencer in his grasp. The hand he had just used to symbolically brush Minoru out of the laboratory was now precariously close to being broken as Minoru twisted up in a way it was not meant to be twisted. Spencer was screaming from the pain, but was also screaming that if Minoru broke his hand, he would be unable to do his research work. Minoru was no fool, and knew better than to damage Spencer's hand. As Minoru let loose of Spencer's hand, he stomped down of Spencer's foot, breaking several of Spencer's toes.

"It appears you will have to do your work sitting down for the next few days." Minoru smiled as he spoke. "This has been a warning. Next time it will be more than just a few broken toes if you continue with such arrogance. Do you understand?"

Spencer grimaced in pain, but managed to nod his head.

"I didn't hear you," Minoru said. "I asked if you understood the message."

"I understand." Spencer was able to say as he took deep breaths to try to control the pain pulsing in his shoe.

"Good then," Minoru responded. "I'll have one of my men help you to the infirmary. You need to have those toes taken care of."

Minoru turned to leave the room. He stopped and thought for a moment, then turned back to Spencer to say something else.

"One more thing, Mr. Spencer," Minoru continued. "I do not like you, but Taka sees value in the services you are performing for us. But even Taka has a limit to how much he will tolerate from you. If you reach that limit, and you are getting close, I will take pleasure in killing you myself." He paused for a moment to allow his message to sink in. "Good day, Mr. Spencer."

Chapter Sixteen

"**F**ind your own Niche with Niki … Lipstick and cosmetics… by Nishiki Matsuura." The commercial ended and everyone sat quietly for a moment looking at Niki.

"I don't like it." Niki finally blurted out. "I'm just not sold on the name 'Niche'."

"What is it you don't like about the name?" the advertising executive asked in obvious frustration.

"It just doesn't sound right. What thirteen-year-old girl will even be able to pronounce it, let alone know what it means?" Niki asked the group gathered around the table.

"Now if it were a perfume, I think 'Niche' might be a good name, but we are talking about a lipstick here. I want an exotic name. Something easy for them to read and remember. Something powerful. You people have to do better than this or I will find another agency that will." It was an empty threat because the agency did have a contract with Taka Industries, none-the-less, they did get the message Niki was not happy.

"Give us a couple of days to come up with some other ideas," the executive told Niki. "Let's get together on Friday and we'll have some new names and ideas for you to think about."

"I certainly hope so," responded Niki as she got up and left the room.

Things were not going as well, or moving as fast as Niki had hoped. The cosmetic business had been her idea and she and Taka had invested a lot of time and money in trying to make it work. It was going to work, but just not as fast as she wanted it to. They had encountered several problems along the way. First, they had that shipment of bovine amniotic fluid confiscated by customs. Fortunately, the shipment was not traceable to anyone associated with Taka Industries. When they did finally get it back, much of it had become unusable. That was part of the reason Taka moved his operations to the United States. Now there would not be the stringent inspections as there were before, when the products had to be imported from Japan. Having to move the businesses out of Japan, and to the United States, had caused quite a delay. It took much too long to purchase the property in Hawaii and get the facilities there up and running. Only now was the Paleaka Ranch beginning to produce sufficient base ingredients to manufacture the lipstick and cosmetics.

Niki had learned a lot as she developed into a world-class model. One of the things she learned was the importance of cosmetics. She had learned which cosmetics were best at protecting her skin by keeping it moist and smooth, which ones made her skin glow with 'luminosity', and which colors were best for highlighting her natural beauty. She also learned which ingredients and chemicals in these cosmetics were natural and which ones depended on artificial ingredients and potentially harmful chemicals to create the desired affect. There were those women who desired to have only natural ingredients in their cosmetics, while others shunned the animal-based natural ingredients for the synthetic chemical compounds. There was always the argument as to which type of formula was the safest and healthiest. Niki had learned long ago that when it came to the majority of consumers, it made little difference. Marketing is what determined if a product would be successful over another product. Most consumers never read the ingredients. All they cared about was if the color looked right or if it felt good on their bodies. They usually didn't even care about what damage the cosmetics may be doing to their lips and skin. The fact is, eighty percent of American women regularly wore lipstick or make-up. That is a lot of chemicals and dyes being put on the skin on a daily basis. Who knows how much is absorbed each time you put on rouge or wash your hair. It is known that the average woman who regularly wears lipstick will ingest up to four pounds of lipstick in her lifetime. That is a lot of lipstick.

Niki had taken the time to read the ingredient lists on her cosmetics. She had learned which ingredients made the cosmetics look the best and which ingredients felt the best on her skin. It was only logical that one day she should use this knowledge to put out her own cosmetic line. It was also only a matter of time until she would have her opportunity to get back at men. Men just like those men who had abused her as a child. It was this anger in her which inspired her part of the plan that she and Taka were close to bringing to fruition.

Taka had bought a manufacturing building in a suburb of Los Angeles. He was having the refrigeration equipment installed, as well as the machinery required to make and package Niki's new line of cosmetics and lipsticks. They had made small batches of the lipsticks and rouge at the laboratory in Hawaii. These had been used for market testing in several cities in the United States and for the Food and Drug Administration approval testing. They were close to receiving FDA approval for all of their product line, and in the marketing tests, the lipstick had proven to be a big hit. The rouge and other makeup formulas did not prove nearly as popular as the lipstick did. Within days the factory would be producing the first batches of the 'clean' line as Niki liked to refer to it. The biggest hang-up was finding a highly marketable name for the advertising blitz Taka and Niki had planned. Hopefully the agency would have the solution to that problem come Friday.

One of the biggest disappointments so far in Niki and Taka's plans was the lack of progress on the absorption research going on at the laboratory in Hawaii. They had not foreseen that the trials to prove the effectiveness of toxic absorption of the cosmetics through the skin would take so long to verify. They had wrongly assumed results would be forthcoming in a matter of weeks. Now it seemed it could take several years before Spencer gave them definitive results. Not that it really mattered. The preliminary findings were so positive they had absolutely no doubt they would be successful with their plan. It was becoming more and more evident that Spencer's research was no longer pertinent. As Taka explained it, it was becoming no longer cost effective to fund Spencer's research, or for that matter to continue to fund Spencer himself. For now, he did help with the harvesting and production of Prion affected tissues and was good at identifying and isolating possible affected animals through his DNA analysis techniques. Spencer also had helped set up the equipment for the weaponization of the anthrax. This did make him somewhat of a valuable asset. Still, he was on Taka's watch list. He was spending way too much money on his gambling addiction and his usefulness was coming to an end.

Niki was living and spending most of her time in the Los Angeles area. That was where her new cosmetic company was located and that was the area where the initial marketing would take place. They would test market it for six months in Los Angeles and then take it nationwide. It had been several weeks since she had been with Taka, although she talked with him almost every other day. They had grown apart and now were more business partners and fellow terrorists than they were lovers. She had a difficult time calling Aioka by the name Taka and often slipped in their private conversations. Aioka would be quick to reprimand her for the slip up, but it continued to occur. Niki had truly loved Aioka when she was young. She worshipped him and did everything he asked her to do. As she now grew older, and as her fame grew, she came to realize that Aioka as well was just using her as most all the other men in her past had used her. She was able to justify his use of her as a means to further their political cause and beliefs. As she matured, she too began to question the righteousness of those beliefs. Much of her doubting directly had to do with her new-found wealth and fame as a world-class model. Still she tried to hold on to her terrorist beliefs. That was why she agreed to Aioka's plan. That was why she grew close to, and eventually married, Taka Matsuura. She did it because Aioka told her to do it. What she had not counted on was falling in love with Taka. He had treated her better than any other man had ever treated her. He gave her freedom and allowed her to be the person she wanted to be. Now she was beginning to question how she could have such anger that she was willing to kill thousands and possibly hundreds of thousands of people. Was it really her terrorist beliefs, or was it the hatred for her father she had translated into a hatred for mankind? Most of all, she was questioning why she had participated in the killing of Taka. Her dreams haunted her every night. Frightening dreams. Bursts of lava flying in the air with visions of Taka's body dancing on the molten lava like bacon in a frying pan. It was the years of brainwashing that kept her on the path of what Aioka called their 'Righteous Plan'. She had contributed much to the plan. It was hard for her not to complete something she had started. It had been that way her whole life. Now she was starting to have some doubts. She told herself she must stay strong in her beliefs.

The paparazzi continued to follow Niki. It didn't matter if she was in Japan or in the United States. The cameramen were ever present. Weekly, Niki's picture would turn up in an American tabloid as well as in the Japanese tabloids. So was the case for Taka. There was still much gossip and accusations this writer Ono Saito continued to tout in the Japanese tabloid. Taka too, was constantly followed by the paparazzi. He had remained in Japan where he was closing out his businesses and shifting his assets to new ventures. There was much speculation in the tabloids that Niki and Taka were splitting up. This was probably due to Niki having not been seen in Japan with Taka for quite some time. There were pictures of Taka with other women, as he dined, and came and went from his Aioka Steakhouse restaurants. In several of the photos the same woman was seen with Taka, and she seemed overly friendly. The tabloid also had pictures of Niki in what they described as being 'in a rage' over Taka's alleged infidelities. These made Niki laugh when she read them. Had she still cared for Aioka, these photos and accusations may have indeed troubled her. She no longer had the feelings for Aioka she once had. However, these photos did trouble Aioka. In fact, the tabloid articles were troubling Aioka greatly. He knew he must have Minoru solve that problem soon.

Niki returned to the advertising agency on Friday. She was hoping they had come up with a better name for her lipstick and make-up line of cosmetics. She and Taka were anxious to get moving on the marketing and retailing of the cosmetics. Niki was always in the news and therefore a hot commodity. They needed to use her fame to promote her new line of cosmetics before that fame began to fade. The tastes of the public were very fickle and dependent upon the media to tell them who was hot and who was not. Taka and Niki knew they needed to act quickly. They had crews waiting to start filming commercials just as soon as the marketing people, along with Niki, could decide on the right name for the products. They all knew the name of the lipstick would either make or break the company. "Niche' was not a bad name for her lipstick, but it was just too difficult for the young girls to read and pronounce. Their target market was the thirteen to eighteen-year-old age group, who were just starting to buy their own make-up and who were not concerned about the animal right issues regarding the animal byproduct ingredients being used, or the health issues regarding the chemical ingredients used in the make-up. They wanted buyers who only cared about how it looked on their lips and faces, and if it felt good when they put it on and wore it. They knew if the name was right it would sell, because they planned to undercut the competitor's price, even if it meant taking a huge financial loss. Their goal was to get as many young girls as possible putting it on their lips and faces. Making a profit was never one of their goals, or part of their plan. They knew the company would not be around for long. They needed to do as much damage as quickly as possible.

As Niki sat waiting for the presentation to begin, the reality of the plan finally coming to fruition and then ending was beginning to sink in with her. What would happen to her when the company folded? Would she go into hiding? Would she be arrested? Would she be able to plausibly deny knowing what was happening in the manufacturing of her cosmetics? She hadn't really given much thought to what the aftermath of her and Aioka's plan would bring. She needed to meet with Aioka and discuss her concerns. She knew she had to be careful though. She did not want Aioka to think she was weakening in her ideals.

Niki was suddenly jarred back into the present as the agency personnel started their new presentation. Several large posters had been placed at the front of the room. They were placed on easels each with its own covering hiding the contents of the poster. The agency wanted to dramatically unveil the posters to hopefully create a positive impact on Niki. The spokesman rehashed what their goals in coming up with the new name had been. Basically, they were just repeating what Niki had told them she wanted earlier in the week at the previous presentation.

"We think this new name is bold and signifies power," The spokesman recited. "It will be easy to recognize and easy to pronounce. It has an exotic flair to it and represents the epitome of Niki Matsuura. We think this name is the essence of Niki. It is a name people already associate with you and will not ever forget."

The sales pitch was good. Niki was growing very curious as too what kind of name could do all they were claiming.

The buildup continued, "Now ladies and gentleman, let me introduce you to the next number one selling brand of lipstick and make-up by Niki Matsuura Cosmetics."

He triumphantly pulled the veil off the first poster. Everyone turned to look to Niki for her reaction.

Niki burst into tears. The room grew silent as everyone stared in disbelief at her reaction. The spokesman was nearly in shock, not knowing what to do. He tried to slink behind the easel to hide. He was sure his career with the ad agency was over. Everyone stopped looking at Niki and started looking down at the table or the floor, not even wanting to make eye contact among them.

After almost a minute of crying, Niki looked around the room and finally spoke.

"It's perfect," she said. "I think it's the perfect name."

Niki got up from her chair and hurried from the room.

Everyone in the room looked around stunned. No one knew for sure how to react. Then smiles began to break across the faces of all the participants. They knew they had a winner. They were all talking rapidly among themselves. Finally, the spokesman quieted the room down.

"All right folks, we have a lot to do." The spokesman continued. "You all know your jobs and I expect you to do them well. Let's go make 'TAKA' the lipstick on everyone's minds as well as their lips."

A cheer went up from the room as they all headed to their phones to begin the marketing campaign.

Chapter Seventeen

"You know, I just don't think I'll ever figure out what that woman is thinking." Jotty said to Jim as they were boarding the jet to fly back to the United States.

"I know what you mean," Jim responded. "I was sure she was going to join up with us. You could sure tell she wanted to."

"I thought so too," Jotty said. "But something," he paused as he thought, "something just wasn't right. She was holding back. It was like she had just found out something important and needed to check it out really bad."

"Well, they sure as hell don't want her around there. You can tell they were hoping she would go with us too," Jim commented.

"And she knows that. That is why I know she would have come with us. Something really important must be about to happen." Jotty was convinced he was right.

"Well, there's nothing we can do about it now. I'm just glad as hell to be getting out of here. I don't like people kidnapping me and making plans to kill me." Jim said in a disgusted tone. They were both quiet for a while as they found their seats. "Now what surprises do you have planned for us when we get back to America?"

"Well, I'm going to sit at my desk and try to figure out what Haruko is up to as well as what the Red Summit is up to. Obviously, they are making some plans to use that affected beef. That's what you are going to figure out for us. Just what the hell can they use the stolen meat and those stolen animal byproducts for? They must be related. I want you to tell me

136

how. And what do you think about this Spencer Tyler situation? Could his disappearance be in any way to the Red Summit? Just what is his expertise? You knew him. What is he capable of doing besides selling anthrax to enemy agents? Is he capable of murdering his boss and faking his own death? And where is he? We need to find him as soon as possible if you think he is any way connected to these terrorist acts. Also, I'm going to need some reports to give to my boss. I need to know what the worst-case scenario could be regarding these thefts. Hell, I need everything, and I need it as soon as possible. But right now, I need sleep, so don't bother me till we get back to the United States." Having said that, Jotty buried his head in a pillow and turned to fall asleep.

"Hell, it sounds like you're just jealous Haruko took a liking to me too," Jim said with a laugh.

Jotty just flipped him off and fell asleep.

Jim had mixed feelings about being back in Washington. Although he had told Jotty he was glad to be leaving Japan, the truth was he really enjoyed the action of being back in the field. There was nothing like the adrenaline rush you get when someone is about to put a bullet in your head and you have to somehow stop it from happening. Sure as hell beat what he was now assigned to do. Jotty needed Jim to write some reports to show to the bosses. They needed to let the bosses know the seriousness of the situation to assure the funding kept coming in. Writing the reports was a drag, but wouldn't be hard. Jotty also had reports to write, and they both had debriefings to go through to explain just exactly what happened in Tokyo. The FBI doesn't like having its agents kidnapped and almost murdered. At least the kidnapping guaranteed Jotty would most likely get as much funding as needed to follow-up on his investigation, even without Jim's scare tactic reports.

Jim had no problem describing the worst possible scenario regarding the theft of the tainted meat in Britain. There really wasn't much meat stolen. It was affected with BSE contamination, and there was a considerable amount of Prion contamination on the brain and nervous system tissue, but not enough to do serious damage to the population if it was put directly into the meat products for direct sale to consumers. At most, several dozen people might contract the human form of mad cow disease, but we wouldn't know for at least five years. It takes anywhere from five to ten years for the symptoms to begin to show in humans. Jim speculated that it seems more likely the tainted tissues were used to taint ruminant feed products which in turn would affect a larger number of cattle and in turn eventually affect a greater portion of the population, assuming those cattle were all eventually slaughtered and the tissue from their nervous systems mixed in with the meat for commercial distribution. That, however, would take several years to come to play out and seemed highly unlikely as a goal of any known terrorist cell, specifically the Red Summit. It would take at least four to six years before the disease became apparent in the affected cattle, and then another five to ten-year before it was passed on to the human consumers. Such long-range planning was contrary to the goals of most terrorist organizations. The purpose of most terrorist organizations was to create immediate terror in the minds of their target population. Although the thought of the eventual devastation from such a long-range plan did bring fear into Jim's heart, he realized the government and the citizenship in general would fail to see the terror aspect in such an undertaking. Jim did discuss in his report some of the recent research and speculation regarding how Prion affected tissue could be cultivated to maximize the replication of mutated proteins as well as acceleration of the mutation. He emphasized these were simply theories that were being explored at various research universities around the country. He did list several researchers who were in the trial phase of testing these theories. He made a note to himself to visit some of these research facilities to monitor the success and progress of these trials.

On his report concerning the theft of the animal byproducts in Los Angeles, Jim went into detail of the various uses for these products, with the most likely use being the base ingredients for lipstick and cosmetics. He included in his report that the product in question was never tested for any contagions or contaminants. The shipment was just routinely pulled as part of the importation inspection process that was mandated by the USDA. These new import inspection restrictions were part of the punitive action Congress authorized against Japan in retribution for Japan's refusal to accept citrus fruit, specifically oranges from California that may have been subject to Med-fly infestation. It was all part of the gamesmanship countries like to play when it comes to international trade. Jim's report continued by saying what was most troubling about the theft was that it was obviously conducted by the same terrorist organization responsible for the BSE tainted theft in Britain. This could leave one to theorize that the material stolen from the warehouse in Los Angeles may indeed have been Prion contaminated material. That being the case, this theft was much more significant than the theft in Britain. The possibility of mass distribution of Prion contaminated tissue was much more likely given the fact that, based on the amount of material stolen, could in fact be used as the basis for a large quantity of cosmetics. The effectiveness of Prion contamination through cosmetics via skin absorption was also a matter of theory which several researchers were presently trying to prove and quantify through experimental trials with swine and mice. This supplied the lead-in to Jim's next report. That report concerned Spencer Tyler. It was that very theory Spencer Tyler was trying to prove when his sentencing to prison abruptly interrupted his research. Now that the FBI knew Spencer Tyler had not been murdered in Dallas, several questions regarding his previous research needed to be answered. That was pretty much one of the main reasons Jim was asked by Jotty to join his task force. If you can call two people a task force. After Jim wrote and submitted his first two reports, Jotty sent Jim to Texas to see what he could find out about Spencer's faked death, his disappearance, and his previous research. Jim was thrilled with the opportunity to get back to his beloved Texas and was scheduled to leave that afternoon. Before he left, Jotty called him to go over some things he needed to know about this mad cow disease.

Jotty had been busy writing reports as well. He had written and submitted the report to his bosses about the incident in Japan. He also had to report Haruko's reluctance to join the team at this time. He included that in his opinion he felt she had pertinent information regarding the Red Summit, and for some reason, she was not yet willing to share that information. Jotty had spent much time analyzing Haruko's database, and noticed the inordinate amount of information, both from the past and recent, regarding the Japanese industrialist, Takaishi Matsuura, better known as Taka. Jotty could understand the past documentation since Taka's brother Aioka was alleged to have been one of the founding members of the Red Summit and responsible for several terrorist acts. Aioka, however, was killed several years ago in a bombing raid of a terrorist training facility in southern Lebanon. His death had been confirmed by the Israeli military who orchestrated the bombing. Jotty made a mental note to contact his cohort responsible for researching terrorist activities in the southern Lebanon area and check the validity of the Israeli military report. Maybe Haruko thought Taka was also somehow affiliated with the Red Summit. As Jotty further read the information about Taka, a light went off in his head. Taka had made his fortune, or at least his grandfather had, in the cattle industry in Japan. That seemed like too much of a coincidence to Jotty. Of course, it made perfect sense that Haruko would believe Taka was mixed up in the recent Red Summit activities. He had the perfect business which would allow him to create Prion-affected meat products. Jotty shared this information with Jim, who agreed the opportunity did indeed seem to be there, but pointed out that, in Japan, every cow slaughtered for meat was individually inspected at a government facility for BSE contamination, as well as a multitude of other possible diseases, viruses, and bacteria. It would be virtually impossible for Taka to distribute Prion-affected beef in Japan.

"Could he export affected beef out of Japan?" Jotty asked Jim.

"I don't see how," Jim responded. "Japan has some of the strictest and tightest export and import laws and regulations in the world. Not only do they have the laws, they have the personnel and facilities to enforce them. Nothing comes or goes out of a Japanese port without it undergoing several inspections, by multiple levels of inspectors."

"Why so many inspections?" Jotty asked.

"History." Jim replied. "History shows that without those several independent inspections, somebody would be paid off to let something slip by. Not that there still are no payoffs, but it just makes it harder for somebody to get away with it."

Jotty nodded his understanding.

Jim continued, "Now if this Taka was doing business in the United States it would be a different story. Our USDA and customs inspection departments are so understaffed, and our regulations and penalties for breaking those regulations are so not enforced, that someone could get away, and in fact usually do get away, with just about anything they want in the United States."

"What do you mean by that?" Jotty wanted to hear more.

"Did you read my reports?" Jim asked.

"I scanned through them," Jotty replied.

"Well, remember the part where I talked about the possibility of feedlots using dead cows and dead cow parts as part of the ruminant feed given to fatten up the cattle in feedlots right before they are slaughtered?" Jim said.

"Yeah, I do," Jotty responded. "You said it can lead to mad cow disease." Jim nodded.

"You also said it was illegal to do in the United States, and any feedlot caught doing it was subject to fine or closure," Jotty told Jim.

"You read more than I thought," Jim smiled. "What I wrote is true, but in reality, it is happening all the time. Those feedlots may at best be inspected once or twice a year. If everything looks clean and all right, the inspector doesn't even bother to take samples for testing. If he does take samples, it takes weeks to get the results back from the overburdened testing labs. If they do find the feedlot is including the remains of butchered cattle in the feed to fatten up the cattle to be slaughtered, the feedlot is written a citation and told not to do it again. The inspector will then come back in about six months to take another sample for testing. If this sample proves to contain bovine byproducts, then the feedlot might receive a five thousand dollar fine. Not much considering the millions of dollars some of these feedlots are making. Finally, the feedlot will clean up its act before the next inspection and it gets a clean bill of health. Then the whole process starts over again. Now multiply this by the thousands of feedlots in the country that slaughter upwards of thirty-five million cattle every year. My friend, we have no control of what these feedlots are feeding these cattle. That's why I quit eating red meat ten years ago."

Jotty was feeling a little nauseated. "So why do they do it? Why do they take the chance of affecting so many people with mad cow disease?" Jotty asked.

"The mighty dollar," Jim responded solemnly. "A feedlot can save tens of thousands of dollars by throwing in the remains of slaughtered cattle in with the ruminant feed for the new cattle. They save money on buying other protein substitutes to add to the feed and they save money on not having to dispose of the old parts or even the cattle that died."

Jotty had heard enough. He decided he needed to do his own research on this Takaishi fellow while Jim was checking in Texas. He wanted to know exactly what research Spencer was doing at Texas A & M when he was arrested, and where Spencer might be today.

That afternoon, Jim flew into Dallas where he was met by a local FBI agent. That agent took him to the strip mall where the bodies were discovered in the rubble of the fire. It was not in a very prosperous part of Dallas and the part of the strip mall building that had been burned was still vacant. The owner had decided it was not in his best financial interest to rebuild. Actually, the owner received quite a little profit windfall when the structure was burned down. An insurance fraud private detective initially investigated him, but no evidence was ever found which could possibly link the owner to the fire. The local FBI office had been kept in the dark about the discovery that the body found was not Spencer Tyler. Jotty thought it might be beneficial if the fewer people who knew the truth, the easier it would be to try to discover what actually happened. Jim questioned some of the occupants of the adjoining buildings in the strip mall, using his Texas 'good ole boy' method of questioning, but nobody was able to give him any information other than what he already knew. After about an hour he and his escort headed to the local Dallas FBI office where Jim reviewed the file on the murders. That too was basically a waste of time, for Jim had already seen a copy of the file back in Washington. It wasn't a very friendly place for Jim to visit either. The local agents knew he wasn't really an FBI agent. They had run across Jim before when he had pulled some of his cowboy antics in taking down bad guys the FBI should have been in charge of taking down. He had made a few of them look bad in the past and they had not forgotten. Jim really didn't care what they thought about him. "Hell," he thought, "ninety percent of the agents at the Dallas office weren't even Texans. They were just a bunch of East coast college boys with law degrees." Jim decided it was time to head over to College Station, Texas, the home of Texas A & M.

Jim knew a few of his 'good ole boy' buddies still lived in College Station. He would have to stop by and have a drink with them. His first stop, however, was to go see Susan Tyler, Spencer's ex-wife, and Jim's ex-girlfriend. She apparently had not remarried since she still went by the last name of Tyler. Jim had gotten her address from the FBI file. It wasn't the old address Jim was familiar with. The IRS had seized the house she and Spencer had owned for back taxes. They said the couple owed taxes on the money Spencer received for selling the stolen anthrax. Fortunately, Susan's parents had a little money so she was able to buy another small house near the university. It was a good thing her parents had some money, for the IRS took just about everything she and Spencer had ever owned. Which in reality wasn't very much. Spencer had managed to put them in pretty heavy debt because of his gambling addiction. There wasn't much left for the IRS to take, but they managed to find most all that was left.

Susan hadn't changed her last name. She would have, but for the longest time, she didn't want to spend the money to legally change it. When she finally had the extra money to pay for the name change, she just never got around to actually doing it. She had gotten over her marriage to Spencer with reasonable ease, and felt no shame in keeping the last name. She had hoped she wouldn't have it for long though. She was still a beautiful woman and there were many suitors who would gladly like to see Susan with their last name. She just wasn't ready yet to make that kind of commitment. Then when Spencer was killed, there was no need to change her name.

Jim found the house and knocked on her door. They were both surprised when they saw each other.

"Wow," Jim exclaimed. "You are more beautiful than I remember."

"I bet you say that to all your ex-girlfriends," Susan replied. She gave Jim a big hug and a kiss, and Jim gave her a kiss back. "God," Susan whispered hoarsely, "it's been years since I've been kissed like that."

"Probably not since you dumped me for that guy who stole my research job," Jim teased.

"As I recall," Susan said rather rudely, "It was you who up and left me and your research job at Texas A & M for the stupid Marines. I have never forgiven you for that. I still blame you for me ending up as Mrs. Spencer Tyler." Her rage over what a fiasco her life had become after Jim had left her welled up inside of her as she burst into tears. "I hate you Jimbo Rikey," Susan was screaming. "I hate you, I hate you, I hate you..." She was beating on Jim's chest as she continued to cry.

Jim wrapped his arms around Susan and she collapsed whimpering in tears as he carried her inside the house.

"Why did you come back, what do you want?" Susan finally asked as she started to calm down.

"I came to see you," replied Jim.

"Don't lie to me," Susan screamed. "You don't know how often I have thought about you. Thought about how great my life would have been as Mrs. Jim Rikey. Instead I live with the shame of my former husband's name and the memory of how he betrayed me and my country." She once again began to cry.

"I came to ask you about Spencer," Jim finally told her.

"Of course you did," she said softly. "I knew you didn't come to see me."

"Maybe that's true, but now that I am here, I kick myself for not having come see you before now," Jim replied.

Susan stood up and kissed Jim passionately. "Make love to me," She pleaded.

Jim took her hand and followed her into the bedroom.

Later in the evening Jim took Susan out for a gourmet dinner. She ordered prime rib, while Jim ordered salmon. As Susan ate her steak, Jim became fixated on the sauce she was using was called 'The World-Famous Takaishi Steak Sauce'. Susan noticed Jim staring at the bottle.

"It's the best steak sauce I've ever tasted," she said. "Haven't you ever tried it?"

"I quit eating steak several years ago," Jim replied.

"You…, Jimbo Rikey, not eat steak? What kind of Texan are you?" She laughed.

"One that I hope will live a long time," Jim replied. "You know, you are one of the only people who I let call me Jimbo. Most people who call me that get the crap beat out of them."

"Well thanks for not 'beating the crap out of me'," Susan said. "And thanks for this afternoon too." Susan was blushing.

"Shucks, it was nothing, ma'am." Jim said in his Texas hick accent. They both laughed.

"Now what is it you need to know about Spencer?" Susan asked. "I assume you know he was killed by one of those terrorists he sold the anthrax to. You know, one of those men that he turned into the FBI."

"I heard about that," Jim responded. He decided it best if he didn't tell Susan Spencer might still be alive. She seemed so relieved he had been killed. "Did Spencer contact you after he got out of prison?" Jim asked.

"He tried to, but I never responded," Susan told Jim. "As far as I know, he never left the Dallas area. I think his probation wouldn't allow him to come here, to College Station. And if he had shown up here, I would have had him arrested."

"Do you know anything about the research he was doing when he was arrested?" Jim asked.

"Only that it had to do with skin absorption of Prions." Susan replied. "You should check with the university. I'm sure they kept his research papers and logs."

"Do you have any of Spencer's old notes or diaries?" Jim queried.

"None that have anything to do with his research. The FBI took all of that! I threw everything else of Spencer's out when the IRS took the house from me. The only thing I kept was his gambling debt ledger and diary. You know how Spencer was meticulous about keeping track of everything. He kept a running log of his Internet gambling wins and losses. He even kept track of what his hands were on the games he played. I kept those diaries just to remind me never to get mixed up with another jerk like Spencer." Susan became solemn once again.

"I'm sure you never will," reassured Jim. "Do you think I can get a look at those diaries?" Jim asked.

"You can have them as far as I am concerned. I think you have finally helped me put Spencer behind me." Susan replied. "Why don't we go back to my house? I'll give you the books, and you can help put Spencer a little more out of my mind." Susan had a twinkle in her eye as she smiled provocatively at Jim.

"The things I do for my country," Jim said to himself as he took Susan's hand and headed for the door.

Back in Washington Jotty was busy researching Taka Matsuura. His files told him Taka was selling off much of his business enterprises in Japan, but didn't say why he was selling off his assets, or what he intended to do. The FBI files just didn't have sufficient information for Jotty. What he did learn from the files, and it concerned him, was Taka Industries had been supplying Sizzle Burger with their hamburger meat for over a year. Jim's comments about the stringent Japanese inspections eased Jotty's fears somewhat, but things were starting to add up in Jotty's mind, and he didn't like the answer he was coming up with one bit.

The next morning, Jim left Susan's house and headed for the university. Instead of going to the biology graduate research laboratory, he went straight to the advanced computer lab. Several old friends still worked at the university and one of them was still the professor in charge of the 'Monster Computer' as Jim liked to call it. The computer was part of the IRL program at Texas A & M. IRL stood for the Internet Research Lab. After a few minutes of reminiscing and catching up on old times, Jim convinced his old professor to help him do some Internet research using the 'Monster Computer'. The professor thought it an interesting challenge and assigned two of his assistants to the task. He assured Jim that, by late afternoon, Jim would have the information he was looking for. Jim thanked him and headed to his old research laboratory, the same one Spencer took over when Jim left for the ranch and ended up in the Marines.

As Jim had expected, no one had seen or heard from Spencer after he was sent to prison. Nor had any of the researchers or professors heard from Spencer after his release from prison. They all knew of his death. News crews came to interview acquaintances and rehash the scandal soon after Spencer was murdered. News crews tended to always stir things up just when they were beginning to quiet down. All of Spencer's research papers and logs had been copied and sent to the FBI previously, so Jim saw no need in reviewing that data. His old professors were pleased Jim had finally completed his PhD and told him whenever he got tired of working at the graduate school of the USDA, he was welcome to come back and teach and research at Texas A & M. Jim thanked them for the offer and assured them he too would love to get back to Texas. He then made the rounds, said his goodbyes, and went back to the IRL laboratory.

The two lab assistants were smiling when Jim got back to the IRL laboratory. Not only did they have the historical information Jim had asked for, but they had correlated their findings to active Internet usage that fit the criteria and had several options available for Jim to investigate as well. Jim couldn't have been happier. Although he wanted to stop by Haskell and check to make sure his farm was running properly, he was too excited about the information he had discovered. He wanted to get back to Washington as quickly as possible and tell Jotty what he had discovered. He caught a commuter flight out of College Station and was back in Dallas within the hour. He used his credentials to bump a first-class passenger off the next American Airline flight to Washington D.C. "A matter of national security," he explained to the ticketing agent.

When he landed at Dulles, he headed straight to Jotty's office. Jim knew it was late, but he also knew Jotty was married to his job and would still be at the office. Jim was right.

"I thought you were going to be gone for at least five days. What the hell are you doing back so soon?" Jotty asked in a surprised tone.

"Well, you sent me to find out what happened to Spencer," replied Jim. "And I found out."

"What do you mean you found out?" Jotty asked abruptly.

"I found Spencer." Jim was smiling.

"In only two days you managed to find Spencer in Texas?" Jotty was in shocked disbelief.

"Nope," Jim responded. "I found him..., but he's not in Texas."

Chapter Eighteen

Haruko was at the tabloid office a half an hour early. She couldn't wait to meet this Ono Saito in person. The editor having predicted she would arrive early had scheduled his attorney and Ono to both arrive an hour early to go over what they were willing to say, and what they were not going to tell the National Police Agency. Haruko needed only to wait less than five minutes before the editor called her into his office.

"Ms. Ozawa, a pleasure to meet you," the editor said as he showed Haruko into his office. "Allow me to introduce you. This is Mr. Otani, my attorney, and this," as he gestured across the room, "is the infamous Ono Saito, better known as Byron Downing."

Haruko was shocked at seeing the dapper Mr. Downing. "It is a pleasure to meet you," she responded politely as she bowed. "Excuse me if I seem a little confused, but you are Ono Saito?" She asked of Mr. Downing.

"I am," Byron responded, "And I would appreciate it if you helped keep our little subterfuge a secret. You see, I don't think the tabloid readers would be so apt to read my stories if they knew I was an Englishman."

"That is unfortunately most likely true, Mr. Downing. I promise not to share your identity. That is, if you promise to help me." Haruko explained to him.

"Help you, help you how?" Byron asked.

"Before I say, do I have the assurance of all of you gentleman that what I am about to share with you, will not end up in a future edition of the tabloid? At least not without my permission." After conferring with the attorney, they all agreed, though reluctantly.

"I am sure you have already researched my background, and you are aware I am a Special Investigator for the National Police Agency in charge of investigating the terrorist group known as the Red Summit. You of course would have told everyone already, Mr. Downing, because you have illegally accessed my secured database regarding the Red Summit." Haruko stared at Byron with contempt when she made the accusation.

Before Byron could respond, she continued, "Please do not try to deny it. I have a video of you arriving and leaving the suburban police station where, somehow, you were able to access the commander's secured computer system. I hope we will be able to reach a mutual assistance agreement so I will not have to have you arrested. It could prove quite embarrassing for the tabloid as well as the officers at the police station who allowed you to access the secure information."

The editor looked at the attorney who just shook his head. "Just what kind of assistance do you want from us?" asked the editor.

"I want to know where Mr. Downing gets his information and what information he may have that has not been made public in the tabloid," Haruko told the three men.

"Something we have printed obviously has raised some concerns at the National Police Agency," the editor stated.

"Am I to assume the information you are seeking has to do with Taka Matsuura?" asked Byron.

"Your assumption is correct," responded Haruko. "As to why I am interested in the information, I cannot say at this time, but I assure you, when I am free to talk about our concerns, you, Mr. Downing, will be the first one to receive the information."

"Did the incident at the hotel yesterday with the two FBI agents have anything to do with this?" asked Byron.

Haruko just smiled. "As I said Mr. Downing, until I am free to talk, you will just have to write your stories based on speculation."

After conferring with the attorney, Byron agreed to help Haruko with her investigation of Taka. He informed her he had plans to fly to Hawaii the next day to meet with an informant who claimed to have proof Taka was not really Taka. "Whatever that means," Byron said. "The informant is the head chef on the cruise ship Taka and Nishiki honeymooned on. He also claims to have corroborative evidence from the ship's photographer showing what he says to be two distinct men both claiming to be Taka. For a rather substantial sum of money, that my editor has so graciously agreed to pay, the chef and photographer were willing to share their information."

Haruko's heart was racing. This was more than she had hoped for.

"If you don't mind," Haruko told Byron, "I would like to join you on your trip to Hawaii. This could be precisely the information I have been seeking for my investigation."

"Just as long as the tabloid gets your story first," said the editor.

Byron stared at the editor in shock disbelief. "Excuse me, but I believe I am the one to decide if I want her to join me in Hawaii," Byron said to the editor.

"Bullshit," the editor responded. "You can't fool me, Byron. All you are thinking about is how you are going to get this police officer in your bed."

Haruko blushed at the editor's bluntness. She was surprised when Byron failed to deny the accusation.

"Please allow me to book both of our flights and both of our rooms." Haruko stressed both when she referred to their rooms.

"That will be fine," responded Byron, "but make sure you book us into the Hilton Waikoloa Village on the big island. That is the only place I will stay when I go to Hawaii."

"That will be fine," responded Haruko. "Now please tell me when you are to meet the chef, and everything he has already told you."

For the next half an hour, Byron told Haruko the little he knew about the cooking demonstration and about the photographer's 'before and after photos' of Taka and Niki going on their helicopter ride. Haruko suggested they interview the pilot of the helicopter as well. Byron said it had already been arranged. When he and Haruko were to arrive on the island, the ship would still be finishing an island cruise. It would be two days before they could meet with the chef and the photographer. During that time Byron planned to meet with the pilot and see the Kilauea volcano. Just this week the volcano had become quite active once again. It was actually spewing and blowing lava up into the air, and there were several surface level lava flows. Haruko said she would love to see the volcano, just as long as she didn't have to fly in one of those helicopters. That made Byron laugh.

"Well, I guess you won't be interviewing the pilot with me then," Byron said.

"Why is that," Haruko replied.

"The only way he would agree to talk to me was if I paid for a private helicopter tour," laughed Byron.

"You are right about that," Haruko continued. "You will just have to fill me in on what he has to say."

Haruko left the tabloid office and returned to her police headquarters cubicle. She pulled up JAL flight schedules and booked her and Byron on a morning flight to the big island of Hawaii. She also booked two rooms at the Hilton Waikoloa Village.

Chapter Nineteen

Taka had been busy closing his businesses and shifting his assets to banks in Switzerland and the Bahamas. He was careful to keep adequate money available for his ongoing new enterprises. He was negotiating with Sizzle Burger to try to expand his network to supply some of their western United States restaurants with beef. So far, he was hitting roadblocks, but he was confident that soon they would purchase his meat to meet their fast food needs. His agent was also making inroads in supplying many of the independent restaurants as well as several of the major hotel catering and food service divisions with prime cuts of meat from his burgeoning Paleaka Ranch slaughter house. Several of the larger hotels had agreed to replace their present meat supplier with Paleaka Ranch meat as soon as their present contracts expired. Many of the local independent restaurants did not have such contracts, and were already using the meat supplied by Taka's Paleaka Ranch packinghouse.

Taka had bought and built the new ranch enterprises, listing David Paleaka as the majority owner. The contracts David had signed took his majority ownership away and assigned it to a variety of shell companies which eventually led back to Taka. In actuality, Taka had made only one trip to the big island to visit his Paleaka Ranch facilities. That trip was made aboard his cattle ship and was done under a false identity. He thought it best he not be seen at the ranch in case something went wrong before his plans were in full operation. Minoru was in charge of overseeing the daily ranch operations as well as much of Taka's planned terrorist activities. Minoru had a small select team of terrorists who supplied security for the ranch, and kept tabs on David Paleaka and Spencer at all times. Minoru made sure the Japanese workers hired to perform daily operation of the feedlot, slaughterhouse and, as ranch hands, were kept unaware of the true purpose of the Paleaka Ranch. The Japanese workers were prohibited from leaving the ranch during their stay, but were well taken care of while working there. Minoru ran the operation as if it were an off-shore oil derrick. He would shuttle in the workers from Japan to Hawaii via Taka's cattle ship for four months at a time. He would then rotate them back to Taka's remaining feedlot and slaughterhouse facility in Japan or to work on the cattle ship. They were paid very well to do the work and keep their mouths shut.

The ranch was losing a good deal of money. Taka expected this and was not concerned. However, the ranch was starting to concern many of the local Hawaiian ranchers. At first, they thought the opening of the feedlot and slaughterhouse was just foolishness, and fated to fail. Now that the Paleaka Ranch was beginning to supply meat to several of the restaurants on the island, it was beginning to affect the small family slaughterhouse operations that processed an average of four or five cows a week. It was now cheaper for their customers to buy their meat from the Paleaka Ranch agent than to pay these smaller slaughterhouses to do their custom butchering as they had done for years. A lot of resentment was beginning to grow among some of these small ranchers and complaints were being heard at the island rancher association meetings. The larger ranches remained unaffected by the Paleaka Ranch operations. The Parker ranch which was by far the largest on the island continued to ship their calves to the mainland where they were sent to feeder farms, then to cooperative feedlots where they were fattened then slaughtered along with thousands of others from all over the United States. There was concern that if the Paleaka Ranch took over supplying the entire Hawaiian Islands with their meat, it might affect the price the larger ranches received from the cooperative sales on the mainland. However, their accountants assured them the loss in sales for the amount of meat consumed on the Hawaiian Islands would have no affect on the prices the ranches belonging to the cooperative would receive. So the larger ranchers paid little attention to what was going on at the Paleaka Ranch. They knew it would eventually fail. It had to.

Minoru continued to travel back and forth from Hawaii to Japan to confer with Taka. Taka was not pleased with the results of the kidnapping and attempted murder of the two FBI agents. He was also not pleased that they had even come to Japan to confer with Haruko. Minoru had wanted to handle the killing of the two agents himself, but Taka had needed him to oversee more pressing concerns elsewhere. Minoru had reluctantly agreed to Taka's wishes and issued orders to one of their trusted terrorist cell members in Tokyo. It should have been a simple job, but obviously it went terribly wrong. Minoru swore to Taka such a mistake would never again occur. Minoru would see to that.

Taka and Minoru next discussed the information about Ono Saito going to Hawaii to meet with the ship's chef and photographer. Minoru wanted to kill both the chef and photographer, but Taka insisted both of their deaths would look too suspicious to the tabloid. He instructed Minoru to convince the chef to not meet with the journalist and to destroy the pictures and negatives belonging to the photographer. He told Minoru to kill the photographer as a means to persuade the chef not to meet with Ono. Regarding the killing of Ono, Taka was not sure if killing him would stop or increase the stories in the tabloid. He advised Minoru to monitor the situation and, if necessary, he had Taka's permission to kill Ono. Usually, Taka wanted the final say over the decision to kill someone, but he was heading to the United States to finalize the plans for the new cosmetic company with Niki and might not be available if Minoru needed to act quickly. Taka told Minoru he had complete trust that Minoru could handle the situation in Hawaii and gave him permission to act as he felt the situation compelled him to do. Minoru told Taka he understood and would choose wisely if it became necessary.

It had become obvious to both Taka and Minoru that they needed to direct Haruko's attention away from Ono and his Hawaii connection. They could not afford for Haruko to somehow stumble across the Paleaka Ranch facilities, or disrupt their plans in any way. As well, they needed to create a diversion in the United States to keep the FBI away from the Hawaii slaughterhouse, feedlot, and laboratory. Taka devised a plan that he was sure would divert both Haruko and the FBI from interfering with their activities any further. His plan would also bring the Red Summit's terror campaign to the United States and place fear in the hearts of all Americans. Taka just needed to be sure not to overplay his hand just yet. He explained the details of the plan to Minoru before he left for the United States to meet with Niki. Minoru understood Taka's instructions and this time, personally made all the necessary arrangements to carry out Taka's new terror campaign.

Later that day, after Taka had left Japan and became unavailable to Minoru, their plans for dealing with Ono became somewhat more complicated. Minoru received information from one of his men who monitored the National Police hacked computers, that Haruko Ozawa had scheduled an appointment at the same tabloid Ono Saito wrote for. She had also spent much time at her computer accessing old tabloid articles, written by Ono Saito. These stories all related to the activities of Taka and Niki. Then two hours after her scheduled meeting at the tabloid office, she booked a flight for two people to Hawaii, along with two rooms at the Waikoloa Hilton Village. This news was very troubling to Minoru. "Perhaps Haruko already knows of the Hawaii facilities," he thought to himself. Of the two flights and rooms Haruko had booked, one was of course booked under her name, while the other was under the name of a British citizen named Byron Downing. Minoru recognized the name, but couldn't remember from where. He did a web search and came up with the information he needed. Suddenly, it all made sense. Byron Downing and Ono Saito were one in the same. "Of course," Minoru said to himself. "That is why we have been unable to find out anything about Ono Saito. There is no Ono Saito." That brought a smile to Minoru's face. Minoru was pleased Haruko and Byron were staying at the Hilton Waikoloa Village. He already had men there with Spencer. Those men would also be able to watch Byron and Haruko.

Haruko had done another search on her computer. She had run a search through police databases on the name John Greer. She found that John had been charged with several crimes throughout his life, but had somehow always managed to avoid conviction for any of those crimes. Where she got his name and why she was looking it up meant trouble for Taka and Minoru. John was on Minoru's payroll in Hawaii. John was also trouble. He recently had been spending a lot of time and money partying with David Paleaka. Minoru had not minded, because he thought John would help keep an eye on David. It allowed Minoru to assign one less security guard to David. Unfortunately, it seemed John was beginning to like the Peruvian flake as much as David seemed to like it. His behavior was coming into question. Minoru could not afford to have one of his men acting in such a manner. John was becoming more of a concern for Minoru than David or even Spencer. Haruko had to have gotten John's name from Ono. Ono, or Byron, in turn had to have been tipped off to John's involvement from the chef or the ship's photographer. Or could John himself possibly be the one who first contacted the journalist? Regardless, Minoru needed to return to Hawaii immediately and prepare to deal with Haruko and Byron, as well as the chef and photographer, and now John Greer. It was Haruko who troubled Minoru the most. Maybe it would become necessary to kill Haruko as well, Minoru thought. He knew Taka would not approve of her death quite yet. They were still receiving much valued information by continuing to monitor her computer. Minoru decided not to try to contact Taka to inform him of this new information. He would wait to see what developed in Hawaii. Then if necessary, he would contact Taka. It would be Taka's decision as to what, if any, action would be brought against Haruko. As for John Greer, he may have flown his last helicopter tour for Minoru. Minoru called Hawaii and told his men to keep an eye on John and to prepare for Byron and Haruko's visit. He told them what to have prepared for his arrival, and he would be returning immediately to Hawaii. Minoru next turned to his laptop computer and booked a first-class cabin on the *Grand Maui*. He was in the mood for a short cruise.

Minoru left Japan that afternoon on a chartered jet. He needed to get back to Hawaii as quickly as possible. He had a lot to do to prepare for Haruko and Byron's visit. But first he thought he just might take a relaxing cruise.

Chapter Twenty

Ever since he had had his toes broken by Minoru, Spencer had been staying at the Hilton Waikoloa Village recuperating. That meant he spent most of the day in his room with his laptop playing poker. Spencer was logged on to the Pan-American Poker website. It was one of his favorite on-line poker sites, mostly because it was the largest Internet poker gambling casino, with the most players playing his favorite game, 'Texas Hold 'Em'. It had become an extremely popular game every since ESPN started showing the 'World Championship of Poker' at least twice a week on their network. In 'Texas Hold 'Em' each player is dealt two cards and then they bet. After all bets are placed, and those wishing to fold, or not play the hand have done so, the dealer deals what is known as the 'flop'. The 'flop' is three community cards everybody uses, along with the two cards they were initially dealt, to build the best possible hand. Once again, the players either bet or fold. Then the dealer deals the fourth community card. This card is called the 'turn'. Again, all the remaining players either bet or fold based on their now best hand. Finally, the fifth community card is dealt. This card is called the 'river'. After this card is dealt, there is a final round of betting. What makes this game, like all poker games, exciting, is the possibility that one of the players is bluffing and really does not have a good hand. He just has a lot of 'juevos', or guts, to try to fool his opponents into thinking he has the winning hand and tricking them into folding. It often works, netting the bluffer a lot of money. It can just as easily backfire, costing the bluffer a lot of money. That is what makes the game exciting. Spencer is fairly good at seeing when someone is trying to bluff. What he is not good at, is trying to bluff. He like most gamblers has certain superstitions he brings to the game. There are certain combinations of cards, that if they are originally dealt to you as your first two cards, odds are you had better fold, because you just are not going to win. Unfortunately for Spencer, one of his biggest wins ever was when he was dealt a ten of clubs and a four of diamonds. Normally, a knowledgeable poker player would fold, knowing his chances to win with these two cards were slim and none. Spencer stayed in and won several thousand dollars when the flop contained a pair of tens and another four. On the fifth card another ten was dealt, assuring Spencer of a huge payoff. Every since that experience Spencer foolishly continued to bet the ten and four combination, even though he knew, as a professional player, his chances of winning were almost nonexistent. It was his continuance to bet that hand as well as other questionable hands that caused him to lose more than he won. Much more.

When you play on-line poker, you always play under an alias. When Spencer played online poker prior to his arrest, he went by the name of 'TheProfessor'. When he started losing too much, he changed his on-line alias to 'Prof1959'. These days he used the name 'Tex75222', which was the zip code for Dallas. While you are on-line playing, there are several options available on the screen. The Internet web-casino keeps track of the number of players during each hand who stay in for the flop, the amount of money bet every hand, the average pot won at a table, as well as the amount of money each player has showing on the table. It is this information which helps a player decide which table to join and play. Also on the screen, if you are playing at a table, there is a chat button that allows a player to have a conversation with other players or viewers or even with a specific player who is also at the table. Some players use the chat button as a way to type messages in hopes of bluffing an opponent. Spencer used this option often. Not only did he use it as a strategy in his game, but as a means for talking with someone outside the immediate area. Minoru had denied Spencer email privileges on his laptop. Minoru could not afford for Spencer to either accidentally or purposely let someone know he was still alive. Minoru was unaware of the chat option on the gambling website. Spencer had made quite a group of acquaintances who played poker with him on-line. He was very careful not to reveal his real name to any of these online friends. Often, when he played, he would join a table based on how many of the aliases he recognized at a particular table. That was when he wanted to chat. When he was serious about trying to win, he looked for newcomers to the casino site. The professional players and the regulars considered these new comers to be 'dead money'. They were called 'dead money' because, when they played with the professional players, like Spencer, their money was dead to them. That meant they were sure to lose it.

Spencer was playing at a table with a lot of 'dead money' that day. None of the names he was playing against were familiar to him. That was why he was a little surprised when the chat icon started flashing on his screen. He assumed it was 'dead money' trying to set him up for a bluff later on. When he clicked on the chat icon, Spencer got the scare of his life. Someone who went by the screen name of 'TWOACRES' had sent him a message. All it said was "Be seeing you soon Spence." Spencer felt like puking. Someone had found him. Or maybe it was Minoru testing him. Either way he was in big trouble. He knew Minoru hated him and would just assume he was dead. If he responded, and it was

Minoru, then Minoru would know he had been chatting to people on the casino website. That alone would be reason enough for Minoru to kill him. If it wasn't Minoru, then someone knew Spencer was alive, and that too was reason enough for Minoru to kill him.

Spencer had totally forgotten about the hand he was playing. The computer automatically folded Spencer's hand when he waited too long without calling or raising a bet. Losing what would probably have been a winning hand was of little concern at the present to Spencer. He knew he was about to become a dead man. "Who the hell is 'TWOACRES'?", Spencer kept repeating over and over to himself. He recalled the only time he had heard that name before was in a Clint Eastwood movie. Clint told some cowboy in a bar he was going to give him two acres and then kicked him in the balls. That was how Spencer was feeling right now. Like somebody had just kicked him in the balls. Spencer didn't respond to the message and immediately signed out of the casino website and off of the Internet. He needed to think. He needed to figure out who sent him the message and what he was going to do about it. He was just glad Minoru was still in Japan on business.

Chapter Twenty-one

Haruko met Byron the next day at the airport. She brought a small carryon bag with her. Byron came with two very large suitcases. He intended to make this trip somewhat of a vacation as well. Especially since the National Police Agency was picking up the tab. Or at least that was what he had thought. In reality, Haruko was paying for the flight and hotel expenses. After what had happened when Jotty and Jim had come into town, she did not want her supervisors knowing what her plans were. Somebody had tipped off the Red Summit about their visitation. She did not want the Red Summit tipped off again.

When they got to Hawaii, Byron called the chef's cell phone from the airport. The chef told him they were out on a cruise and he and the photographer would be in the Kona harbor in two days. He asked if Byron had his money. Byron assured him he did. Byron told him there would even be a bonus if the information were as good as he claimed it to be. That seemed to excite the chef.

"It will be," the chef assured Byron.

"Good, then I and my associate will see you in two days," Byron responded. "We will come to the ship when it is moored at the harbor."

This caught the chef by surprise. "What do you mean your associate?"

"My secretary," Byron said while smiling at Haruko. "I brought her along to keep me warm at night while visiting the island." Byron winked at Haruko as he said this.

Byron could hear the chef laugh into his cell phone. "I understand completely," the chef told Byron. "There is no better place than Hawaii for such a tryst. Enjoy yourself. I will welcome the two of you aboard in two days," the chef added.

"Believe me I will. We will see you in two days," responded Byron as he looked at Haruko for a reaction. Byron was hoping that just maybe he would get the lovely National Police Agency officer bedded before they had to leave Paradise. At least he could always hope. Haruko ignored his smile and turned away.

Haruko was not so amused by Byron's conversation. She was more concerned about meeting with the chef and photographer to see if maybe they did have information that would prove Aioka may still be alive. At least she wanted to somehow connect Taka to the Red Summit. That was the hope that brought her to Hawaii. She had left Japan without giving proper notice to her superiors. If she did not return with sufficient reason for having left, her career with the National Police Agency would no doubt be in jeopardy. She had left in the middle of an active investigation of the kidnapping and attempted murder of the two visiting FBI agents. There would be trouble when she got back to Japan. Her supervisors seemed to be looking for a reason to get rid of Haruko. Now she was questioning if she herself had given them the opportunity they needed to justify firing her.

Haruko rented a car and they drove the half an hour drive from the Kona Airport to Waikoloa. Byron wanted Haruko to have him designated as a driver on the rental car as well, but Haruko insisted that if he needed to drive somewhere, she would take him. Byron was not happy about this, but realized Haruko would always be around him. "And who knows what that might lead to," he thought to himself.

There was quite a line of guests checking into the hotel. Many more than would normally be visiting at this time of year. It seems Kilauea, only three days earlier, had started a series of spectacular eruptions, spewing molten lava up to one hundred feet into the air. Several large lava flows could now be seen flowing down the south side of the island. Families in several of the still occupied houses that lay in the path of the new flows were now being forced to evacuate. The road running from the park observation center down to the ocean had once again been covered by a new lava flow. When such a spectacular event occurs, tourists who normally would not visit the island this time of year seem to pour in to witness Mother Nature's fury. Haruko and Byron were aware of the recent volcanic activity, but had given little thought to it until they heard people talking about it in the check-in line.

"Too bad you are afraid to fly in a helicopter," chortled Byron, "It sounds like you are going to miss quite a show."

"If we have time, maybe I will drive over and have a look at the lava," replied Haruko. Someone in line overheard their conversation.

"Oh, you can't get close enough to see it by driving. You have to fly if you want to see the lava," the stranger said. "You better make reservations, because all the helicopter trips are filling up fast. Even the helicopters aren't allowed to get too close now that lava is shooting out of Kilauea. They say it's shooting hundreds of feet into the air."

The excited stranger would probably have kept talking had they not been called to the counter to check in.

"Remember, book your helicopter trip soon," the stranger called out to Haruko as he and his family walked to the counter.

Haruko checked both her and Byron into their respective rooms. She insisted the rooms be next to each other. She didn't want Byron trying to sneak away without her knowledge. Their rooms were at the far northern end of the resort in the area called the Ocean Towers. The Ocean Towers are a series of three connected concentric towers with either an ocean view or a mountain view. In the center of these towers is a lagoon surrounding several small islands. On these islands are a variety of rare tropical birds. The lagoon is part of the transportation design of the resort. Several classic wooden boats ferry passengers and luggage from the hotel lobby to the one of the three main tower areas or to the convention center on the property, through a series of canals and lagoons. There is also a tram that goes the length of the property and stops at several stations along the route. On much of the route the tram parallels the boat canal. Along the route are several restaurants, shops, and gardens. If you are in no hurry, there is a walkway that also pretty much parallels the tram. It is a good twenty-minute to half-hour walk from one end of the property to the other, but well worth it. All along the walkway is an art display valued at over seven million dollars.

The Ocean Towers are more adult-oriented since they are situated furthest from the children's swimming pool and water park. "At least things will be a little quieter on this side of the resort," Haruko thought to herself as she watched the man who had talked to her in line try to corral his brood of children onto the tram. Byron was disappointed their rooms were not in the Palace Tower. That tower has an oriental theme and is located across from a Zen garden and the Flamingo Preserve. Byron felt it was the most beautiful area in the entire resort. He also thought the Palace Tower was in the most romantic area of the resort. He had stayed at the hotel on numerous occasions, and always seemed to be 'lucky with love' when he stayed in the Palace Tower.

Byron's meeting with the helicopter pilot, John Greer, was not till tomorrow, and they were not going to the ship for two days. Byron suggested they have dinner at The Kamuela Provision Company Restaurant, which was at the opposite side of the resort from their rooms. The Kamuela Provision Company offered an unsurpassed view of the sunset and was one of the finer restaurants at the resort. Byron also offered to pay, which made Haruko a little happier. At dinner Byron turned out to be extremely charming, witty, and surprisingly much more desirable than Haruko had imagined. They had wonderful dinner conversation and the food was exquisite. The dinner was topped off by a truly postcard picturesque sunset with several Humpback whales frolicking in the ocean, just off shore from the restaurant. They had shared a bottle of wine during dinner, but Byron insisted they share another bottle after dinner as they sat for almost an hour enjoying the warm trade winds and each other's company. After they finished the second bottle, they decided to walk back to their rooms along the ocean rather than the art walkway. It was a beautiful Hawaiian evening and the walk took them past several of the resort's spectacular pools. As they passed one of the waterslide pool areas, one of the children of the man who had talked to them in line splashed water on Haruko's dress as she and Byron walked past. It was just an innocent prank by a child, and Haruko, though taken aback, was not angry. Parts of her dress had become soaked, and her breasts now highlighted through the wet dress material on her chest. Byron commented on how lovely her dress now looked, causing Haruko to blush. Haruko's head was spinning from the wine and from the feelings of lust she had so rarely allowed herself to experience in the past. They walked hand in hand past the Dolphin Learning Center and paused to watch several of the dolphins playing what seemed like a game of tag with one another. After a few moments, they continued along the ocean path and crossed the bridge over

the turtle lagoon. They stopped on the bridge and looked
across the lagoon at the lights of the Grand Staircase which
ended at the lagoons edge. There were several young couples
kissing on the balcony of the Water's Edge Ballroom located
near the Grand Staircase. A local school was holding their
formal dance at the ballroom that evening. Byron was
wonderful company and Haruko found herself embracing
Byron in a passionate kiss as they stood on the lagoon bridge.
Had any of Haruko's coworkers been watching the resort web
cam, they would have been shocked to see Haruko's passion
that night. Without further conversation, they continued
their walk, hand in hand, towards The Ocean Towers. As they
walked past the pools that separated the Ocean Towers from
the Pacific Ocean, Haruko stopped at one of the giant statues
of zodiac animals associated with the years of the Chinese
calendar. According to the Chinese calendar, Haruko was
born in the year of the dragon. They searched the other
sculptures until they found one that listed Byron's year of
birth. Byron was the year of the cock. This made both Haruko
and Byron laugh. Haruko had never felt so enamored to a
man before. When they arrived back at their Ocean Tower
rooms, they paused in front of Haruko's door. Byron once
again embraced her and they shared a deep passionate kiss.
Haruko unlocked her door and they both entered her room.

Chapter Twenty-two

As Haruko and Byron lay in each others arms across Haruko's bed, two seemingly unrelated events on opposite sides of the world were unfolding.

In Atlanta, Georgia, a man in a white refrigerated delivery van waited next to his driver's side door at a cold storage warehouse on the outskirts of the city. He smoked a cigarette as three Japanese men unloaded crates filled with large packages of frozen meat and then placed these large packages of ground meats and steaks in the back of the van. The driver worked for a local delivery service and had been hired to deliver the meat to various food banks and homeless kitchens throughout the Atlanta area. An anonymous donor had generously provided close to a ton of freshly frozen ground round along with another ton of prime cut steaks and roasts to be distributed among various agencies in the greater Atlanta area. These charities would use the donation to help feed Atlanta's homeless population. As the deliveryman dropped his cargo at the various charity sites, one of Taka's private planes made the return trip back to Hawaii. No record of where the meat originated from would be found. The names on the receipts for the rental of the space in the cold storage warehouse and the receipt for the hiring of the driver from the delivery service would prove to be a fake. Both were paid in cash and in advance. The happy charities would begin cooking and serving the meat that very day. Several homeless men and families had not had such a treat in many months.

In Tokyo, a young man boarded the Keio Line of the Tokyo subway system at the Mizue station. He looked like dozens of other student passengers with packs on their backs headed home from school. There was nothing unusual about the young man that anyone would notice or remember. The digital video cameras monitoring the subway stations would record him entering the station platform and boarding the train. Unlike the other student passengers, his backpack did not contain the books he needed for his studies. Instead, his backpack was filled with four pounds of a highly explosive commercial gel. Wrapped around this gel was another ten pounds of screws and ball bearings. Attached to this bomb was a trigger device made from a cell phone. The student was given instructions to board the subway at the Mizue station, and then place the backpack under his seat when the train stopped at the Funabori station. He was to exit the subway at either the Sumiyoshi station or the Kikukawa station. He had to be sure to exit at one of those two stations. As soon as he left the train, he was to call his handler who would in turn detonate the bomb. Which station he exited depended on when he could safely exit and leave the backpack under the seat without being noticed. He understood that he must be off the train by the Hamacho subway station.

The young man like many other young students in Tokyo was not happy with his prospects for success in today's Japan. That was what led him to become an activist in the student rebellions in Tokyo. He had studied and followed the ideals of the Red Summit and was happy to have the opportunity to help turn Tokyo away from its Americanization policies. He thought he would now be welcomed to join the Red Summit as an active terrorist cell member. He was mistaken!

A call came into the National Police Agency headquarters from a payphone near the Mizue subway platform. The caller asked to speak with Haruko Ozawa. They were told she was not in her office. The caller then insisted he talk to her supervisor. When Haruko's supervisor answered the phone, the caller informed them that the Red Summit was about to strike at the heart of Tokyo. They also said Haruko would never be able to stop them from their reign of terror. Then the caller told the supervisor to listen closely. An explosion could be heard over the phone line.

The student with the backpack entered the train as instructed and was holding the backpack as he was also instructed to do until he reached the Funabori station. The train was just leaving the platform when the caller detonated the bomb. The student and eight people near him were blown into hundreds of pieces. Another twenty passengers lost limbs or were seriously injured in the explosion. Several of those injuries would prove fatal in the following days. Another sixty-three passengers sustained minor to moderate injuries.

Before hanging up the caller warned of more attacks to come.

Haruko's supervisor was furious. Haruko had left without informing anyone of where she was going or when she would return. She left abruptly in the middle of the investigation over the kidnapping of the two FBI agents from the United States. The FBI had requested her assistance and asked Haruko to become a member of an international team formed to investigate the Red Summit. Jotty and Jim were almost killed by the very terrorist cell they came to investigate. The National Police Agency knew of the FBI's request and had agreed to release Haruko to join the team, but she refused the offer. Now she was not even around to do her job. Things did not look good for Haruko's future with the National Police Agency.

Haruko awoke in the arms of Byron. They had breakfast in their room as they sat watching the golfers out the window. They could see the humpback whales that continued their migration in the waters just off shore behind the golfers. Haruko had forgotten to bring her cell phone and Byron had not bothered to turn his on since arriving in Hawaii. His appointment with John Greer, the helicopter pilot, was in just over an hour so he and Haruko quickly showered together and left her room. Byron had called ahead to the valet, so their rental car was waiting when they reached the lobby. It was a short drive to the Mauna Lani heliport where Byron was scheduled to meet John for his private tour and conversation. Haruko debated taking a Dramamine and joining Byron on the flight, just so she could see Kilauea actively spewing lava as the stranger in line at check-in had told them about. When she arrived and saw the helicopter, she thought better of joining Byron on the flight and agreed to come back in an hour to pick him up. Byron in turn promised to share all of the information he learned concerning the pilot's flight with Taka and Niki. Haruko watched as the helicopter lifted off and headed southeast towards the volcano.

Haruko drove back to the King's Shops near the Waikoloa Hilton. She entered the Starbucks and was having a cup of tea when she picked up a copy of the Los Angeles Times and saw the headline regarding the bombing of the subway in Tokyo. The blood drained from her face as she continued to read the newspaper account of the tragedy. When she reached the part about the caller claiming the attack was the work of the Red Summit she gasped for breath. She sat there dazed. Her hand was visibly shaking as she pondered what next to do. She felt angry and ashamed that while she was making love to Byron, the Red Summit had attacked near her own home. It was her job to find and stop the Red Summit. She had failed the people of Japan. She questioned if she would ever be able to face her coworkers again. Haruko decided to wait until she picked up Byron and discussed her options with him before calling her office. She would wait to see what information Byron obtained from the pilot. Deep in her heart, she knew somehow all of these events were connected to Taka.

Chapter Twenty-three

"Just what makes you so damn sure we will find Spencer in Hawaii?" Jotty asked Jim as their plane taxied down the runway at Los Angeles International Airport preparing for takeoff.

"Cause I've talked to him," Jim responded smugly.

"What the hell do you mean, you've talked to him?" Jotty asked demanding an answer.

"Just what I said," continued Jim. "I chatted with him on the internet. He never exactly responded to my greeting, but he did respond as I expected. He quickly signed off his computer when I told him I'd be seeing him real soon."

"He knows you are coming to see him?" Jotty gasped in disbelief. "He's probably gone to Argentina by now."

"I don't think so,' Jim responded. "And he doesn't really know who sent him the greeting. All he knows is that somebody with the screen name 'TWOACRES' sent him a little surprise wake up call in the middle of a poker game."

"Very funny," Jotty replied, "TWOACRES' as in a kick to the balls?"

"You got it partner," Jim replied as he eased back his seat to take a little nap.

During the flight Jim explained to Jotty how he was able to find Spencer.

"You should have read his file a little closer. I'm sure even you would have been able to put it together," Jim said mockingly to Jotty. "It was all in the files. What you forgot was that Spencer was a compulsive gambler, and once a compulsive gambler always a compulsive gambler. That's all I needed to know to find him. The FBI had all the information about where and when he gambled, and how much he loss. You got all that information from the Internet casino's website records. Every poker hand ever played on-line, how it was played, by whom it was played, and how much was bet, is recorded somewhere in a monster computer on the Internet. That was how the FBI was able to track down Spencer's losses the first time. That time was easy though, because he told you what his online name was. All you had to do was have the casino do a search of his on-line poker name. Now this time, it was a little trickier. I took the information you guys had, and the information I got from his ex-wife about his betting patterns, and fed it into the computer. Then I had 'the mother of all computers' at the IRL lab at Texas A & M compare the information I gave it to all recent activity at the Pan-American Poker website. That was the site Spencer always played. I couldn't imagine him playing somewhere else on-line. In no time at all, the computer kicked back the answer I wanted. It gave me a 98% match to my inputted information with a player named 'TEX75222'. That happens to be the zip code of Spencer's old house in Dallas, Texas. The computer gave me a few other matches in the 60% to 80% range. I did check those out as well, but I was sure the first one was our man. It also told me 'TEX75222' always logged on through a mobile line connection from the big island of Hawaii. That is, except when he logged on through the server at the Hilton Waikoloa Village Resort." Jim paused so his next statement would amaze Jotty. "Room 1342, Palace Tower," Jim smiled.

  "You even know what god-damned room he's staying in?" Jotty gasped in disbelief. Jim just kept smiling that shit-eating grin which got him in so many fights.

  "He was there yesterday when I sent him my little greeting. Immediately he logged off. I have no doubt he is still there. Mostly because I called the hotel and a Mr. Karl Spencer is still staying there." Jim had thoroughly impressed Jotty with his sleuthing skills. "You know though," Jim said in a curious tone, "something about it just ain't right. I get the feeling Spencer isn't here on his own free will. I got a feeling somebody needed Spencer's knowledge and forced him to go there with them."

"What makes you think that?" Jotty questioned.

"Just a hankering gnawing at my gut," Jim replied.

"Jesus, I hate it when you start talking like a hick, Jimbo." Jotty teased.

Jim slugged Jotty hard in the arm. "I told you never to call me Jimbo."

When they arrived at the Kona airport, the FBI had a car waiting for them. They had made reservations at the Waikoloa Marriott Hotel, which was just south of the Hilton Waikoloa Village Resort. Jotty was afraid Spencer or someone with Spencer might be watching for anyone suspicious who comes and goes from the Hilton. Jotty figured they could easily walk along the beach to get to the Hilton from the Marriott. That way they could avoid the lobby area. Jim knew if Spencer wasn't in his room, he would be at one of the bars trying to pick up on women. That was another old habit of Spencer's Jim knew would be hard for Spencer to change. That was one of the reasons he hated Spencer. He heard from friends, that, after Jim joined the Marines, Spencer started dating and eventually married Jim's old girlfriend Susan. Several of his buddies told him that even after the marriage, Spencer was still hitting the bars and cheating on her. "That just wasn't the right way for a married man to act," thought Jim as old feelings of rage began to rise in his heart. When Jotty and Jim got to the hotel, there was an emergency message waiting for Jotty. He was to call his office in Washington D.C. immediately from a secured phone.

"Hell," said Jotty, "The closest secured phone is probably in Hilo and that's two hours away. I'll just have to call them from a land line to see what the big emergency is," he told Jim as he headed out the door.

"The hotel probably has a secured line in the business center," Jim called out after him. "Look there first."

When Jotty asked at the concierge desk, he found out Jim was right. There was a secured line at the hotel business center.

As soon as Jotty was out the door, Jim pulled out his laptop and signed on to the Internet. He went to the Internet web casino where he discovered Spencer playing Texas Hold 'Em the previous day. There were more than fifty active poker games, each with at least seven players playing at each game, taking place when Jim began his search. Jim knew there was no need to check the small limit games. If Spencer was there, he would be playing at the large stake games. Jim found 'TEX75222' playing at the third table he viewed. All the seats at the table were taken, so Jim had to wait almost ten minutes before he was able to join the game. Jim had to be actively playing in the game in order to access the chat button on the screen. He knew as soon as he joined the poker game, Spencer would see the name 'TWOACRES' show up as one of the players now playing. Jim didn't know how Spencer would react, but he had a feeling he wouldn't sign off this time.

Spencer had just lost $1200 on a full house of queens over sevens. What he had thought was 'dead money' had picked up their fourth seven on the 'river' card, giving them the winning hand. Normally, Spencer would have gone into a rage when some 'dead money' got such a lucky draw and beat what normally should easily have been a winning hand. Not today. Spencer was very troubled by the message he had received the previous day in the chat room from 'TWOACRES'. He had spent much of last night brooding over his new dilemma. He had decided it wasn't Minoru trying to trick him into responding. Minoru needed no reason for such a ruse. Spencer was sure Minoru hated him and needed no such fabricated reason to justify killing him if he wished to do so. No, Spencer was sure it was not Minoru. Spencer was equally convinced there was also no way it could be anyone who used to play poker against him prior to his arrest and sentencing to prison. Back then, Spencer was very careful not to reveal his real name to anyone in a poker chat room on-line, or to anyone in his non-internet reality who knew of his excessive gambling. Even Susan, his former wife, knew nothing about his online gambling addiction. At least not until right before his entire life collapsed because of it. Spencer became sad for a moment as he thought about Susan. While he was in federal prison, he dreamed that when he was released, Susan would take him back and they could start a new life together. Spencer was hoping to contact her, but Minoru and his men changed Spencer's plan unexpectedly. Spencer realized that very soon Minoru would have no further use for him and he would be killed. Spencer knew he needed to act, but he had no idea of what to do. He was constantly under the scrutiny of Minoru's two men assigned to watch his every move. They were always looking over his shoulder as he did his online gambling. The only time they left him alone for any amount of time was when he was able to pick up some women in the hotel bar. When that happened, Minoru's men would discretely follow Spencer back to his hotel room and keep watch over the room until his lady friend left to return to her own room. Spencer knew most of the women he was able to get back to his room were professional call girls hired by Minoru to keep Spencer and his men happy. Lately, Spencer had noticed these professionals were not as readily available. Spencer thought this too was not a good sign for his continued employment with Minoru.

Spencer's mind had drifted. He was concerned about the message he had received in the poker chat room. He was now feeling sorry for himself because of the terrible situation he seemed to be in thanks to Minoru. He was posting his ante for the next hand when he was suddenly jarred back to reality. 'TWOACRES' had just joined the game. At first Spencer thought about signing off immediately. Then he realized whoever this 'TWOACRES' was, he was smart enough to find him, and maybe, just maybe they would be smart enough to help Spencer get out of the awful predicament he knew was leading to his premature death.

Spencer had only one guard with him in his room. That guard was sitting on the bed watching Sumo wrestling on a Japanese language station. He was paying little attention to Spencer's online game. The chat icon began to flash on Spencer's computer. Spencer looked nervously at the guard sitting on the bed. He used his mouse to click on the button to read the message.

"Told you I would be seeing you soon, Spence", was the message 'TWOACRES' had typed. Spencer wanted desperately to reply, but his guard would have noticed him typing on the keyboard. Playing online poker only required the use of a few mouse clicks once a player was signed on. If Spencer typed, the guard would know something was going on. Minoru had advised the guards to watch for just such a thing.

Jim was puzzled when there was no response from 'TEX75222'. His computer indicated the message had been read, but 'TEX75222' didn't respond nor did he quickly sign off as he had yesterday. 'TEX75222' continued to play the hand as Jim watched the action waiting for a response. As the poker hand developed, several players folded. Jim had not yet got involved in playing and had chosen the 'sit this hand out' option on his screen. 'TEX75222' stayed in the hand calling the bets of the other players who remained. At the conclusion of the hand and the players cards were revealed, Jim was astounded 'TEX75222' had not folded. He had losing cards from the very beginning, yet continued to play out the hand, with no hope of winning. Spencer hadn't done it as a bluff, it was just terrible card playing. Jim couldn't understand what Spencer was doing. Jim sent 'TEX75222' another message. "What kind of poker playing is that, Spence" Jim could see the message was read, but still, no response. Jim continued to sit out and watch the next poker hand being played. Once again Spence had remained in the hand when he should have folded. Still he failed to respond to Jim's messages. "Maybe he can't respond," Jim started to think. Especially if he is not here on his own free will. Jim decided to run a little test. He sent another message to ''TEX75222'.

"Spence, I know it's you. I'm betting for some reason you can't answer my messages. If that is true, fold on the next deal." Jim sat back to see what would happen. The dealer dealt the players their two down cards. When the bet came around to 'TEX75222', he folded. A big smile came across Jim's face. He had guessed right. Spence was being held against his will and was unable to type any messages back in response. Somebody had to be watching him closely. Jim suddenly realized Spence had no idea who was sending him the messages. Jim also realized Spence must be desperate if he is responding to a stranger in a chat room at

184

an online poker casino. He decided he better let Spence know who was writing the chat messages.

"Spence, its Susan's ex writing to you. I'm here to get you out. Do you need help? Fold again if you do." Jim waited for the next hand to be dealt. Just like the previous hand, 'TEX 75222' folded immediately.

Just then Jotty came back into the room.

"We got big trouble, my friend. We need to catch the first flight out in the morning back to the mainland. Someone who claims to ..." Jim shushed Jotty.

"Shut up for a minute, I'm talking to Spencer," Jim yelled at Jotty.

"You're what?" Jotty answered as he looked over Jim's shoulder at the computer screen.

"Shhh...," Jim scolded. "Just be quiet a minute."

Jotty stood quietly behind Jim as he typed in the next message.

"Is there just one person guarding you? Fold again if yes." Jim wrote.

This time when the cards were dealt, Spence didn't fold, but continued to play the hand.

"Hell," Jim swore. "That means there is more than one person guarding him."

"What are you talking about?" Jotty questioned. "How do you know that? The guy never responded."

"He can't respond," Jim told Jotty. "At least he can't type a response. I worked out a code with him to get responses. He's being watched or guarded, and, according to his last response, there is more than one person doing the watching."

Jotty was so fascinated by what Jim was doing, he forgot the urgency of the message he just got from

Washington. Actually, he decided it could wait a few minutes. There was nothing they could do about it right now anyway.

Jim sent Spencer another message. "Can you get out of your room and into an open area? Fold if you can."

Jotty and Jim waited as the next hand was dealt. When the bet came around to 'TEX75222', the hand was folded.

"That's good," Jim said to no one in particular. Jim then turned and spoke to Jotty, "How are we going to get him out of there, buddy."

"It's simple," Jotty told Jim. "We are just going to go meet him at the bar."

"Sounds like a plan to me," Jim responded. "Now what is the big emergency back in Washington?"

Chapter Twenty-four

Minoru had flown to Oahu where he boarded the *Grand Maui*, which was already halfway through a cruise. Several people actually boarded the ship halfway through the present cruise, so they could be on board when the ship went to the big island and view the fiery activity of Kilauea's recent eruption. Seeing the spectacular eruption of Kilauea at night from the deck of the *Grand Maui* was one of the best and most sought-after ways to see the volcano. The streams of flowing lava snaking down towards the ocean and the fiery explosions from the caldera were sights one never forgot once viewed.

Minoru had made arrangements to take care of several of Taka's problems over the next two days. He was on the ship to personally handle the photographer and chef. After dinner on his first evening aboard the ship, Minoru sought out Hiroshi to convince him he would live a safer, happier, and rewarding life if he went back to Japan immediately without speaking to any journalists. Hiroshi was shocked by Minoru's comments. He could tell Minoru was not the type of person to make an idle threat. Minoru was offering him much more money than the tabloid to forget what he knew and move to Japan where he was guaranteed the position of head chef at one of Japan's premiere 'Aioka' Steakhouse restaurants.

Hiroshi did not even hesitate in his decision to take Minoru up on his offer. He agreed to leave the ship the next day at Hilo, before it went to Kona where he was scheduled to meet Byron.

"I thank you for such a generous offer and opportunity," Hiroshi said as he bowed to Minoru.

"You made a wise decision," Minoru responded as he bowed in return. "Just remember, never be so foolish you speak of such things again, or your life may take a sudden turn for the worse." It was a blatant threat Hiroshi understood completely.

"What of the ship's photographer?" Hiroshi asked. "He too was to meet with Ono when the ship arrives in Kona."

"Do not concern yourself with him. I have made arrangements with him as well," Minoru told Hiroshi. "And please do not contact him or speak with anyone else about our meeting." With that, Minoru took out an envelope from his jacket pocket. It contained a guaranteed cashier's check for a large sum of money, several thousand dollars in cash, and a first-class airline ticket to Japan on a flight scheduled to leave the next day from Hilo.

Hiroshi was shocked at the contents of the envelope. "I will speak of this to no one. Thank you for your generosity." Hiroshi bowed as Minoru left the room.

Later that night, the ship's fire alarm began sounding. The monitor in the bridge showed there was a fire in the photography studio and lab. By the time the fire crew arrived, the lab, studio, and all of its contents were destroyed. They were able to contain the fire to just that area. When the fire was out, they discovered the charred remains of the photographer lying in what used to be the studio darkroom. Fire inspectors were flown to the ship from Oahu. It was determined a freak explosion of chemicals used in developing film caused the fire. They ruled the fire and death as accidental. Hiroshi knew better.

With the ship moored in Hilo, Hiroshi left with his few possessions to return to Japan. He told the captain he had to return to Japan immediately due to the severe illness of his mother. The captain hated to see Hiroshi leave, but understood his need to go so suddenly. After all, the captain had a much more serious issue to deal with. One of his crew had just perished when a fire gutted the ship's photography studio.

Minoru also left the ship when it docked in Hilo. A car was waiting for him at the pier to take him to the airport. When he arrived at the airport, he boarded a waiting helicopter. John Greer was not the pilot.

Chapter Twenty-five

aruko left the Starbucks at the King's shops and headed back to the heliport at Mauna Lani. She was a little early, so she waited in the rental car for Byron to return. She watched as the helicopter flew in from the direction of Kilauea. When it landed, two Japanese men exited the copter with the pilot. It was obviously not Byron's helicopter. Haruko watched as a rather well-dressed Japanese gentleman walked to a car parked near the helicopter service hangar facilities and climbed into the back seat. The other man that exited the helicopter was large and muscular. He grabbed a small suitcase from the storage compartment of the helicopter, carried it to the car, and placed it in the car's trunk. He then opened the driver's side door, entered the car and drove away from the heliport. Haruko continued to stare at the car. There was something familiar about both the Japanese men. She was sure she had seen them before, but she had no idea where. A moment later, another pilot came running from the office with two other workers in overalls. Haruko had seen both the men in overalls working on a helicopter when she had dropped off Byron. They all jumped aboard the helicopter that had just landed. It took off quickly and headed towards Kilauea.

Haruko continued to wait checking her watch every couple of minutes. She had no patience for Byron being late. She had a lot on her mind that she needed to talk to Byron about. She especially wanted to know what the pilot had to tell him. She continued to wait. It was almost thirty minutes past the time Byron and the pilot were scheduled to return. A car pulled up next to her that held a husband and wife and three children. The children were dancing around excited about their flight over the volcano they were about to go on. Haruko watched as the family entered the helicopter tour office. Three minutes later they exited the office and came back to their rental car. The children were no longer dancing and the parents had a look of disbelief. Haruko rolled down her window so she could hear their conversation as they climbed back into their car.

"I just thank God it wasn't us," the father was saying.

"I told you we shouldn't have signed up for a helicopter tour. I told you I heard they are always crashing here on the islands," the wife added.

Haruko's brain went numb as she stared at the family as they got into their car and drove out of the parking lot. For the next ten minutes Haruko sat motionless in the car trying to get up enough courage to go in the office to verify what she already knew had to be true. When she finally did enter the building, a man behind the desk confirmed one of the helicopters had crashed, but that there was no news regarding the condition of any passengers who may have been on board. As the man was telling Haruko it was still too early to make any assumptions, the radio monitoring the other helicopters that were involved in the search was blaring out the bad news.

"Jesus Christ, he crashed right into the caldera. Look, look, you can still just see the tail of the copter sticking out of the molten lava. Oh my god...." The man behind the desk turned the volume of the radio low so Haruko couldn't hear it.

"I'm sorry, but there is still no confirmation anyone was injured in the crash," the man behind the desk said trying to reassure Haruko.

Haruko just turned away and left the building without saying anything else. She knew Byron was dead and didn't want anyone to see her cry. She went back to the car and waited. Why or for what she was waiting for, she had no idea. When the police arrived about twenty minutes later, Haruko left her car and identified herself as a Japanese National Police Agency special officer. She informed the police officer she was a friend of Byron's, and had come to Hawaii with him. The officer told Haruko Byron, along with the pilot, John Greer, perished. According to eyewitnesses, their helicopter flew too low above the lava spewing from the caldera causing an explosion on the helicopter. The copter plummeted into the molten lava pool inside the caldera and disintegrated.

"Are you sure the explosion was an accident?" Haruko questioned the officer.

"Why do you ask that? Is there something we should know?" the officer responded.

Haruko remained silent. The police officer had a look of concern as he tried to evaluate what Haruko had asked.

"Of course it was an accident," said the officer. "Anyway, there is nothing left of the copter for the FFA to collect to even examine. Everything melted into the lava. All we have is the eyewitness report from another helicopter full of tourists doing the same thing the crashed helicopter was doing, looking at the volcano," the officer explained to Haruko.

"Not exactly doing the same thing," Haruko thought to herself.

For the next hour, Haruko answered questions about what she and Byron were doing in Hawaii and why she didn't go on the flight with him. They were very curious as to why Byron was the only passenger on the flight. Haruko told them they would have to ask the helicopter service about that.

While she was being questioned, another officer was following up Haruko's story. The police had confirmed Haruko and Byron did arrive together from Japan and Haruko had paid for both flights and both hotel rooms. They sent an officer to check Byron's hotel room. He called the officer questioning Haruko to tell him that he had found Byron's room had not been slept in or even used as far as the investigating officer could tell. The officer now started asking some very personal questions of Haruko. His insinuations and tone of voice angered her and she told him she was through answering their questions. She told him if he needed to know anything else about her, he could call her supervisor at the National Police Agency. That was when he informed her he already had called her supervisor. The officer told Haruko he had no more questions for her right now, but not to leave the island for a couple of days. He also told her she may want to give her supervisor a call. Apparently Haruko's supervisor was more than a little surprised to learn Haruko was in Hawaii.

Haruko didn't answer or thank the officer. She knew her career as a special officer, for that matter, as any kind of officer was now definitely over. She had blown her career, but she was still determined to prove Taka was not who he seemed or claimed to be. She would meet with the chef and the photographer the next day when the *Grand Maui* docked in Kona. She hoped if she got the proof she needed, maybe the National Police Agency would take her back, If not, then she would call Jotty and see if his offer was still on the table. She had a feeling it would be.

Haruko went back to her room at the Hilton Waikoloa Village. The police had already removed Byron's belongings from his room and the hotel maid was just finishing with her cleaning. That meant Haruko did not have Byron's phonebook with the chef's cell number in it. She would just have to meet him the next day as originally planned. Haruko couldn't imagine things getting worse and turned on the television as she lay on the bed to unwind. She was channel surfing the available choices when she came across a local news station talking about a fire on the *Grand Maui*. It seemed during the night there had been a chemical explosion and fire which killed the ship's photographer and destroyed the photography studio on-board. The newscaster continued telling the viewers that despite the on-board tragedy, a representative from Hawaiian Island Cruises had announced that the *Grand Maui*, which was now moored in Hilo, would continue its present cruise schedule and undertake the rebuilding of the destroyed studio while at sea. Haruko could not believe what she was hearing. She grabbed the phone and called information for Hawaiian Island Cruise Lines. She told the receptionist who answered the phone she needed to contact the kitchen on the *Grand Maui*. She told her it was a matter of life or death that she gets in touch with the head chef immediately. The receptionist informed Haruko the kitchen did not have a separate phone number and was unable to help her. When Haruko finally identified herself as a police officer, the receptionist gave Haruko the radio room operator's cell number. She told Haruko the radio operator would be able to transfer her call to the kitchen. Haruko thanked the receptionist and placed her call.

The radio operator answered after two rings.

"This is Scott," he answered.

"Hello. This is Haruko Ozawa. I am the secretary for a Mr. Ono Saito. Could you please connect me to the head chef in the kitchen?" Haruko felt foolish calling herself Byron's secretary, but knew if she said she was a police officer, the chef may refuse her call.

"The new head chef isn't on board yet. He will be coming aboard when our sister ship 'The Kauai Princess', docks in about an hour. He has to finish up that cruise first. Would you like to talk to the chef temporarily in charge?"

"No, I would like to speak to whatever chef was in charge yesterday," Haruko said desperately.

"Then I won't be able to help you," the radio operator replied. "He quit suddenly this morning and has already left the ship. From what I hear, he has already left the island."

Haruko saw no point in questioning the operator any longer. She knew the chef was gone and there would be no point in trying to find him. It would only get the chef killed. That is, if he was still alive, which Haruko doubted.

Haruko brooded in her room for almost an hour trying to decide what her next move would be. After all that had happened, she didn't even want to go back to her position as special investigator in Tokyo. She knew, even if they accepted her back, her future at the National Police Agency was not going to be too promising. She also did not want to face her coworkers and bosses with the shame she felt. She would call her supervisor later that day to discuss what her plans were. That is, as soon as she figured out what her plans were.

Chapter Twenty-six

Spencer couldn't believe his luck. He also couldn't believe Jim had been able to track him down. He thought Minoru had pulled off the perfect crime when he had faked Spencer's death. There was never any hint in the newspapers that the authorities thought anything but what Minoru wanted them to think. That is why he was so astounded and elated. "Boy, will Minoru be surprised when Jim shows up," Spencer thought to himself. Then Spencer started to get nervous. He knew Jim had gone to the Marines and been in a covert special operations group. That meant Jim would be able to handle himself in a fight. Spencer had no doubt there would be a fight. He also knew his guards carried guns. He prayed Jim still carried his six-shooters. He also knew Jim had quit the Marines and now worked as a Farm Service Agent in west Texas. "What in the hell was a Farm Service Agent doing tracking me down in Hawaii," Spencer said to himself. There had to be more to this picture than Spencer was seeing. Regardless, Spencer planned to be at the Malolo Cocktail Lounge at three o'clock that afternoon. That was the time Jim told Spencer to meet him and that was the time Spencer hoped he would finally escape Minoru's death grip.

Jim was able to find out from Spencer that there were two guards watching over him. He also found out Spencer was allowed to visit the bars and restaurants in the hotel. That was good news for Jim and Jotty. It would be a lot easier to get the jump on the two guards in a public area than trying to get into Spencer's hotel room. In the bar, they could casually walk up behind the guards and disarm them before they knew what was happening.

"If we are lucky," Jim told Jotty, "Maybe these two guys will fight back. I haven't been in a good barroom brawl for ages."

Jotty just shook his head and smiled.

"Well, let's hope this is easy. We have to get to Atlanta as soon as possible. We need to see what we can find out about an incident there," Jotty explained.

"You mean the terror attack?" Jim asked.

"What do you mean, terror attack?" Jotty responded.

"Check out the television, Bud," Jim responded.

There was a breaking news banner across the bottom of the television screen and a very serious looking broadcaster was talking about the Red Summit's terror attack on the United States and Japan.

"Hell, I didn't hear the Red Summit was behind the Japanese train bombing," Jotty exclaimed. "I need to call Haruko right away."

"After we get Spencer back," Jim replied. "The news seems to have better information than the FBI. At least a ton of mad cow affected beef donated to fifteen homeless shelters, food banks, and church kitchens in and around downtown Atlanta, and seventy percent of it already cooked, served and eaten. Man is somebody going to get sued."

"They are still testing the meat," Jotty insisted.

"It doesn't matter," said Jim. "As far as the public is concerned, the cows have left the barn. And you know as well as I do, that meat will be tainted."

"What will happen to everybody who ate the meat?" Jotty asked Jim.

"Nothing for several years. Then one day they will wake up with a twitch in their arm muscle. The twitches will grow gradually more severe. They will start forgetting things. Then they will start forgetting a lot of things. Their balance will be a little off. Then they will start falling down a lot. Their muscles will constantly spasm. Pretty soon, they will be in a wheelchair unable to walk, sit up straight, talk, or for that matter control any of their muscles or body functions. They will be too far gone to wish to die, but all of their loved ones will wish that for them." Jim looked at Jotty. "And there is no cure."

"You paint a pretty grim picture, my friend." Jotty responded solemnly.

"It is a pretty grim picture," Jim replied, "but the good thing is it isn't contagious like a thousand other diseases that can cause the same type of damage. The only way you are going to get the human form of mad cow disease, is to ingest mad cow affected tissue. Unfortunately, several hundred people apparently just did in Atlanta."

Jotty and Jim headed for the bar at the Waikoloa Hilton. They left early so they could be in place when Spencer and his two guards came into the bar. They decided it would be safe to drive over to the Hilton Waikoloa since both of Spencer's guards were with him in the room. At least that was what they thought.

Haruko had not been the only one to recognize a familiar face at the heliport. As he was exiting the helicopter, Minoru also recognized Haruko sitting in the rental car. He had actually expected to see her there waiting for Byron to return from his flight. She would be waiting for a long time. It was Minoru who caused John Greer's helicopter to crash. He had one of his men place a small explosive device in the engine compartment of John's copter. It was Minoru's helicopter that reported witnessing the crash of John's copter, along with another tour copter in the area. It was Minoru's pilot who lured John over the caldera by telling him of a fabulous view of the flowing lava. When John's copter approached Kilauea's caldera, Minoru denoted the explosives by remote control. It was a well-timed denotation that plunged John and Byron into the molten lava along with the helicopter. There would be no wreckage to inspect. John had a reputation as a pilot who took chances. He also had a reputation as a heavy drinker and partier. It would not take much for the local police to rule it as an accident based on John's behavior. The cocaine Minoru had one of his men place in John's apartment in Waimea would also help lead the police to the conclusion Minoru had designed for them to reach. His plan would work to perfection.

When Minoru left the heliport, he dropped his suitcase at the Paleaka Ranch, made sure all was going as planned, and then headed to the Hilton Waikoloa Village Resort to check on Spencer and his guards. He also needed a massage after all of his recent traveling to help him relax and focus on the next steps in Taka's plan. When he and his driver arrived at the hotel, they saw Spencer with his two guards having drinks in the Malolo Lounge. Spencer did not see Minoru arrive. Minoru told his driver to keep an eye on Spencer and the guards while Minoru went for his massage. Minoru reminded his driver not to let them know they were being watched and left him at the far end of the lounge. The Malolo is a huge lounge right off of the lobby area of the Hilton. It has several open rooms all connected, yet it allows a person some privacy if desired. There is a large stage where a giant television screen shows televised sporting matches during the day and local jazz singers perform with their combos in the evenings. There are two outside seating areas. One area is by the valet parking lot for smokers just outside the door from the pool table, while the other is on the opposite side across the hotel passageway next to the tram and canal.

Haruko had decided she needed to get in touch with Jotty immediately. She had been watching television when the program was interrupted by the breaking news of what the media was calling the newest terrorist attack on the United States by the Japanese terrorist cell the Red Summit. She had left her laptop at home along with her cell phone. She did know his email address and decided to walk to the business center at the Hilton and email him. She also would use the secured phone at the center to call FBI headquarters to try to reach him there. She began her walk down the hallway that led from the Ocean Tower to the business center at the far end of the resort. As she left her room and walked past the boat landing area, she noticed a large crowd gathered around the edge of the canal. Haruko stopped to see what was going on. A hotel worker was explaining to the crowd who had gathered and was pointing at something in the water, that the canal and lagoons were indeed filled with ocean water and, yes, there were several species of fish swimming in the waterway. He confirmed the big long fish everybody was pointing at was indeed a barracuda.

"That big barracuda goes by the name of 'Elvis'," the hotel worker told the crowd. Several people laughed as the people talked among themselves.

Finally, somebody spoke up and asked, "Why do they call him 'Elvis?"

"They call him 'Elvis' because of the way he eats. He is quite plump for a barracuda. Kind of like Elvis Presley plumped up when he grew older," the worker explained.

"Who is Elvis Presley?" a young boy asked. Most of the adults in the crowd laughed.

"Ask your mom that question," the worker answered. That drew a laugh from several other people in the crowd.

"How big is 'Elvis'?" another man in the crowd asked.

"He's over five and a half feet long and weighs over forty pounds. Which is huge for a barracuda," the worker continued.

"Does he bite," a little girl asked.

"He probably would if we didn't feed him so well," the worker responded.

Haruko left the crowd and started walking down the passageway towards the business center. The passage is filled with several million dollars worth of native Hawaiian art and artifacts, as well as antique paintings, sculptures, and furniture from around the world. Haruko wished she was in better spirits so she could take her time and enjoy the artwork as she had with Byron the night before. Thinking about Byron made her tear up, but she refused to cry.

Jotty and Jim had planned to get to the Malolo Bar before Spencer and the two guards. That was the message Jim had sent to Spencer. He was to wait at least an hour before heading to the bar. Spencer, however, was much too anxious to get out of the predicament he was in and immediately left his room and went to the bar after Jim's last message. The bar was much more crowded than usual for being so early in the afternoon. The hotel was totally sold out and there were two conventions being held at the hotel convention center that day. The afternoon sessions had ended and dozens of conventioneers had descended on the Malolo Lounge. Jotty and Jim used their FBI credentials to park in the valet parking "A" lot which was right next to the

Malolo. When they entered, they knew they were in trouble. The bar was almost full. They found two seats near the pool table and started surveying the room in case Spencer was already there. Spencer was there, but Jim didn't recognize him right away due to the plastic surgery Spencer had undergone. It was Spencer's voice that made Jim realize Spencer was already in the room. Spencer had seen Jim come into the bar and knew Jim would not recognize him. His guards were being unusually protective of Spencer today because of the large crowd and wouldn't allow Spencer to wander around the lounge as they normally did. Knowing he had to let Jim know who he was and where he was, he bellowed to the waitress to bring him and his two friends another round of drinks. The two guards looked at Spencer in surprise. They had never heard him be so loud and demanding before. They looked at each other and laughed as they discussed in Japanese how Spencer must already be drunk to act so foolishly. Spencer's ploy did work as Jim turned quickly at the sound of Spencer's voice. Their eyes met in a fleeting glance acknowledging they were both aware of each other's presence. Jim's sudden turning to see from where the bellowing voice originated startled Jotty. Without being told, he knew it was Spencer getting Jim's attention.

Jim and Jotty were not the only people in the room who recognized Spencer's loud demand for more drinks was more than just a drunken man's desire for more alcohol. Minoru's driver whose job it was to keep an eye on Spencer's guards noticed Jim's reaction to Spencer's call. He also noticed the furtive glance between Spencer and the very tall American who had just entered the room. Minoru's guard studied the two Americans and decided they both looked like police or FBI agents. They were not dressed as a typical tourist in their Aloha Hawaiian shirts and shorts, nor did they wear the badges of the conventioneers who dominated the crowd. He did notice they both had their shirttails untucked and each had the bulge of a concealed gun in their waistbands. Minoru's driver slowly started shifting his position in the room to afford him a clear shot at the two FBI agents if it became necessary.

His movement caught someone else's attention at that very moment. Haruko was in the passageway along the edge of the Malolo Lounge. She saw it was the Japanese driver from the heliport. She didn't see his companion anywhere near him in the crowd. Minoru's driver was staring across the room. Haruko could tell he was moving and positioning himself in the same way a police officer stakes out and moves in on an armed criminal. When she looked to see whom he was stalking, she gasped. Jotty and Jim were sitting on the other side of the bar. As she watched, she could tell they too were watching and stalking someone. They were completely unaware they in turn were being watched. She tried to see who their prey was, but was unable to due to the crowd. Almost immediately Jotty and Jim left their seats at the bar and headed across the lounge. The man from the heliport also moved towards Jotty and Jim. Haruko then saw the three men Jotty and Jim were focused on. One of them, who looked American, saw Jotty and Jim coming and was almost pleading with his eyes for their help. He was beginning to rise from his stool as if to meet Jotty and Jim on their way. The other two looked to be Japanese and they too started to rise as if to stop the other man from fleeing. Haruko watched as Jotty and Jim began to reach towards their waistbands for their guns. Simultaneously, the Japanese man from the heliport pulled his own weapon and took aim. Haruko screamed 'gun' as loud as she could while grabbing a drink off the table next to her and throwing it at the Japanese man about to pull the trigger. The drink hit the man's wrist just enough to cause his first shot to go astray. The bullet grazed Jim's back and hit a waitress standing behind Jim in the shoulder. Jotty and Jim dove to the ground, as did dozens of startled patrons in the bar. Several others ran for the exits and into the Hilton lobby, out the back door to the valet parking area, or down the passageway towards the Lagoon Tower. Before the Japanese man could get off a second shot, Haruko grabbed a martini out of the hand of a man standing next to her who appeared to be too scared or too drunk to react. In one movement, she shattered the top of the martini glass as she leaped at the shooter and buried the stem of the glass in his throat. She than began wrestling with the much larger man and knocked the gun out of his hand. They continued to wrestle as the Japanese man struggled to beat off Haruko and grab his gun from the floor of the bar.

Jotty immediately recognized it was Haruko who had screamed 'gun'. He turned to look in the direction of the gunshot and saw Haruko as she stabbed the man holding the gun in the throat. Jotty's mind started swirling with hundreds of questions that needed answering, but he knew now was not the time to ask them. He would sort things out later. When he turned back towards the two guards and Spencer, he saw the guards had drawn their guns and were pulling Spencer out the door towards the lobby. Jim had grabbed the injured waitress and several other patrons and pulled them down to the floor. As they were going out the door, one of Spencer's guards fired three rounds into the ceiling in hopes of encouraging everyone to stay down. The exit towards the lobby was blocked by screaming people who had fallen while trying to run out of the bar and were then trampled by more stampeding patrons trying to escape. They couldn't escape through the door leading to the valet parking lot and they were on the opposite side of the lounge trying to getaway by heading down the passageway towards the Lagoon Tower area. The tram was approaching from the Lagoon Tower area and preparing to stop at the lobby. The two guards holding Spencer darted in front of the tram, separating themselves from Jotty and Jim as well as the rest of the people attempting to run from the bar. The driver of the tram hit the brakes when the three men ran in front of the tram. It took a few seconds for the tram to come to a stop. When it did finally stop, it made a very effective barrier allowing the two guards holding Spencer time to start their get away. There were two sets of tracks at the point where the tram came to a stop. That allowed room for the three men to head away from the bar towards the Lagoon Tower, while they stayed hidden behind the tram.

Spencer was unable to keep up with the guard because of his broken toes. The guard smashed the butt of his gun against Spencer's mouth breaking two of his teeth. He then stuck the barrel into Spencer's mouth and told him to run faster or die. Spencer got the message and quit struggling against the guard. The guard pulled Spencer into the boat canal waterway. The water was only three to four feet deep, except for the two guide channels on either side of the waterway that served as steering guides for the canal boats. These channels were about two feet wide and another three feet deep. They crossed at one of the wider sections of the boat channel. It was almost forty feet across and there was a small island in the middle with several exotic birds chattering noisily. The two of them were careful to not slip into the guide channels and they were quickly able to cross and climbed out into the bushes on the opposite side of the canal. The second guard had stayed behind the tram to provide cover for the first guard as he crossed. By the time the second guard began to cross the boat canal Jotty had circled through the lobby in front of the tram and was standing on one of the lobby bridges that crossed the channel to the grand staircase. The bridge where Jotty stood was about sixty feet from where the second guard was attempting to cross the canal. Jotty yelled to the guard to stop. The first guard turned from his hiding spot in the bushes and quickly fired off four rounds at Jotty to provide cover for his partner. Jotty was well protected by the high cement walls of the bridge and ducked behind it for safety. As the guard fired at Jotty, the second guard continued to wade cross the canal. Suddenly, a large fish flashed through the water and rammed into the guard's leg. The guard looked down to see 'Elvis', the six-foot barracuda that lived in the canal, turning to charge him again. The guard let out a scream in fear of the fish. The guard holding Spencer turned to look when his partner screamed. Jotty used the distraction to fire two shots at the second guard who was struggling to exit from the water, hitting him twice in the chest. The guard died instantly.

In the Malolo Lounge, Haruko had subdued the large man who had fired the initial shot at Jotty and Jim. He was lying on the floor gurgling as blood poured from the severed artery in his neck. Haruko was exhausted from her struggle with the large man and was bleeding from her nose and mouth, where he had managed to strike her several times before she was able to take him down. She sat in a chair next to the man and held his gun on him in case he tried anything else. It was an unnecessary precaution. The man would die before paramedics could arrive to try to save him.

Jim had run down the passageway towards the Lagoon Tower to try to cut off the first guard who was holding Spencer. He had cleared the stopped tram and was behind the passageway wall when he heard gunfire. When he looked around the corner, he saw Jotty shoot the second guard. When the guard collapsed into the water, Jim jumped in the boat canal and waded quickly across. He had managed to get in front of the first guard and Spencer who were at the bottom of the hill next to the turtle lagoon. They were moving away from the grand staircase, carefully trying to avoid open areas. Jim was able to stay on a trail above them and out of sight. From his position, he was also able to see Jotty running down the grand staircase and closing in on the guard holding Spencer. The guard also saw Jotty approaching and prepared to ambush Jotty when Jotty reached the bottom of the stairs. Jim saw this as well and jumped from his position above the waterfall. He yelled for the guard to drop his gun. The guard turned to see Jim pointing a gun at his head from above. By that time Jotty had reached the bottom of the steps and had a clear shot at the guard as well. Instead of dropping his gun, the guard placed the barrel of his gun under Spencer's chin.

"Let me go or I will kill him," the guard yelled to both Jotty and Jim.

Spencer was crying and pleaded to Jim, "For god sakes, Jim, do what he says or he will kill me."

"How can he kill someone who is already dead, Spencer," Jim replied. Jim's reply confused the guard. For a split second the barrel of his gun wavered from Spencer's throat. That was all Jotty and Jim needed. They both fired at the same instant striking the guard on the side of the head that was facing each of them. The guard's head was unable to give with the impact of the two bullets striking almost simultaneously from opposite sides and virtually exploded. Spencer was splattered by tissue from the guard's exploded head and started screaming uncontrollably as the partially headless body collapsed next to him.

Minoru had finished his massage and was walking up the steps of the Kohala Spa when he heard the gunshots and saw the people running from the Malolo Lounge. He knew his men must be involved with the shooting. He reached the passageway in time to see Jim cross the canal and take a position above a target down by the grand staircase. Minoru ran up a flight of stairs to a canal overpass that led to near where Jim was hiding behind a rock. Minoru could tell Jim was tracking someone with the pistol in his hand. As Minoru crossed the canal, he saw the body of one of his guards floating face down about fifty feet away. The water around the body was rapidly turning red. Minoru worked his way behind Jim as he removed his own silenced pistol from his briefcase. Before he was in a position to see who Jim was watching or in a position to get a clear shot at Jim, Jim jumped to the other side of the rock he was using for cover and started talking to someone. The nearby waterfall made too much noise to allow Minoru to hear what Jim was saying. A second later Minoru heard what he thought was one very loud shot with a slight echo. Jim ran down the hill and Minoru took Jim's previous position behind the rock. Minoru saw the body with most of the head missing lying on the ground next to Spencer. He knew the body belonged to his other guard. Spencer was still alive and screaming as he lay on the ground with blood running from his mouth. Minoru smiled knowing he could at last kill this man, Spencer, who had caused him so much unnecessary grief.

Jotty and Jim went over to pick Spencer up. He was in shock and unable to speak coherently. As they lifted him to his feet, Jotty heard a muffled pop. Instantly, blood started pouring from the center of Spencer's forehead. Jotty and Jim dropped to the ground and frantically looked around to see where the shot had to have come from. All they saw was a crowd of people who had begun to gather to watch the spectacle.

"Looks like we let the big one get away," Jim said as he shook his head,

"Hell, we got less than nothing," Jotty responded.

Minutes later, police swarmed the hotel, cordoning off the entire upper lobby, bar, and grand staircase area.

Jotty ran up the staircase and found Haruko still sitting in the chair next to the now dead initial shooter. The police officer who had questioned her earlier in the day was once again questioning Haruko in not a very friendly manner. Jotty took exception to the way the officer was treating Haruko and roughly pulled him away.

"This officer saved our lives," Jotty yelled at the local officer. "Treat her with respect."

"I'm sorry sir, but this lady has no authority here in the United States and, based on all the trouble she seems to have been a part of or around today, I am going to treat her like I would treat any other suspect in a murder investigation," the officer responded back to Jotty.

"For your information, this officer is on loan from the Japanese National Police to the FBI and is part of an international team trying to deal with the terrorist activities of the Red Summit. Or have you not watched TV today? Don't you know the United States was attacked by that terrorist group this very day? There was also an attack in Tokyo, but she came to assist us." Jotty was lecturing the officer sternly.

The officer turned back to Haruko. "If this is true, Ms. Ozawa, please forgive my arrogant method of questioning. Is what this FBI agent said true? Are you working for the FBI?"

Jotty turned to hear Haruko's response. Haruko turned towards Jotty as she answered the officer's question. "Yes. Yes, it is true. I am working for the FBI."

The local officer thanked her and apologized again for the way he had treated her. He also told her she should have said something earlier that day and it would have saved both of them a lot of time and embarrassment.

When the officer left, Haruko and Jotty joined Jim on the far side of the Malolo Lounge. Haruko told the two of them how she came to be in Hawaii, and how everything fell apart. She told them about the helicopter crash, about the fire on the ship, and about the chef disappearing. She told them how she happened to stumble upon the Japanese pilot she had seen earlier in the day stalking someone as she was headed to email Jotty from the business center. She told them she was surprised to find it was Jotty and Jim he was stalking. Everything happened so fast she never had a chance to really think about it till now. She did remember to leave out the part about sleeping with Byron.

Jotty in turn told Haruko all about Spencer. How Spencer was apparently kidnapped and his murder faked by someone who needed his skills here on the island. Jim added the part about how he had found Spencer through the Internet gambling website. Haruko was impressed by Jim's investigative skills. When they had all finished filling each other in on what they each were doing in Hawaii, they mutually concluded that it all tied together.

When the local police, under the supervision of the local FBI office, searched the rooms of Spencer and his guards, the now formed international team was sure they were dealing with the Red Summit. In the guard's room next to Spencer's hotel room, the police found two black ninja outfits that were identical to the outfits worn by the burglars in both the burglary and murders at the British Health Laboratory and the bonded warehouse in San Pedro.

Now Jotty, Jim, and Haruko had to decide what next to do. Obviously, the big island was key to the Red Summit's operation, but how? There had to be a laboratory in the area where Spencer had worked. It only made sense, Spencer had used his knowledge of Prions and mad cow disease to assist the Red Summit with their so-called terror attack on the homeless in Atlanta. The Taka connection was also very obvious. He was a cattle rancher who supplied meat to the Sizzle Burger chain of fast food restaurants in Hawaii. Could Taka possibly have facilities on the island? If he did, where were they? Haruko pointed out that the meat for Sizzle Burger came from Japan and had to undergo stringent testing, so it would be impossible for Taka to taint that meat. Still, somehow, tainted meat had showed up in Atlanta, and Hawaii was their best lead for the possible origin of the meat.

Haruko mentioned the bombing of the subway in Tokyo. Jotty had been briefed about the bombing and told Haruko the caller called specifically asking for her prior to the explosion. Jotty also told Haruko she made a wise decision in agreeing to join the FBI team. Jotty got the impression from his briefing that Haruko may not have a job waiting for her back in Tokyo with the National Police Agency. Haruko had still not called to inform her supervisor of where she was and what she was doing. That was not a good thing.

Jotty made a suggestion to Haruko. "Call and inform your supervisor you have been working a covert operation for the FBI and were unable to contact him until now. Tell him about the shootout here at the hotel today which involved three Japanese nationals who were members of the Red Summit. That way, when you are ready to go back, they will have to take you back. You will be a hero. You may have already killed the people responsible for the Tokyo bombing."

Haruko smiled at the suggestion. "I cannot tell him such a lie."

Jotty replied, "It is not a lie and, as your new boss, I am ordering you to tell him that, for security reasons. Also, let him know it may be a while before you get back to Tokyo. You have to fly to Atlanta in the morning to work on the Red Summit terrorist attack there along with me."

Jotty turned to Jim, "I want you to stay here on the island and see if you can find the lab where Spencer may have been working, and try to find the man who shot Spencer. Talk to the local ranchers and see what you can find out."

Jim looked at Jotty and eyed him up and down. "I think I would enjoy spending a little time here on the island. A little ranch time sounds great right now. But you can't fool me," Jim continued, "I know you just want the woman for yourself."

Now it was Jotty's turn to slug Jim on the arm. Fortunately, Haruko had already left to call her supervisor or she would have confirmed that Jotty and Jim were just two overgrown teenagers in heat.

Chapter Twenty-seven

Minoru was angry. Very angry. He felt his guards as well as his own bodyguard had let him down by being killed. The entire operation at the Paleaka Ranch was now jeopardized and even though Taka was prepared for just such an occurrence, Minoru was not happy it had come about so soon, especially since Taka had put Minoru in charge of handling the situation in Hawaii with Haruko and Byron. Minoru was troubled by how the FBI agents had found Spencer. Could Haruko have known about Spencer or was it shear coincidence she and the two FBI agents arrived in Hawaii at the same time following different leads? Regardless, it had happened, so now Minoru had to dismantle part of the operations at the ranch immediately. He also knew he had to leave the island as soon as possible, but not until the Prion-affected cattle were destroyed and some special equipment in the upper laboratory was transferred to the hidden secured laboratory below it. He also needed to destroy the Prion-contaminated ruminant feed stockpiled at the ranch's feedlot. As soon as he felt it safe to return to the ranch, he would direct the workers to begin the tasks.

After he shot Spencer, Minoru blended into the crowd gathering to see what the disturbance was all about. He slowly made his way away from the lobby area and towards the beach to the south of the resort property. He heard several sirens wailing as police cars, fire trucks, and ambulances all converged on the Hilton. Minoru continued down the beach until he reached the Waikoloa Marriott property. He entered the lobby and joined the line of tourists checking into the hotel. When it was his turn, he told the receptionist he was supposed to check into the Hilton, but something was happening there and he was turned away. He was there to inquire if the Marriott might have an available room. They were able to accommodate Minoru and he was checked into a room. He told the receptionist he would have his bags sent over from the Hilton later. Within minutes, several other real tourists who were turned away from the Hilton because of the shootings also arrived to request rooms. Minoru was pleased with this turn of events. The tourist story would help cover his departure from the Hilton. He would be safe for the time being. He decided he would hide out in his room at the Marriott for at least a day and wait to return to the ranch the next evening. His car was in the valet lot at the Hilton. He would need to rent another vehicle the next day from the car rental agency in the lobby of the Marriott. Until then, he would relax and play the role of a tourist.

Minoru knew there were video cameras monitoring all areas of the Hilton. It would only be a matter of time until the FBI was able to match his picture in the hotel video to the pictures of him on the two burglary videos of him killing the security guards. He also knew Haruko had seen him at the heliport when he returned to Mauna Lani. Minoru heard on the news it was Haruko who had killed his bodyguard in the Malolo Lounge. She must have recognized him from the heliport as well. She too would soon discover it was Minoru who had fired the shot that killed Spencer. That was a killing Minoru was happy to have performed. He did not like Spencer. He thought Spencer was a weak man for selling out his country to pay for his gambling addiction. Minoru laughed as he thought that maybe the United States should consider him a hero for having eliminated such a despicable traitor.

Taka would not be happy Minoru killed Spencer. Spencer had a lot more work to do to prove his absorption theory and Taka still had hopes to use that knowledge as well as Spencer's knowledge of anthrax in later terror attacks. Taka did realize the experiments were taking too long and would soon have to end prematurely anyway. The escalating pace of the present terror plans was to blame for that. Spencer's usefulness in the weaponization of the anthrax they were culturing was in reality no longer important either. Spencer had helped design and put into operation the equipment necessary for the weaponiztion. That part of the operation took place in the hidden laboratory. In the regular lab, the culturing of the anthrax still took place. Minoru would have to have the equipment moved to the hidden laboratory right away. They had managed to weaponize enough anthrax to infect a population of several million people. That was if the winds distributed the powder as hoped. The anthrax was stored in a vault in the lower secret laboratory. Minoru decided that, when he left Hawaii the next day, he would take with him a thermos size container of the weaponized anthrax. He would store it in another vault in Taka's house next to the Paleaka Ranch. Taka may find a use for it sooner than planned and it may be a while before Minoru or Taka would be able to once again access the secret laboratory.

Minoru wanted to contact Taka, but knew he would be unable to reach him for another two days. That was when they had prearranged a time for secure communication. When they had spoken the previous morning, Minoru had assured Taka all was going as planned. The chef had left the ship and the photographer was killed. Minoru told Taka it had become evident they needed to remove John Greer as well as Byron Downing. Minoru explained his plan to Taka about causing the helicopter to crash into the volcano. Taka agreed to the killings and approved of the plan. He had also told Taka the results of their actions in Tokyo were having the desired affect on Haruko. She was being discredited with her supervisor and would have no choice but to soon leave the island and return in disgrace to Tokyo. As far as the FBI agents were concerned, he had not had any information as to their whereabouts since they had left Tokyo after the botched attempt to kill them. Minoru told Taka he could only assume they were in Atlanta dealing with the terror attack there. Taka seemed pleased and told Minoru they would speak again as arranged in three days.

Minoru rented a car and left the Marriott late in the afternoon the next day. The activity around the Hilton Waikoloa Village had seemed to return to normal. Minoru had called the ranch to see if everything was still alright there. His security guards reported nothing out of the usual had occurred and no visitors had come by. Minoru was somewhat reassured as he left the Marriott towards the mountains above Waimea.

When he arrived back at the Paleaka Ranch, it was late in the evening. He decided the workers could wait to destroy the Prion affected ruminant feed and cattle early in the morning. There would be too many questions asked if he asked them to do such a task in the middle of the night. Minoru also decided he would move the laboratory equipment himself, with the help of the two other researchers who lived in the lab. This he would do as soon as he got back to the lab. They would also destroy the active anthrax being cultivated in the upper laboratory. He would then have one of the researchers prepare the thermos of the weaponized anthrax for him to take to Taka's house vault. The Prion affected bovine byproducts had all been shipped to the facility in Los Angeles several days ago. The holding vats still needed to be cleaned and sterilized so there would be no trace of the Prion affected materials having been stored at the Paleaka Ranch. The security team on duty met Minoru when he entered the ranch property. He explained to them that he expected there could be trouble during the night and to be prepared for it. The security guard in charge asked if Minoru wanted a second shift of guards to be put on duty, but Minoru declined. He wanted fresh men for in the morning when he knew the chances for unwanted visitors would be far greater.

Minoru stopped by the workers' sleeping quarters and advised the foreman of the tasks he wanted performed first thing in the morning. He told them to forgo their regular duties until Minoru's orders were followed completely. He then went to the lab, woke up the two researchers who resided in the laboratory's living area, and gave them instructions as to moving equipment, cleaning the storage area, and preparing the anthrax. The researchers were not the least bit pleased to be awoken in the middle of the night in order to perform what they considered to be janitorial duties. Like Spencer they feared Minoru and knew about Minoru breaking Spencer's toes. They did not wish to enrage Minoru and possibly suffer the same fate as Spencer, or possibly even worse. They agreed to his orders and began getting dressed. Minoru left the lab and drove off the ranch property. He drove to the house Taka had built down the road near to the Paleaka Ranch. The drive took longer than usual due to the heavy cloud cover that seemed to be moving into the mountains surrounding the ranch. He parked the car at the house and passed through the house into the hidden entrance that led through the lava tube back to the secret laboratory. When he arrived back at the laboratory the two researchers were busy moving the equipment from the upper laboratory through the secret entrance to the hidden lower laboratory. They were surprised when Minoru appeared in the lower laboratory. They had not seen him come into the upper laboratory, let alone go through the secret passage from the upper laboratory to the lower one. Minoru noticed their puzzlement and realized he had made an error in judgment that it would be necessary to correct at a later time. Taka would not be happy that Minoru had allowed the situation to get so out of hand.

Chapter Twenty-eight

Taka was in Beverly Hills attending a photo shoot of Niki. They were taking photographs to be used in the magazine advertisements for the new 'Taka' line of lipstick and cosmetics by Niki Matsuura. He liked the name the advertising agency had come up with. It seemed to just roll off the tongue when you said it. "TAKA…" He was confident the millions of young girls throughout America would think the same thing as they lined up to buy 'Taka' at their local shopping malls. This photo session featured Niki and several up-and-coming young Latina models. There were several large billboards, including a primetime billboard on Sunset Boulevard that featured a 90-foot blowup of Niki's lips with the word 'TAKA' next to it. A television commercial featuring Niki had already begun showing in several major markets like Los Angeles, Dallas, and Chicago. The commercial would be aired nationwide as soon as more of the product was available to be shipped around the country.

That was the part that excited Taka. At that very moment, at the manufacturing plant in Cudahy, a small city in East Los Angeles, the workforce was producing and packaging over a million tubes of 'Taka' lipstick. All of it using the Prion affected amniotic fluid from the Hawaii laboratory as the primary base ingredient of the lipstick. Other Prion affected byproducts were being used in the lotions and facial creams as well. Taka knew it would be the lipstick that would do the most damage. They may be able to market it for several years before they are caught in their terrorist act or until Taka decides to reveal his terrorism master plan. Then, at exactly the right moment, Taka will reveal to the world how he has potentially killed millions of women with his mad cow tainted products. Thus, fulfilling the goal of all terrorists by filling the minds of Americans with a never before known fear and terror. Osama will then know they have succeeded in their planned campaign against the unrighteous Americans. Then Taka will have rightly proved the Japanese ideal, that through time, their cause will conquer all.

Niki was not so happy about how the plan was going. She was beginning to have second thoughts about the entire plan. Her success had softened her terrorist ideals. From the beginning, she had been following her own agenda. Not the agenda of Aioka and the Red Summit. She participated in the terrorist plot to pay back the men she had grown to hate. Those same men who had used and abused her so often when she was but a child. Now those same men were giving her unheard-of opportunities. She had been offered a major role in a new motion picture starring two of last year's academy award winning actors. She had a major cosmetics company that was guaranteed to be a success. She failed to see it was the terrorist money that made all of this possible and would continue to make it possible. She was beginning to see Aioka as one of these men who had used her for their own pleasure then discarded her like trash when they had gotten what they wanted from her.

Taka was due to hear from Minoru that morning. During their last conversation Minoru had reported all was going very well correcting the problem with the ship's photographer and the chef. Taka had read about the fire aboard the ship in the paper and the photographer's death. Taka was pleased Minoru was able to avoid killing the chef fearing too much attention might have been focused on his business holdings in Hawaii. He was sure Minoru was just as careful in dealing with John Greer and this journalist, Byron or Saito, whoever he was. Taka had listened to Minoru's observation of Spencer's behavior, and was tending to agree with Minoru that Spencer may be outliving his usefulness. They would discuss that more today when Minoru called. The shipment of tainted cosmetic ingredients had arrived from the ranch and was already being processed, packaged, and prepared for shipment. All seemed to be going well with Taka and Osama's plans. The big news on the television stations and in the newspapers, was of course, the so-called terrorist attack on the homeless in Atlanta. The President had even spoken to the nation on live TV about this cowardly act attributed to the terror cell the Red Summit. Newsmen around the country were scrambling to find background information on the Red Summit and its former deceased leader Aioka Matsuura. There had already been several calls placed to Taka's secretary back in Japan requesting interviews with the brother of the founder of this terrorist group. There were also reports from CNN that the FBI already had a task force in place specially assigned to finding and dismantling the Red Summit terrorist cell. CNN continued to report that a senior agent led the new task force. They also reported the name of this senior agent, Jotty Joplin.

"They should have said the deceased former agent Jotty Joplin," Taka said to himself. He was still upset Minoru's men had failed to kill the two FBI agents when they came to visit Haruko in Japan.

The newscasters also told of numerous unsubstantiated reports of mad cow tainted meats showing up in several other cities in the mid-west and how dozens of food banks had closed down in major cities all over the United States. Congress was calling for an investigation into the situation and was recommending stricter government oversight of the charities that ran these food kitchens and homeless shelters. Beef futures had plummeted on the Chicago Futures Exchange, as had the share price of the larger fast food retailers on the stock exchanges.

Taka could not have been more pleased. "All of this for such a minor act," Taka again said to himself. "Just wait till I unleash the full horror of my terrorism plan." He smiled as he continued to watch the newscast.

Niki had been pacing in the hotel room next to Taka's. They had not been intimate for a long time and for several months had slept in separate rooms. She needed to talk to Taka about their plans. The plan to sell the tainted cosmetics had been Niki's idea from the beginning. Now she was not so sure she wanted to follow through with it. Things were going well for Niki and she wanted to stop her involvement with the Red Summit. She was worried as how to approach Aioka about stopping the distribution of the mad cow affected products. She needed to convince Aioka that the tainted cosmetics were not important in achieving his ultimate goal. She hoped the massive amount of media coverage regarding the tainted meat in Atlanta would be enough to make Aioka see her part in the plan was no longer important.

Niki knocked and entered Aioka's room. She was acting demurer than Aioka had seen her behave in quite a while. He knew she was trying to manipulate him with her shyness and beauty. She had tried this in the past and Aioka had always twisted it to his advantage sexually. Maybe today it would be the same, he thought.

"I have a favor to ask," Niki said in a purring voice. Aioka did not answer. He remained aloof waiting for Niki to ask her favor.

"I want to stop with the production of the tainted cosmetics," Niki finally said.

Taka laughed, "It is much too late for you to have a change of heart. Stopping now is impossible and I will not even consider the idea."

"It was my idea and I want it to stop!" demanded Niki.

Taka stood up quickly and slapped Niki hard across the face. "You are foolish to think you have any say in the plans of the Red Summit. You have served the cause well and will continue to do so. Only Taka makes the decisions as to what and what not the Red Summit will do."

Niki spat on the floor at Aioka's feet. "You are not now, nor will you ever be, the man Taka was. You are not deserving of such an illustrious name."

Aioka grabbed her by the hair and pulled her to her knees before him. He pushed her face forcefully into his groin. "I should treat you like you are used to men treating you. This is the position that has got you where you are today and don't you forget it. You will never leave the Red Summit." Aioka pushed Niki roughly away and she fell crying on the floor. Her face was already beginning to bruise where Aioka had struck her.

Chapter Twenty-nine

As soon as Haruko and Jotty had left for Atlanta, Jim made a phone call to Parker Ranch. He set up an appointment to meet with the ranch foreman. He knew a ranch on Hawaii would be run just the same as a ranch in Texas and, in Texas, the ranch foreman knew everything going on at the other ranches near him. He had to know. If trouble were brewing at the ranch down the road, it could mean trouble brewing for your ranch too.

Dusty Talbot looked to be the spittin' image of Jim. At least what Jim imagined he'd look like in twenty more years. Dusty was just as lanky and muscular as Jim, but about twice as weathered. Dusty was only about an inch shorter and, from a distance, you wouldn't be able to tell the two of them apart. The only difference was Dusty was about thirty years older than Jim. However, it was hard to tell Dusty's age just by looking at him. His weathered face and skin hid his age well. He also carried himself like a man half his age. Dusty still spent at least three days a week riding his horse while checking on the ranch operations.

Dusty had been the foreman of the Parker Ranch for the past twelve years. Before that he spent seven years running the feedlot and slaughterhouse at the ranch until they were both closed down. The economy started changing on the island and they both became money losing operations. Parker was the last big feedlot and slaughterhouse operation on the island and the last to have to close down. Now Parker Ranch concentrated on its cattle business. There were over 17,000 calves born each year on Parker Ranch. The ranch kept a few and shipped the rest to feeder cattle farms in

Texas and Northern California. Jim had first heard of Parker Ranch a couple years back while checking up on boll weevils at a ranch up near Abilene. Jim came to find out several of the ranches in his Rolling Plains Farm Bureau region grazed feeder cattle that came from the Parker Ranch here in Hawaii.

When Jim met with Dusty later that afternoon, it was like two old friends getting together. Dusty was fascinated hearing about Jim's experience in the Marines and loved Jim's tales about getting stuck behind a desk several times for his cowboy style of justice. Dusty couldn't understand how a Farm Service Agent could end up working for an FBI terrorist task force unit. That was until Jim told him he also had a PhD in biology with a specialty in Prion research and bovine contagions.

"So you were picked up by the FBI because they think this terrorist group is going to try to pass off mad cow infected meat?" Dusty asked Jim.

"Affected meat, not infected," Jim corrected. "You need to watch a little more television news," Jim continued. "The Red Summit already has passed off affected meat. They did it the other day in Atlanta, Georgia."

"Well, ain't that the just a shitty thing for someone to go and do. How many people do you think are going to come down with this here mad cow disease?" Dusty asked.

"We got people trying to figure that out right now," Jim explained to Dusty. "Actually, they call it Creutzfeldt-Jakob disease when it affects people. All I know right for sure is three Japanese men loaded about two tons of tainted meat into a delivery truck at a cold storage warehouse in Atlanta. The driver was paid in cash to delivery the meat to several homeless shelters and food banks. We figure over two thirds of the meat was cooked up and fed to the homeless before we got the phone call from the terrorists."

"So why are you here in Hawaii and not in Atlanta," Dusty asked Jim.

That's when Jim told Dusty the story of what happened the day before at the Hilton Waikoloa. "We all followed leads to Hawaii trying to track down these terrorists. It seems now all our leads were either killed or have disappeared. But there had to be a reason they brought Spencer here. They had to have some kind of a laboratory for him to work in and a supply of cattle for him to work with, which is why I came to talk to you Dusty. I figure you being the ranch foreman of the largest ranch in these parts would know if anything strange or out of the ordinary was happening on any ranches around here."

"You got to be kidding me, right?" Dusty responded. "Hell, everybody on the island knows about all that crap going on up at the Paleaka Ranch."

"Well I must have been in the barn when they made the announcement," Jim replied jokingly. "Just what the hell is going on up at this Paleaka Ranch?"

"What's going on is they are pissing away money, a lot of it. They're also pissing off the residents by not hiring any local paniolos or ranch hands to help out up there."

"What do you mean pissing away money?" Jim asked.

"I mean exactly what I said," Dusty said impatiently. "David Paleaka sold half-ownership in his family ranch to some Japanese business group run by this Minoru guy. They brought in all these workers in from Japan who rebuilt the feedlot and packinghouse. They also built what David called a big laboratory they use for testing the meat. David doesn't know much about it though, 'cause they don't let him go near the building. Even if they did let him near it, he would probably be too doped up to know what he was looking at. They didn't hire a single local to do any of the work rebuilding the place or any of the work running the ranch now. That don't set well with local island folk. They had to spend a fortune doing all that. And for what? There's no way in hell they can turn a profit running a feedlot and packinghouse here on the island. The Parker Ranch tried for years and we finally had to throw in the towel. There is just no way you can make a profit in that business. They can make money raising cattle, but certainly not grazing them then slaughtering them."

"Run by some Japanese fellows you say? I guess I need to take a look at this ranch and this Minoru fellow," Jim told Dusty. "Think you can arrange it for me?"

"I've been wantin' to see that ranch for a long time myself. A couple of local boys went up there one night with David and almost got themselves killed. Seems to be this Minoru fellow has hired several other of his fellow Japanese to keep guard on the place. They all carry some kind of machinegun or automatic rifle. At least that is the story two drunken local boys were blabbing to anyone who would listen and buy them a drink. I do know there are some video cameras on the roads approaching the ranch and the ranch buildings. That's a little more trouble than I want to mess with," Dusty explained to Jim.

"Maybe you could introduce me to this David Paleaka," Jim said to Dusty.

"You know, maybe I could. Matter of fact I would kind of like to ask him a few questions myself," Dusty was telling Jim.

"You know Dusty," Jim said, 'its mighty fine talkin' to someone else who can speak Texan. Makes me feel right at home."

That night around ten, Dusty met Jim at the Clipper Bar at the Waikoloa Marriott Hotel. "There's a good chance David will show up here. Some of my ranch hands, who spend too much of their time and money drinking and partying with David, told me he always shows up here first, usually between ten and eleven, If there are too few women, they say he will then head over to the Malolo Lounge at the Hilton to continue his partying. It will be best to talk to him here before he gets too drunk or too high to make any sense."

Jim and Dusty continued to drink and tell stories while they waited for David to arrive. It was very breezy in the open-air patio of the bar. The wind was not the typical trade wind breeze. For some reason, the air was thick and heavy. It was also much more humid than it had been. Dusty thought the temperature seemed cooler, but with the humidity it seemed hotter.

Dusty seemed to sense Jim was puzzled by change in weather. "It's the Kona winds," Dusty said. "They sometimes blow this time of year. Winds from the southern hemisphere kick up and out blow the trade winds. Makes you wonder if you are colder or hotter when they blow. Blows all the clouds up to Mauna Kea and holds them there. Thickest damn fog you have ever seen."

Jim nodded his understanding. They continued their conversation and it turned towards horses and guns. It turned out Dusty also preferred a six-shooter to a semi-automatic pistol and had a matched pair of pearl-handled series one Colt Army pistols. Jim got excited talking guns and was about to take Dusty up to his room to show him his pair of Colts when Dusty pointed to a young man who had just walked into the bar.

"Let's go meet David," Dusty said to Jim.

David was a very personable man when he wasn't too drunk or too jacked up on cocaine. Fortunately, the Clipper Bar was his first stop that night and he was yet to show the affects of the cocaine he had just snorted in his car before he had walked in. David knew and was a little afraid of Dusty but was cordial. Dusty was one of the ranch association leaders who were really upset when David sold half his interest in the ranch to that Japanese company. Dusty was also an icon on the island. His family had been involved with ranching longer than David's family had been. Dusty introduced Jim as a rancher friend from the mainland. He didn't want to scare David off by telling him Jim was an FBI agent. They had a light general conversation about ranching to put David at ease. Slowly Jim started moving the conversation to what was going on at the Paleaka Ranch. The cocaine David had snorted earlier combined with the drinks Jim was now buying David started to loosen his tongue and he began to complain about the way Minoru treated him at the ranch. He told Dusty and Jim the story of him and his two buddies being run off the road and held at gunpoint for just driving around on his own ranch. Jim kept pushing David for details about the laboratory and asked if any cattle were kept next to it.

"Only the sick cows are kept there," David said.

This sparked Jim's attention. "What do you mean, sick cows? How do you know they are sick?" Jim asked.

"The cows by the lab are always falling down or can't stand up," David told the two men.

Dusty and Jim both looked at each other. "Are there a lot of these sick cattle?" Dusty asked.

"Sometimes," David continued. "Two weeks ago, there were several that couldn't stand up and a couple even looked dead to me. The other day there were about half as many, but they seemed to be different than the ones in the corral last week. I have to be careful when I go over that way. Minoru doesn't like me wandering around the ranch."

"Tell me about this Minoru," Jim asked David.

"He used to be a really nice guy. He was the one who negotiated the deal to buy half the ranch from me." David looked at Dusty who was shaking his head. "Minoru was very fair to me. At least he was at first. Now he scares me. He seems to travel a lot and spends a lot of time at the Hilton when he comes into town. I saw him yesterday. He stopped by the ranch in the early afternoon when he arrived back from a trip somewhere. He was just checking on everything. One of his men told me he went down to the Hilton for a massage. Funny thing was he never came back to the ranch last night. At least I don't think he did. But I did see him come back tonight just as I was getting ready to leave, but I never talked to him. He seemed like he was in a hurry or something."

Jim was getting excited and looked at Dusty who was smiling back.

"Hey. Maybe it had something to do with all shooting they had at the Hilton yesterday. Did you guys hear about it?" David asked the two of them.

Dusty and Jim both nodded.

"Well, the good part is Minoru won't be around here for a while anyway. By the time I climb out of bed tomorrow afternoon, he will be long gone." David continued. "I heard him telling a couple of his security people he was leaving the island for a while. He told them to close down the laboratory and to get rid of the sick cattle in the morning."

Jim got excited at David's last comment. He bought David another drink and told him it had been a pleasure talking to him. David wasn't paying too close of attention to Jim and Dusty anymore. A group of women who were at the

Marriott for a massage convention had walked into the bar and David couldn't take his eyes off of them. He just nodded as Dusty and Jim started back to their table.

"One more thing," Jim said to David who was too preoccupied looking at the women to even turn towards Jim. "Can I have your permission to take a little ride to the ranch and check out that laboratory?"

"Sure, anything you want," David responded even though he hadn't really heard the question. Jim knew David really wasn't listening or paying attention. He had counted on that when he asked for permission to visit the ranch.

"Looks like I am going to get my chance to see the Paleaka Ranch after all," Jim said smiling to Dusty.

"I think you mean 'We'," Dusty responded. "And from the sound of things we need to make that visit first thing in the morning before they can get rid of any of those sick cattle."

"Yeah, but the problem is we can't take the police in with us. We have no probable cause for a search warrant. I could probably get one, but not before everything and everybody was gone." Jim told Dusty.

"We don't need the police or any probable cause. If there is even the chance there are mad cow affected cattle on that ranch, that's all the probable cause I need." Dusty continued. "Besides, David just gave us permission to visit the ranch."

"True, but you seem to be forgetting about those armed guards patrolling the ranch. If we are going in, we are going to need some back-up and a plan," Jim said. "I'm sure this Minoru fellow is the one Haruko saw at the heliport with the Japanese man she killed in the bar. He has got to be the one who killed Spencer at the Hilton. He must be connected to the Red Summit like Haruko seems to think."

"Well, let's go find out," Dusty replied, "And why don't you bring those Colts of yours along for the ride."

"With pleasure," Jim said as the two of them headed out of the bar.

Chapter Thirty

Jotty had to admit he wouldn't mind spending a little time alone with Haruko. Even if that time together was for business purposes. Both Jim and Jotty were pleased Haruko had decided to join their team. As if she really had a choice. She had burned her bridges at the National Police Agency when she left with Byron and did not inform her supervisor where she was going or what she was doing. When the Red Summit claimed the bombing in the Tokyo subway system and Haruko was not there to take the call or investigate the bombing, her career was pretty much over in Japan. That was until Jotty told her to make the call to her supervisor and explain to him she was working undercover for the FBI, just as previously agreed to by the National Police Agency. Haruko had been told not to inform her supervisor she was leaving because the FBI feared there was a mole in the counter-terrorist division of the National Police Agency. They believed it was that mole who had leaked the information of Jotty's and Jim's trip to Tokyo, which in turn led to the two FBI agents being kidnapped and almost murdered. The FBI couldn't take the chance of Haruko's trip to Hawaii being leaked to the terrorists. Unfortunately, it appeared that somehow the terrorists did seem to find out about her trip with Byron and that led to at least three deaths and the disappearance of the ship's chef.

Haruko's supervisor was advised to do a thorough investigation of his staff as well as a complete check of their computers and communication system to see if the integrity of those systems had been compromised. It was obvious there was a confidentiality problem within his department.

Now it was Haruko's supervisor who was in hot water, not Haruko. The supervisor was also asked to forward a copy of the investigation regarding the subway bombing to Jotty's team. Haruko insisted it wasn't a typical Red Summit type of terrorist act. As Haruko thought about it, it seemed the bombing, in relationship to the call to her office, was designed to either keep her in Tokyo or get her to return to Tokyo from Hawaii quickly. Such a scenario seemed likely to be true now more than ever, based on the fiasco in Hawaii. Obviously, the Red Summit, or someone claiming to be the Red Summit, knew Haruko was going to be in Hawaii and why she was going to be in Hawaii. It was apparent someone did not want her there.

Jotty was under orders to get back to Atlanta as soon as possible. He had scheduled a flight for Jim and himself to leave early the next morning. Jotty decided it would be best for Haruko to now join him on the flight before the local police had a change of heart and decided they needed to question Haruko a bit more, even though Jotty claimed she was assigned to his FBI task force. Jim would remain in Hawaii and see what he could turn up there. Haruko and Jotty took copies of the Hilton video surveillance camera tapes to see if they might help them identify the person who killed Spencer. They would review the tapes on their flight back to Atlanta. Haruko had a strong suspicion it was the Japanese man she saw get off the helicopter in Mauna Lani. The same man who left in the car along with the man she killed in the Malolo Lounge.

Haruko still believed Taka Matsuura was the key to the Red Summit. His connection to the Red Summit through his younger brother Aioka, as well as the fact some of his businesses included the processing of beef for retail sale and for use in his own restaurants, logically made him a prime suspect in the Atlanta tainted meat terrorist act. At least it seemed like a logical assumption to Haruko. Now that she had the resources of the FBI behind her, Haruko was confident she would be able to connect Taka to this attack and hopefully other attacks attributed to the Red Summit. On the flight back to the mainland, she explained her suspicions regarding Taka Matsuura to Jotty. She told Jotty Taka was the reason she came to the big island with Byron. They were there following up on tips Byron had received that concerned Taka's behavior while here on his honeymoon with Niki Matsuura the famous model. Jotty agreed it did sound highly suspicious. As Haruko explained the details, Jotty decided he had better phone his office to have them research Taka Matsuura's business holdings and dealings in the United States. He told the staff worker to have the file on Taka, with the information he had requested, waiting for him and Niki when they arrived in Atlanta.

Jotty and Haruko changed from a commercial flight to an FBI jet when they landed in Los Angeles. As they exited the commercial flight, they were escorted down to the tarmac where a car was waiting to whisk them to an outlying private terminal. There, an FBI Lear jet was warming its engines in anticipation of Jotty and Haruko's arrival. As soon as they were aboard, the plane was cleared for take off and was on its way to Atlanta. On board this plane, Haruko was able to view the videos provided by the Hilton. It did not take long for her to discover the Japanese man she had been sure she would find. There was no doubt it was the same man she had seen at the heliport. The videos showed him arriving at the Hilton with the man she had killed in the Malolo Lounge. Another camera's video showed the man entering the Kohala Spa, and a short time later leaving the spa. Another camera showed him in the passageway going against the flow of the crowd that was obviously running to get away from the gunfire in the lounge. He could be seen leaving the passageway near the canal and going out of the area recorded by any cameras. He showed up again later on another camera's videotape, mixed in with a crowd leaving the central area of the resort and heading towards the south end of the resort property. The last recorded image that showed the man was when he was walking on the beach trail leaving the Hilton property headed towards the Marriott Hotel. Haruko showed the images to Jotty when he returned from making a phone call from the front of the jet. Jotty was stunned at the image of the man Haruko suspected.

"I recognize that man," Jotty said in surprise. "I saw him at breakfast this morning in the Marriott. He sat just two tables away from Jim and me."

"Are you sure it's the same man?" Haruko asked.

"I'm positive," responded Jotty. "I'm positive because he looked familiar to me this morning. I even mentioned it to Jim. ...Wait a minute." Jotty paused for a moment as he stared at the picture. "Can you get me a close up of the man's face?"

Haruko was unfamiliar with the software program on the jet's video computer system. One of the jet's crew was called to see if he could enlarge the frame for a clearer view of the man's face.

"That's him, Jotty shouted, "That's the leader."

"What are you talking about," asked Haruko.

"Look at the eyes," Jotty was pointing at the screen and bouncing up and down like he had just won the lottery. Haruko still didn't understand. "Those eyes. I knew I had seen those eyes before. They are the same eyes on both the burglary videos from the Weybridge laboratory in Britain and the warehouse in San Pedro. That man was the ninja leader. I recognize the eyes."

Haruko stared at the enlargement on the screen in front of her. "You may be right," she finally agreed.

"I know I'm right," Jotty replied triumphantly. "I need to call Jim. If this guy is still at the Marriott, Jim could be in trouble."

Jotty tried several times to reach Jim, but there was never an answer. He called the local police and had them go look for Jim at the hotel, but they too were unable to find him. The concierge remembered giving him information about driving directions to several of the ranches in the area and saw Jim leaving to visit those ranches. When the police relayed the concierge's information to Jotty, he began to feel a little better about Jim's safety. He called Jim's hotel room again, but this time left a message on Jim's phone. He hoped Jim would check his messages when he returned and call Jotty back very soon. He also faxed a picture of the Japanese man to the local island FBI office and asked them to stake out the Marriott to watch for the suspect. They said it would be no problem, but after they had agreed to the stake out, they realized they lacked the manpower to do so. The local island office called the main office on Oahu and they said they would send some agents over to the big island later that day.

When Jotty and Haruko arrived in Atlanta that evening, a local FBI agent was there to meet them with a car and the requested information about Taka Matsuura. It seems Taka was at that very moment in Los Angeles with his wife Niki who was filming a commercial for her new line of cosmetics. The Niki Matsuura cosmetic company was a wholly owned business with no shareholders. Niki and Taka Matsuura were the co-owners of the company. The cosmetic company was once a part of a major Japanese cosmetics manufacturer, but through some tricky language in the contract between Taka, Niki, and the Japanese cosmetic's company, Taka and Niki were able to gain sole control of the Niki Matsuura cosmetic line. They had moved the business to Los Angeles. As they read the report, they also learned Taka owned a major interest in a cattle ranch, feedlot, and meatpacking facility located on the big island of Hawaii. The analyst who wrote the report noted this information was a little harder to find, because it was actually owned by a number of shell corporations that eventually led back to Taka. Someone definitely wanted to make finding out the ownership of the ranch difficult. The report also noted Taka had never visited this facility and had a manager who has overseen and run the entire ranch operation from its beginning.

"Let me guess," Jotty said to Haruko. "I bet this fellow here is the manager." Jotty held up the enlargement of the Japanese man from the Hilton video.

"We actually were unable to find out who the manager of the ranch is, but our Hawaii office is working on it," the staff member offered.

"Taka still has several business enterprises in Japan and the Far East, including his 'Aioka' chain of gourmet steakhouses. "Oh," the staff member continued, "here is something that may interest you. Taka holds a contract with Sizzle Burger to supply their Hawaiian stores with the meat for their hamburgers. It used to come from his meat packing plant in Japan, but I believe that is why he opened the facilities in Hawaii."

The more the staff member told them, the more it looked like Taka was the man behind the Red Summit tainted meat attack in Atlanta. It all just seemed to make sense when you considered Haruko's suspicions. Jotty really needed to get a hold of Jim to let him know what they had found out. He called Jim's hotel room again, but there was still no answer. Jotty should have known to try the bar.

It was almost two in the morning in Atlanta. Jotty and Haruko were on their way to the hotel the FBI had arranged for them. They were now sitting quietly in the back seat of the car, thinking about all the information the staff member who was driving the car had told them.

"Why are we here?" Haruko asked Jotty.

"Is that a metaphorical question?" the tired Jotty quipped back at Haruko.

"I mean, why are we here in Atlanta?" she repeated.

"We are here to interview witnesses and to try to figure out who supplied the Prion affected meat to the food kitchens, potentially killing hundreds of the poor and homeless," Jotty replied softly.

"Don't you get the feeling that is exactly what someone expects us to do? Someone besides your bosses, I mean. What do you really think we are going to find out here? Your report already told us the driver was paid in cash to deliver meat to these charity organizations and three Japanese men loaded the meat into his truck and the same three Japanese men also delivered the meat to the warehouse the day before. No one knows where the meat came from or who these men are. At least I believe no one in Atlanta knows. You have dozens of agents trying to track down all possible connections and they are finding none. Yet, I would bet just as someone predicted, the people who know the most about the Red Summit, meaning you and me, are here in Atlanta chasing ghosts and rumors. Don't you get the feeling this Atlanta thing, kind of like the subway bombing in Tokyo, was meant to get us away from somewhere we are not wanted? Somewhere they don't want us looking?"

"Let me guess," said Jotty. "Hawaii."

"Hawaii would be my guess, too," Haruko responded. "Everything we just learned, and everything we already know, points to this Taka's ranch as a source of the tainted meat." She paused for a minute. "That guy Spencer, who was killed at the Hilton, you told me why you and Jim were in Hawaii looking for him, but you never told me much about his background."

Jotty retold Haruko the story about Spencer's faked death and how Jim had figured out where Spencer was. As he was beginning to tell her about Spencer's time in prison and his research expertise, Jotty suddenly stopped mid-sentence.

"Turn the car around," Jotty yelled at the driver. "We need to get back to the airport and back to Hawaii now. Turn around, quickly!"

As the driver complied with Jotty's demand to return to the airport, Jotty called FBI headquarters and told them he needed the jet refueled immediately and fresh pilots waiting at the airport. He and Haruko needed to get them back to Hawaii as fast as possible, before this mysterious Japanese man in the video had a chance to kill Jim and destroy the evidence at the Paleaka Ranch. He requested they authorize a search warrant for the ranch and asked every FBI agent available in Hawaii head to the big island and be armed and prepared to search the facilities as soon as Haruko and Jotty returned. He also told them to get the local police out looking for Jim. This time, Jotty remembered, "Tell them to check all the bars."

Haruko smiled to herself as she realized how easy it had been to manipulate Jotty.

Chapter Thirty-one

Jim picked up his Colts and his holster from the safe in his hotel room. He saw he had a message on his hotel phone, but didn't bother to check it. It could wait until the morning Jim decided. Dusty was waiting in his truck at the entrance to the Marriott. Jim jumped into the truck with the bag containing his six-shooters and his holster. He and Dusty headed up towards Waimea to the Parker Ranch. On the way up, Dusty made a phone call to one of his paniolos. The paniolos are the last true cowboys on the island of Hawaii. They are carrying on the tradition that many of their fathers and grandfathers had followed so proudly before them. Technology had changed the way the paniolos now herded the cattle and handled the ranch chores. Several of them now used ATV's in their daily treks across the various ranches looking for strays or downed fences. Yet tradition was strong and they all still spent part of their day on horseback and caring for the ranch horses. At the Parker ranch, there were nine paniolos, each in charge of six horses. Even as the ranch foreman, Dusty still cared for four of the ranch horses, as well as three of his own. Several other of the smaller ranches still employed two or three paniolos who performed pretty much the same duties and tasks as the Parker Ranch paniolos. A lot of the local residents were very upset when the Paleaka Ranch went back into business and failed to rehire the paniolos whose families had worked on the Paleaka Ranch when it was a big operation run by David's father. There was a lot of animosity and anger towards the Japanese workers employed at the ranch. That was why, when Dusty called on one of his paniolos to organize a group of riders to ride onto the Paleaka Ranch that night, he had almost two dozen volunteers. As they continued their drive back to the ranch, Dusty and Jim formulated a plan to get to the laboratory at the Paleaka Ranch hopefully without any trouble from Minoru's security guards. Just in case, they planned to be prepared with plenty of firepower if Minoru's guards took exception to Dusty and Jim's invite from David.

When Dusty and Jim got to the Parker Ranch, the paniolos were already loading horses into trailers preparing to move them up to the high country near the Paleaka Ranch. Over the next forty minutes eighteen paniolos arrived at the ranch, each heavily armed. It seemed word regarding the ban on assault weapons never reached the paniolos on the big island. They had more weaponry than Jim's unit used to take on special ops assault missions when he was in the Marines.

The owner of a ranch adjacent to the Paleaka Ranch had offered his property as the staging area for Dusty and Jim's plan. At around one in the morning, a caravan of pickup trucks pulling horse trailers headed out of Waimea up Highway 250. It was a slow drive into the hills towards the Paleaka Ranch. The Kona winds had blown a blanket of thick clouds against the mountain and it was making travel very slow. Fortunately, the mists that accompanied the winds had not yet fully formed, but it wouldn't be long.

When they got to the staging area at the adjacent ranch, one of the paniolos who worked on that ranch had already gone out and cut some fence which separated their ranch from the Paleaka Ranch. He also herded a few of the ranch cattle through the break in the fence. Since David had given his permission for Jim and Dusty to trespass on the ranch, it wasn't really necessary to cut the fence and drive the strays onto the Paleaka Ranch property. It was just a little extra precaution Dusty recommended they take. There was an old written law on the books from when King Kamehameha ruled the islands. That law allowed paniolos to go onto neighboring ranches to retrieve cattle that somehow escaped from their own ranch. That way, if someone started shooting at them for trespassing, they could shoot back in self-defense and the Hawaiian laws protected them from being charged or prosecuted for it.

By three in the morning all the paniolos were saddled up and ready to begin their ride onto the Paleaka Ranch property. Dusty and Jim had briefed them as to what they hoped to accomplish and they all seemed to understand their roles in the plan. They also understood the danger involved. The paniolos were divided into three teams. Each team had a former paniolo from the Paleaka Ranch who knew the pastures, the valleys, and the hills of the ranch property. They also knew where the bunkhouse was that housed the Japanese workers brought over to operate the ranch, feedlot, and slaughterhouse. One team of paniolos was to head to the bunkhouse and make sure the workers stayed inside, out of the way, and calm. Several of the paniolos in this team spoke Japanese to help explain to the workers what was going on.

A second team of paniolos was to head to the laboratory to look for Minoru, disarm any guards who might be stationed at its entrance, and then check to see if there in fact were 'downer cows' housed there that may indeed have mad cow disease. Jim would be in charge of this paniolo team of riders.

The third and largest team, which also was the best-armed team, was to take out the armed security force at the ranch. One subgroup from this team would surprise the security guards who were not on duty and hopefully asleep in their housing unit located near the laboratory. The larger contingent of this third team was assigned the task of taking out the guards who were on duty and patrolling the ranch. This would be somewhat of a more difficult task, since these guards were heavily armed and looking for intruders. Dusty was in charge of the third team of paniolos, as well as the leader of the group assigned to take on, and hopefully take out, the guards on patrol. Dusty had borrowed the mobile communication system used by his men at the Parker Ranch and at least three members of each team had one of the walkie-talkies.

Before the group had left the Parker Ranch, two of Dusty's ranch hands who were not paniolos were also assigned a part in the plan. They both happened to be friends of David Paleaka. Jim told them to go back to the Marriott where he was sure David would still be. They were to stay with David and make sure he got back to the ranch safely. They were given a radio and two assault rifles to hide under the seat of their jeep. They were to stay in David's ranch house until they got a call from Dusty on the radio. They were to then leave the house and take a wrong turn towards the off-limits section of the ranch. They were to make a lot of noise in the process as if they were very drunk. This should attract the security guards on patrol. That would give Dusty's team a chance to sneak up behind them.

Dusty's wife was back at the Parker Ranch monitoring the walkie-talkie channel. She had instructions to call the police and the FBI the instant gunfire was reported or she was instructed to do so by Jim or Dusty. As the teams began riding towards the Paleaka Ranch, the Kona Mist hung thick in the hills. When the Kona Winds blow from the south, the clouds become so thick and heavy with moisture, it is as though you are under water. The mist was thicker than any fog Jim had ever experienced. You could not see five feet in front of you. The horses belonging to the old Paleaka Ranch paniolos seemed to be able to sense which way to go. As they made the trek across the pastures, the mist would at times dissipate, allowing the riders to see up to a hundred feet in front of them. Then as quickly as the mist cleared, it would once again become too thick to see the rider next to you.

Around 4:00 a.m., the first team was approaching the worker's bunkhouse. As they neared the bunkhouse they could see the lights coming on inside. For some reason, the workers were getting up early that morning. One of the Japanese workers went outside to smoke a cigarette. As he lit up, he saw several riders on horseback coming through the mist not thirty feet from him. The cigarette dropped from his mouth as he dropped to his knees in fear. He thought the ghosts of the Samurai Warriors were coming to take him away and he was praying and pleading to be spared. One of the riders jumped from his horse and pulled the worker to his feet while covering his mouth to keep him quiet. He told him he was not here to kill him unless he refused to follow orders. The worker anxiously agreed to do as he was told. The paniolo asked him why everyone was up so early. The worker told the paniolo Minoru had ordered them to rise early to destroy the sick cattle by the laboratory and to remove and destroy the feed stored in the locked bin at the feedlot. The paniolo relayed this information to the other teams. The rest of the first team moved into the bunkhouse with weapons drawn gathering the Japanese workers as they went, herding them into the bunkhouse dining room where they explained what was going on. They met no resistance from any of the Japanese workers. These workers were hired to work on the ranch, not fight and die for it. They would cause no trouble.

When Jim heard what the Japanese worker had to say, he was sure this Minoru was definitely the one they were after. The third team called in seconds later and reported all the security guards had left their quarters and were heading towards the front gate of the ranch. Jim told Dusty's wife to call the FBI and local police and have them head to the ranch fast. A minute later she radioed back saying the FBI told her a team of agents were sent to the Paleaka Ranch almost an hour ago and should be there by now. This puzzled both Jim and Dusty. Something was going on and they needed to act quickly. Dusty radioed his two workers who were at David's ranch house and told them to leave immediately and create the distraction as planned. Jim told Dusty's wife to call back the FBI dispatcher and tell them to warn the agents they may be heading into a trap. Jim also told her to tell the agents not to shoot the cowboys in the mist. Jim's team was still a ways from the laboratory and was moving slowly due to the thick Kona Mist. They were also trying to avoid running into either of the security teams now patrolling the ranch.

Minoru was busy urging the researchers to work faster. He too was sensing time was growing short. He got a call from his second security team telling him there were two unmarked police cars now waiting outside the property. They wanted to know what to do. Minoru told them to take cover out of sight near the gate. If anyone tried to enter the ranch property, they were to shoot to kill. The security team understood Minoru's orders. One of the researchers was moving the active anthrax cultures to the secret laboratory. His partner had almost completed moving all the equipment to the hidden laboratory and he was transferring more cultures when he heard what sounded like automatic weapon fire coming from the far end of the ranch. He panicked and dropped one of the cultures, shattering the Petri dish containing the anthrax spores, on the floor of the main laboratory. Minoru became enraged at his clumsiness and shot the researcher point blank in the face. The second researcher began to scream. Minoru turned and smashed the butt of his gun into the nose of the other researcher. Minoru ordered him into the secret laboratory and told him to transfer the weaponized anthrax into thermos-size containers Spencer had specifically designed to safely and discretely carry the weapon grade anthrax. The second researcher nervously followed Minoru's order, spilling some of the finely powdered anthrax on his clothing. Minoru, as had the researchers, had been inoculated with an anthrax vaccine, so he was not too concerned about the spill. The researcher completed the transfer, started to clean the spilled powdered anthrax off of the container, but Minoru grabbed the last thermos full of anthrax away from the researcher before he finished cleaning off the spilled powder. Minoru then had the researcher return to the main laboratory where he too was shot at point blank range, but this time in the back of the head. Minoru went back into the secret passageway towards the hidden laboratory. He locked the passageway and armed a large explosive device designed to self-destruct the laboratory if someone did happen to discover and attempt to open the secret passageway into the hidden laboratory. There was little to no chance anyone would ever find the passage, but Taka had prepared for all possible scenarios. Taka always prepared for what may happen. Minoru then left the hidden laboratory through the other entrance into the ancient lava tube. He followed the tube back to the small house outside the ranch property.

Jim heard the automatic weapon fire coming from the front entrance of the ranch. He had stopped at a cattle corral next to the laboratory that contained several 'downer' cattle. As he was looking in the corral, he had heard what he thought were two pistol shots about three minutes apart, come from inside the laboratory.

"Dusty," Jim called, "is everything okay at the gate?"

About half of Dusty's paniolo team had followed the second security team to the front gate. In front of the gate were two cars with three men in each car. They appeared to be waiting for someone or something because they were parked just outside the gate across the road, making no attempt to enter the ranch. Another car came speeding up to the gate. In this car were a man and a woman. They stopped across the street and spoke with the drivers of the other two cars. They were each handed an automatic rifle and they climbed back into their car. Then one of the cars sped across the road and onto the ranch property. The security team hiding by the side of the road opened fire on the lead car. Fortunately for the FBI men inside, the car that entered the ranch was reinforced with bullet-proof windows and door linings. As two of the security guards opened fire on the car, they gave their positions away and the paniolos behind them opened fire on them. The initial battle was over in a few seconds. The car sustained minimal damage and the agents inside were unhurt, but the two security guards were killed. The four other security guards who were lying in ambush and had not opened fire stayed under cover, hidden by the mist. One of them started randomly firing in the direction the paniolos shot from. He connected on one lucky shot hitting one of the horses causing it to fall on the paniolo rider, breaking the paniolo's leg.

Jotty, who had arrived with Haruko in the third car, fired his own rifle at the muzzle flashes of the security guard shooting into the mist. His first shot struck the guard in the stomach causing the guard to scream and drop his rifle. Two of the other security guards tried to run away into the mist, only to run into the paniolos with rifles aimed at the guards' heads. Both the guards threw down their guns and surrendered. The remaining guard faded into the mist and seemed to disappear for now.

"Everything is now under control at the gate," responded a voice, but it wasn't Dusty's voice. It was Jotty's voice.

"You can tell me what the hell you are doing here when this is over," Jim responded back. He needed to get inside the laboratory.

Meanwhile, the two ranch hands that had left David Paleaka's house were following their instructions and creating quite a scene in a different area of the ranch. They had managed to attract the attention of the security team that was on duty patrolling the ranch. Just as they were about to get out of their jeep to talk to the security guards, the battle at the gate started. The security team on patrol opened fire on the farm hands jeep Cherokee from their own open-air jeep. The two ranch hands ducked down and floored the gas pedal with their hands heading across the pastures. The security team took off in their vehicle in pursuit. The Kona Mist hung tremendously heavy in the air, cutting the visibility down to almost zero. The two ranch workers were sitting up in their seats frantically trying to get away and avoid hitting one of the hundreds of cows grazing in the field. The security guards were doing the same. They were also calling on their radio for assistance, but were receiving no response.

Dusty and his team came upon the guards as they took off in pursuit of his farm workers. The security didn't see Dusty's team of paniolos approaching as they began to speed away. At least speed as fast as the mist would allow them to go. The guards fired a few shots in the direction the jeep Cherrokee had taken, hoping to get a lucky hit through the mist. They only managed to hit two cows that fell in the path of their vehicle slowing them down. Dusty and two of his paniolos spurred their horses into a gallop in pursuit of the security guard's jeep. Dusty and one of the paniolos grabbed lassos from their saddle and began to swirl the lassos above their heads. They were on either side of the jeep and their targets were the two security guards standing in the back seat of the jeep. Dusty and the paniolo each were successful with their first throw of the lassos, encircling their respective guards and stopping their horses to brace them against the strong tug of the lassoed guards. The ropes fell around the chests of both men. In an instant, their arms were pinned against their bodies and their guns flew into the air as the momentum of the jeep caused both men to go flying out the back of the jeep as the ropes pulled tight. The two guards in the front were unaware of what happened to the two in the rear seats. When the guards flew out the back of the jeep, one was knocked unconscious and the other dislocated his shoulder and broke his arm in two places. A few seconds later the two guards in the front noticed that the two in the back were missing and stopped their jeep. They thought they must have fallen out because of the rough ride. When they got out to check, they were met by the remaining paniolos with guns drawn. The two security guards knew it was time to surrender.

Meanwhile, Jim and two of the paniolos on his team entered the laboratory. Three other paniolos remained outside guarding the entrances and the corral with the 'downer' cattle. The three who entered the laboratory were moving carefully, checking each room of the laboratory, and yelling 'clear' as each room was checked for occupants. They continued to provide cover for one another with their rifles, just as a military operational team would do, as they advanced deeper into the building. It was a slow process but Jim wanted to make sure they all came out alive. As they neared one of the main lab work areas, they came across the second researcher with most of his face blown away. The bullet Minoru had shot point blank into the back of the researcher's head took most of his face away as it exited. Around the corner they came across the other researcher in a pool of blood. There was broken glass scattered around along with some small white crystal type material. One of the paniolos picked up some of the spilled material and brought it to Jim.

"What is this? Is it cocaine?" the paniolo asked.

Jim took the white substance in his hand and turned it around staring in disbelief. "This is death," was Jim's reply. "This is anthrax."

Jim got on the radio and told everyone to stay out of the laboratory. He called Jotty and explained what they had found. Someone had killed the two researchers and dropped cultured anthrax spores in the laboratory. He told Jotty to contact the military HAZ-MAT team stationed at Oahu and get them here fast. He also told Jotty they needed a medical team to help the two paniolos who were probably now infected with anthrax. Jim had been given a series of shots to immunize him from anthrax when he was working at Texas A & M. He had also had several boosters, so he was sure he would be unaffected by the cultures.

Jotty and the FBI agents moved onto the ranch and collected the captured security guards from Dusty and the paniolos. The police arrived and took control of the Japanese workers in the bunkhouse. The paniolos all quietly got on their horses and headed back into the mist towards the adjacent ranch and their horse trailers. They did not want to have to answer too many questions about the weaponry they were carrying with them. Jim told Jotty over the radio to let them go. The bodies of the dead guards were collected, but none of them was Minoru. Minoru had somehow disappeared during the night. The captured guards last heard from him when he radioed them from the laboratory and told them to ambush the police at the front entrance. After that, no one heard or saw Minoru. Jim was sure it was Minoru who had killed the two researchers, but had no idea how Minoru could have slipped past them and out of the laboratory. After Jim heard the two gunshots, he and his men had sealed off the exits to the laboratory and no one had left the building. At least he thought no one had left the building.

Jotty and his FBI agents were outside the laboratory talking over the radio to Jim, who was inside the lab entrance with the two scared paniolos. Jim reassured them that the doctors who were on the way would be able to tell if they were exposed to the anthrax. Even if they had been exposed, Jim told them, there was medication to stop it from spreading and make them well. The Kona Mist was still heavy in the air and visibility was still poor. As Jotty was talking to one of his agents, the remaining security guard who had avoided detection came up behind Jotty, aimed his rifle at Jotty's head, and demanded he be driven away or he would kill Jotty. The other agents were ordered to back away or he would shoot. The security guard was very agitated and upset. Jotty knew he would fire the rifle if they didn't cooperate with his demands. The mist was thick and it allowed someone else to come up behind the security guard holding the rifle. Haruko sneaked up behind the guard without making a sound. In a flash, she had the guard's rifle in her hand and smashed the butt of the rifle against the guard's head knocking him unconscious.

"That's two you owe me," Haruko said to Jotty as she walked to a bench in front of the laboratory and lay down. She and Jotty had been flying for almost twenty hours straight, going from Hawaii to Atlanta and right back. As the mist began to clear, dozens of police and military personnel descended on the ranch and began taking over. Jim was quarantined inside the lab with the two paniolos who had helped him search it. Jotty too, was beginning to feel exhausted and needed to get back to the hotel to rest.

"Heh Jim," Jotty said with a smile. "You won't need your room at the Marriott for a few days. Mind if Haruko and I borrow it to catch up on some sleep?"

Jim didn't think Jotty was funny and flipped him off.

"The doctor says you should be released from the building in a couple of days if all goes well. Haruko and I will be up later tonight to check on you," Jotty told Jim. "That is if we can get out of bed by then." Jotty was grinning.

"Maybe we will bring you a bottle of wine or something," Haruko added smiling. She had caught on to Jotty's teasing of Jim and added to it.

The two of them got into the car and headed down to the Marriott.

Dusty said his goodbyes to Jim and the two paniolos locked in the laboratory with Jim. He told them he would be up the next day to check on them and promised to bring them a good home-cooked meal. Jim thanked him for all of his help and told Dusty he was always welcome to come to Texas for a little Texas-style cowboy fun. Dusty laughed and rode off across the fields and disappeared just like the cowboys in the mist.

Chapter Thirty-two

After Minoru killed the two researchers, he quickly sealed the passageways and made his way to the safe house Taka had built on a separate parcel of land down the road from the Paleaka Ranch property. It was a small inconspicuous house designed like several other vacation houses in the area. A lot of Americans and a few Japanese had these houses built as their vacation home on the island. It was a lot cheaper than staying in the pricey resort hotels. This house looked much the same as the others, but was built to keep out any locals who thought they might break in to steal the possessions of the rich absentee owners. There were remote sensors that warned approaching trespassers they were being videotaped and a private security force would be contacted if they came any closer to the house. There was also a tall fence and an electronic gate protecting the property. The house had strong secure locks on the windows and doors making entry almost impossible. Inside, the house was sparsely decorated. Taka had only visited the house once and Minoru did not spend any time staying there. What made the house unique was the hidden indoor passageway that led to the ancient lava tube. That tube ran from the hidden laboratory past the house and down to the ocean. Inside the passageway from the house to the lava tube Taka had installed a large vault-like safe. It was in this safe Minoru now placed the thermoses of anthrax. This safe also contained several million dollars Taka had placed inside in preparation for that day, if it ever came, when he would have to give up his businesses and go into hiding. He would have enough money to continue his terrorist activities.

He would also have the weapon to continue that activity if he needed it as well.

As soon as Minoru had sealed the anthrax safely in the vault, he secured the house and drove the rental car towards the small village of Hawi. In a very overgrown and remote valley, he pushed the car off the road and down the cliff into a lush overgrown tropical valley, hiding the car from the view of anyone driving or walking on the road above. He then called one of the helicopter pilots who was still on Minoru's payroll. The pilot was paid to keep his mouth shut and paid well. Without questioning Minoru, he agreed to fly to Hawi and pick up Minoru in a field near the town. It would be a longer flight than usual because the thick Kona Mist would force the pilot to fly far around the north end of the island, rather than the direct route over the mountaintop. While the Kona Winds still caused the clouds to hang thickly on the south side of the mountains, Hawi on the northern side of the mountains remained clear.

Minoru had the pilot fly him to the Kahului airport on Maui where Minoru had arranged for a car to be waiting to take him to a safe hiding place. In route to the airport Minoru began to worry about what he would tell Taka. He knew when he arrived at the Maui airport it would be time for him to make his scheduled call. He just hoped Taka would understand the egregious turn of events.

Chapter Thirty-three

Niki slowly picked herself up off of the floor. Taka was ignoring her and had gone back to watching the television news reports. Without looking at or saying anything to Taka, Niki left back through the door connecting their two suites. Niki went to the mirror and saw that Taka's handprint blazed red on her cheek. She also noticed it was already beginning to show signs of bruising. She went to the dressing table and started applying makeup to hide her injured face. As Niki tried to cover the handprint, she looked at herself in the mirror and burst into tears. She realized she had been used and abused her entire life. She no longer wanted to live that way. She needed to find a way to stop Aioka from running and ruining her life any longer. Life had been good when the real Taka was alive. With Aioka, she thought things had been getting better, at least Niki had convinced herself they were getting better. And they were, until Aioka refused to cancel Niki's part in his terrorist plan. Niki thought maybe it was time for her to take control of her own life and future. Maybe she should tell someone what Aioka was up to. The more she thought about exposing Aioka's plan the better she began to feel. Then she started thinking how implicated she would be in Aioka's plot. She did have the original idea to taint the cosmetics with the Prion affected cow byproducts. Aioka would no doubt let the authorities know that bit of information if he was arrested. Niki wondered if she could take that kind of risk. Maybe she should just destroy the tainted cosmetics or have them stolen and then destroyed. Niki's mind was working hard on a solution when Taka's secured phone began to ring in the suite next to hers.

Taka was basking in the glow of the confusion and chaos the tainted meat incident was causing in Atlanta. That was why he sounded so cheerful when he answered the phone.

"Good morning Minoru," Taka said cheerfully. "I hope all is well in Hawaii. Have you watched the news, everyone is talking about the Red Summit and the Atlanta terrorist attack?"

Minoru was silent on the other end of the phone. Taka sensed something was not right and he immediately took on a serious tone.

"Tell me what has happened, Minoru, I can tell from your silence something has gone wrong."

"I am ashamed to say many things have gone wrong, Taka. Way too many things. The ranch has been lost. I am unsure exactly who raided it in the middle of the night, but I believe it to be those two FBI agents who we failed to kill in Tokyo," Minoru explained.

"How could two FBI agents take control of the ranch?" Taka questioned. "What about the guards? What about your ninjas? How could this happen?"

"Two of my ninja were killed along with my personal bodyguard at the Hilton hotel yesterday. My ninja were killed by the two FBI agents and my own bodyguard was killed by Haruko, the National Police Agency investigator," Minoru explained.

"What were they all doing at the Hilton at the same time? I thought only this Haruko was there," Taka bellowed.

"As did I," responded Minoru, "but it seems those two FBI agents somehow found out Spencer was in Hawaii and came in search of him."

"And did they find him?"

"They did, but he will tell them nothing," Minoru responded. "I had to kill Spencer myself at the Hilton to keep him from being captured and telling all he knew."

"That is the first good news you have told me," Taka said in exasperation. "Was it these three who raided the ranch?"

"I believe so," Minoru said, "but I cannot be sure. I was busy in the laboratory moving the anthrax and specialized equipment to the hidden laboratory."

"I assume you were successful or you would not be calling me now," Taka replied.

"I was successful in moving the equipment, but one of the researchers dropped a culture of the anthrax spores and they were left in the main laboratory, where it will surely be discovered. I am sorry," Minoru apologized.

"What about the two researchers? Did you deal with them properly?"

"I killed them both and left their bodies in the main laboratory. I sealed the passageway and armed the self-destruct explosives. I was fortunate enough to take with me several thermoses full of the weapon grade anthrax powder. I placed them in the secured vault in the passageway from the lava tube to the safe house below the ranch property."

"I am saddened by these interruptions to our plans," Taka told Minoru, "but I am glad you were able to retrieve some of the powdered anthrax, and I am glad you are safe as well my friend. I had prepared for these events in case they were to happen and unfortunately, they have, but all is not lost. It just requires a few changes to our time schedule. Now I need you here in Los Angeles to help complete the next step in the Red Summit's terror plan. Unfortunately, all is not going as I had planned, either. It seems Niki's resolve is not as strong as yours or mine. You may need to complete her work as well."

"I will come at once."

"Do not be so hasty," Taka told Minoru. "Wait a day or two to see if you can find out what happened at the ranch. I have a feeling I will be coming to Hawaii soon and will meet with you there to discuss what I need you to do in Los Angeles. Are you safe where you are?"

"I will find a safe place and await your arrival," Minoru humbly replied to Taka. "Are you sure it is safe for you to come here to Hawaii?"

I know it will be safe," responded Taka. "I have done nothing that would allow them to place any of the blame for what has happened on me. It is you, Minoru, who will bear the burden of blame for all that occurred. Fear not though, for I will protect you and have plans in place that will keep us both out of harms way. I will contact you when I arrive in Hawaii. Be strong in your faith, my friend." Taka hung up the phone and sat back down in front of the television. The news was now talking about a major gun battle at a resort hotel in Hawaii. Taka turned off the television and called his attorney.

Chapter Thirty-four

Jotty and Haruko slept together that night at the Marriott Hotel. At least they slept in the same room. They shared the same room Jotty and Jim had shared two nights previous. It had two double beds and what the hotel called a 'partial ocean view'. That meant if you went out on the balcony and leaned way out, you might see the ocean, if the tide was in. Actually, Jotty would have loved to have shared his bed with Haruko, but when they got back to the Marriott, they had both been awake for going on forty hours and all either of them could think about was sleep. Jotty's planned offer to Haruko would have to wait until another day.

Jim spent his first night under quarantine in the laboratory sleeping on a couch. He along with the two paniolos quarantined with him. The two paniolos were pretty nervous about all the HAZ-MAT technicians and doctors coming in and out of the laboratory in their white airtight suits. Jim convinced them there really wasn't anything to worry about. They would be allowed to go home in just a couple of days. At least that was the plan until they discovered the weapons grade anthrax powder on the shirt of one of the dead researchers. That absolutely made no sense to Jim at all. Turning those large cultured samples of anthrax Jim had seen on the floor of the lab into weapon's grade anthrax required a lot of very sophisticated equipment. Equipment unlike any Jim had seen in this laboratory. This was something to really worry about. That meant the Red Summit had their hands on some weapons grade anthrax capable of killing thousands and maybe hundreds of thousands of people. This changed the playing field considerably as far as Jim was concerned. That was why they needed and had taken Spencer from Dallas. He knew how to build equipment and process those cultures. "That means there must be another laboratory somewhere on the island," Jim said to himself.

Now that there was weapons grade anthrax in the area, the cleanup became much more intense, as did the treatment of the two paniolos. Fortunately, no spores were found in their bodies and they were allowed to leave to return home the next morning. Jotty and Haruko showed up just as Jim was released from the laboratory.

"Where's my bottle of wine?" Jim asked as they got out of their car.

Jim told Jotty and Haruko about the weaponized anthrax and showed them some of Spencer's journals he had found. The journals made no reference to the anthrax, but did talk about three separate batches of tainted beef sent from the laboratory. Each shipment was about three tons, about the same tonnage as the meat distributed in Atlanta. The date of one of the shipments also corresponded to the date the tainted meat showed up in the food banks in Atlanta. Jim had checked the records of the meat shipped from the slaughterhouse and found that on dates corresponding to the tainted meat dates, a large shipment of beef was sent to a number of restaurants, including the Sizzle Burger fast food chain locations throughout Hawaii. Jotty, Jim, and Haruko all looked at each other wondering whom they should tell this information to.

Jim finally spoke up, "If that meat was eaten, there is not a damn thing we can do about it now. The chances are great that, if eaten, whoever did eat the meat will eventually be affected by the disease. Look at the panic in Atlanta," Jim continued. "Have you guys been watching the news? Have you seen all the crazy things people are saying and doing because of this tainted meat in Atlanta? I don't think telling the media there may be several thousand additional people affected is a responsible thing to do right now."

"Is it responsible to allow these people to die without knowing why?" Haruko asked of Jim.

"That is a decision not for us to make," Jotty spoke up. "Our job is to make sure it doesn't happen any more."

"Once we arrest Taka for producing this tainted meat, we will have put the Red Summit out of business and stopped this form of terrorism," Haruko remarked.

"Unfortunately, it is not Taka who is responsible for this. At least we cannot yet prove his involvement," Jotty explained.

"I don't understand," said Haruko in a perplexed voice. "He owns this ranch. He is the one responsible."

"Not according to his attorney," Jotty continued. "It seems Taka has never even been to this ranch. It is just one of his many investments. This ranch and its feedlot and slaughterhouse were run entirely by this Minoru Sakura. The man in the hotel videos. The same man you saw at the heliport. The same man who killed the two security guards in San Pedro and the three in Britain. Taka blames Minoru for ruining his good name and destroying his businesses. We will have a hard time proving it was anything but that. It is Minoru Sakura we are after, not Taka."

Haruko was devastated. Yes, she did want to catch this Minoru Sakura, but she was sure it was Taka who was the power behind the Red Summit.

"What's our next move?" Jim asked.

"Our next move," Jotty explained, "is to find this Minoru, after we write up about a thousand pages of reports."

"Well, I think Minoru is still somewhere on this island," Jim told Haruko and Jotty. "There has got to be another laboratory somewhere around here with the capabilities of turning cultured anthrax into weapon grade anthrax. That was a specialty of Spencer's. That and his absorption research."

"What is this absorption research?" Haruko asked.

"Spence had this idea that it wasn't necessary for cattle or other animals to ingest Prion affected tissues. He thought the disease could be transferred via absorption through the skin. The military was paying for his research expenses at Texas A & M, hoping to find out if it was possible as Spencer claimed it was." Jim explained.

"And is it possible?" Haruko continued to ask.

"I don't know," Jim told her. "Spencer went to prison before he could complete his research. From the looks of this laboratory, he may have been trying it again. If the lab wasn't still off limits, I would show you."

"Show us what?" Jotty enquired.

"I would show you some of his other journals and samples he was working with. It seems he was mixing Prion affected materials into cosmetics and applying them to different animals," Jim told them.

"Were his experiments working?" Jotty asked.

"Who can tell," Jim replied, "It takes several years for signs of mad cow disease to show up in animals."

"Then why are there so many cows out back that appear to have mad cow disease?" Jotty continued to question.

"Well, either they were affected several years ago and brought here to the island or Spencer figured a way to speed up the affecting process. His journals refer to some experiments along those lines, but that information must have been written somewhere else, because I sure couldn't find it in any of his journals or papers I have found and read," Jim told the both of them.

"Here's what I need you two to do," Jotty said. "Jim, I want you to oversee the cleanup and destruction of all the sick animals here. I understand they found feed that contained a lot of Prion affected tissue, which means all the cattle on the ranch need to be destroyed. I want you trying to figure out just what Spencer was up to and how successful he was at it. Haruko, I want you to start going through the computers and business logs for this operation. I need to know where all these animals came from, where and when meat or live animals left the ranch and where they went. I need to know who was on the payroll and for how long. I want to know everything about this Minoru Sakura. Any questions?"

"Yeah," Jim replied. "Just what the hell are you going to do?"

"I'm going to write this up and get you guys a lot more help. You are going to need it."

Chapter Thirty-five

The batch of lipstick with the mad cow affected ingredients was manufactured, labeled and packaged for shipment. The tainted lipsticks, along with several hundred thousand other tubes of BSE free lipstick, were awaiting shipment in the factory and warehouse facility in Cudahy. It was ironic that the buildings where the 'Niki Matsuura' line of cosmetics were manufactured and stored were previously used as a slaughterhouse for a meatpacking company. Cudahy used to be the home of several meatpacking companies. The name Cudahy itself was once the name of a large pork product manufacturer and distributor. Those industries were now all gone leaving behind dozens of vacant and run-down factories. Some of those factories were being revitalized for other industries as had the old Cudahy plant for the 'Niki Matsuura' cosmetic plant. Most, however, were nothing more than vacant decaying buildings which served as residences for the hundreds of homeless immigrants who seemed to migrate to the East Los Angeles area. Cudahy was one of the poorest and most overcrowded areas west of the Mississippi River. The most popular businesses were the dozens of swap meets, which catered to the immigrants, selling them basic necessities and fake designer items at a fraction of the cost.

Taka did not want to leave Los Angeles quite yet, but the difficulties in Hawaii dictated that he must leave. Taka was very concerned about Niki's lack of resolve. He needed someone he could trust to make sure his plans were followed through. He no longer trusted Niki to do that. That was why he would send Minoru to Los Angeles as soon as they had their talk in Hawaii. First, he needed Minoru to find out what exactly had occurred at the Paleaka Ranch.

Before Taka left for Hawaii, he told Niki to be strong and their dreams would be realized. Niki told Taka she would fulfill her part in the Red Summit terrorist plan. Taka did not believe her, but knew she could not stop what was already in motion. He would have Minoru in charge by that evening. Minoru would see to it Niki cooperated.

Niki was no fool. Aioka did not give her the credit she deserved. It was Niki who had envisioned the concept of the tainted cosmetics. It was Niki who now envisioned a way to get out of her part in the Red Summit terrorist plan. When Taka left Los Angeles, Niki drove to the manufacturing plant in Cudahy. She found the tainted cosmetics and ordered two of the warehouse workers, Ignacio and Leonel, to load them into a truck. Ignacio and Leonel were two high school dropouts hired through a federally funded program to find local residents jobs in the community in which they lived. The program was a double-edged sword. While it did pay half the wages for the workers, saving the employer a good deal of money, it tended to employ lazy unmotivated workers who tended to steal you blind if they were not carefully watched. Such were Ignacio and Leonel. Niki pulled the two workers aside and offered them a deal. She told them she would give them each $500 to load the truck with cases of a certain batch number of the 'TAKA' lipstick and take it to the dump and destroy it. She stressed to them it was extremely important the lipstick be destroyed. They were also to tell no one what she had ordered them to do. Ignacio and Leonel both eagerly agreed to her offer. She told them she would arrange it with their supervisor, so they were not to worry.

Worry was something Ignacio and Leonel rarely did. That would take too much effort.

Taka flew in his private jet to Maui where he met with his attorney from Japan. He and his attorney held a press conference denouncing the heinous crimes of his former entrusted employee Minoru Sakura. Taka apologized to the people of Hawaii and informed the press he was ending his financial support of the facilities at the Paleaka Ranch. He denied knowing anything about the Red Summit or how his ranch's meat packing plant may be connected to the tragedy in Atlanta. Taka assured the retailers who had a contract to receive their meat from the Paleaka plant that one of his affiliated businesses in Japan would continue supplying the retailer's meat product needs. When asked about the rumors of the cattle on the Paleaka Ranch being affected with the mad cow disease, Taka denied any knowledge of that, saying it was highly unlikely, but reminded the journalists present that he had never actually been to the Paleaka Ranch. It was strictly an investment he helped fund. It was owned and run by Minoru Sakura and David Paleaka. He told the journalist any further questions of that type might best be answered by this David Paleaka or Minoru Sakura, if this Minoru was ever found.

Taka and his attorney were very gracious and answered several more questions the journalists asked. One of the journalists present asked about his and Niki's relationship. He told the crowd he and Niki had been separated for a while, but he had just left Los Angeles where she was filming commercials for her new line of cosmetics. He continued by telling them he and Niki had a wonderful time together in Los Angeles and reconciled their differences. They still were both madly in love with each other. As a matter of fact, she was going to be flying back to Japan next week to join Taka. They were leaving together for a trip to New Zealand to celebrate their second wedding anniversary. By the end of the news conference, Taka looked like a saint that this Minoru had tried to rape. Taka definitely knew how to work the public opinion to his favor.

Taka returned to the hangar that housed his private jet. On board the jet, Minoru was waiting. The jet taxied to the runway and took off heading for Oahu. During the flight Taka told Minoru what he needed to do in Los Angeles. Minoru in turn told Taka of what he had found out about the raid on the ranch. Taka knew most of this information already. He had read much of the information Minoru gave him in the newspaper articles or saw it on the national television news reports. Taka knew it would be quite some time before he could return to the big island to retrieve the anthrax hidden there or restart the weaponization process in the hidden laboratory. This did not trouble Taka, for he knew his struggle was a long one. It would take time to achieve his victory, but he knew that through time his ideals would eventually prevail. Besides, he had succeeded in affecting thousands of people with his tainted meat and he would be affecting tens of thousands more when the lipstick was shipped to the retailers throughout the United States. Soon the Red Summit would announce to the world that thousands in Hawaii had eaten the mad cow affected meat. It excited him to think about the terror such an announcement would bring about. Taka couldn't help but smile.

When Taka's jet landed in Oahu, Minoru left the plane dressed as a maintenance worker. He slipped into a private hangar and boarded another private jet that took him to Los Angeles. After refueling, Taka's jet headed for Japan. Taka's attorney said it was wise for Taka to stay out of the United

States for some time to come. Taka agreed as he reclined in his chair to take a well-deserved nap.

Chapter Thirty-six

Jotty, Jim, and Haruko watched Taka's press conference on the television at the pool bar behind the Marriott Hotel.

"The asshole could have at least come to the big island and apologized," Haruko said out loud. Several parents with their children sitting at tables eating snacks glared at Haruko for her choice of language.

"Do I sense a little hostility in your voice?" Jotty said laughingly.

"No," said Jim, "I think you sense a lot of hostility."

Jotty had several FBI agents sorting through reams of papers and thousands of computer files at the Paleaka Ranch. The military was still cleaning up the laboratory and burning the carcasses of hundreds of cattle that had to be killed. Jotty, Jim, and Haruko could no longer stand the smell of the bar-b-cue beef and had to take a break from their work at the ranch. That's why they were sitting around the pool bar having a few drinks and watching television.

"I sure hope David Paleaka has a good attorney. He is in for a few thousand law suits the way this mess is starting to sort out," Jotty told his friends.

"Well if he goes to trial here on the island, I don't think he will have anything to worry about. The locals here seem to take care of their own," Jim commented. The others all nodded in agreement.

"You know," said Haruko, "I would really like to talk to Taka in person."

"Why?" said Jim, "So you could beat a confession out of him."

"We don't treat our suspects in Japan the same way you do in America," Haruko started to say. "We are not allowed to beat confessions out of them by sticking broomsticks up their a....,"

"Not so loud," Jotty scolded Haruko. "There are children present."

The drinks had obviously begun to loosen Haruko's tongue and her inhibitions.

"I think maybe you have had enough to drink," Jim said to Haruko as he moved the drink away from her hand.

In a flash Haruko grabbed Jim's wrist to stop him from taking her drink glass. Their eyes met in a stare. "Damn it feels good when you touch me there," Jim said breaking the silence.

Haruko blushed and quickly removed her hand from Jim's wrist.

"No, no don't stop," Jim said as he pretended to moan.

Parents were now beginning to glare at Jim.

"We need to get out of here," Jotty said. "I can't take you guys anywhere."

"We just need to get out of this hell hole and take a vacation," Jim said sarcastically as he motioned to the incredible Hawaiian surroundings of the Marriott. "Maybe we should all go on a trip to New Zealand like Taka and Niki have planned."

"I wouldn't mind going with Haruko," Jotty laughed, "But you can forget about me taking you along Jim."

Jim and Jotty were both laughing and didn't notice Haruko had stopped and was staring towards the ocean.

"We need to go to Los Angeles," Haruko blurted out. "We need to go to Los Angeles right away. That is where we will find Minoru."

Jotty and Jim looked at each other.

"What makes you think Minoru is in Los Angeles," Jotty asked.

"Niki is not going to New Zealand with Taka. She is about to start a major promotional tour of her new line of cosmetics," Haruko told them. "Jim, didn't you say Spencer had been working in the laboratory on Prion absorption through the skin using cosmetics? And Jotty, wasn't it cosmetic byproducts that were stolen in San Pedro?"

"They plan to try to give mad cow disease to thousands of people using cosmetics," Jotty said before Haruko could say it.

"I hate to tell you guys this," said Haruko, "but I did see several transfers of bovine amniotic fluid and other byproducts, and a couple of them were dated around the same time as those shipments of tainted meat."

"If Minoru is the mastermind behind the Red Summit, he would be in Los Angeles making sure all goes well there," Jim said.

"Or if Taka is the mastermind," Haruko interjected, "He may have sent Minoru to Los Angeles to convince Niki to join Taka in New Zealand or to make it look like Niki planned to distribute the tainted cosmetics herself."

"That, or Niki is the mastermind behind the Red Summit and has been working with Minoru all along to undermine Taka," Jotty conjectured.

They all reflected upon the possible scenarios for a few seconds.

"Regardless," said Haruko, "we need to get to Los Angeles fast. Does anybody know where the 'Niki Matsuura cosmetic factory is?"

"We will know by the time we get to Los Angeles tonight," said Jotty.

"I do know where we will find Niki," said Jim. "I saw on 'Entertainment Tonight' that there is a big gala opening at the Beverly Hills Hotel for her new line of cosmetics. I think that is where we need to go first. Niki may be unaware of any of this. We need to see what she knows first."

Jotty was on the phone arranging for their flight to Los Angeles and telling his office to find the 'Niki Matsuura' manufacturing plant. Haruko had to be right. Minoru must be in Los Angeles. What they didn't know was Minoru was only a couple of hours ahead of them.

Chapter Thirty-seven

Niki was having trouble covering the bruise on her cheek with her makeup. Her skin needed to look perfect tonight. It had to look perfect. That was what she was selling, her beautiful perfect skin and the makeup which made her skin look that way. God, she hated Aioka and what he had done to her. She would be able to hide the bruise and keep Aioka's slap a secret, but she hated the way Aioka had used her. Just like so many other men had used her in the past.

Niki was actually in a much better mood since Aioka had left for Japan and she had managed to get rid of all the tainted makeup. She was now free from Aioka and the Red Summit. If Aioka troubled her again, she would threaten to expose him as the leader of the Red Summit and as the murderer of Taka. If he tried to implicate her in the murder, she would say he threatened to kill her if she ever told what happened. People would believe her. She was scared, any one in her situation would have done the same. She wanted nothing to do with Aioka. Maybe she should go to the authorities now and tell them her story. She would have to think about that. For now, she needed to sell some cosmetics and to do that she needed to cover this damn bruise.

Minoru arrived in Los Angeles and was met by the three members of the Red Summit cell who had been sent from Japan to load the tainted meat in Atlanta a few days earlier. They were all ninjas trained by Minoru and all had been involved in the British burglary of the mad cow tainted meat. They were experienced terrorists who would do whatever Minoru instructed them to do. They all headed to the cosmetic manufacturing plant in Cudahy. Minoru wanted to be sure all was going as Taka had planned. The tainted cosmetics should have been completed by now and ready for shipment. Minoru would have his men mix the tainted boxes of lipstick in with the safe boxes. That way the Prion affected lipstick would be delivered all over the United States.

They arrived at the shipping warehouse that was located behind the manufacturing warehouse. They entered the warehouse and began searching for the cases with the batch numbers containing the contaminated lipstick. There should have been close to two hundred cases of the mad cow affected lipstick, but none of it was there. Minoru looked at the shipping log and saw no product had left the plant or the warehouse that week. The log did show the batch numbers they were looking for had arrived at the shipping warehouse from the manufacturing facility earlier in the week. Yet Minoru and his men could find them nowhere. Minoru noticed one of the company trucks was not where it should be either. He had his men search the plant, but the truck was nowhere on the property. Someone had to have taken the truck out and it was beginning to seem likely they took the tainted cosmetics as well. Minoru told his men he needed to go see Niki. He told them to wait at the plant for the truck to return and hold the driver until he returned.

Minoru knew where to find Niki. Taka had warned Minoru Niki was losing her resolve and feared she may do something stupid to jeopardize the Red Summit terror plans. It now seemed Taka had been correct in his prediction. Taka always seemed to know what people would do or were planning. That is what had made the Red Summit so feared and so successful. Minoru went to the Beverly Hills Hotel. It was still a few hours until the gala opening and security was not yet tight. There were several paparazzi already waiting on the sidewalk outside the entrance drive to the hotel. Several took Minoru's picture as he turned his car into the hotel driveway. Taka still had a suite reserved at the hotel. When he left for Hawaii, he was not sure if he would be returning to the hotel or going on to Japan. Taka had given his room key to Minoru when they met in Maui. Minoru entered Taka's suite, which was next to Niki's suite. He could hear Niki next door as she was preparing for the debut of her 'Niki Matsuura' line of cosmetics at the gala later in the evening. Minoru listened for several minutes trying to decide if she was alone. He finally decided he could wait no longer and went out his suite and knocked on her door.

"Who is it," Niki said without opening the door.

"Room service," Minoru replied. "I have some flowers for a Niki Matsuura,"

That did the trick. Minoru could hear Niki unlatching the door. As soon as she began to open the door Minoru banged solidly into the door using the full weight of his body. Niki was knocked off her feet as the door slammed heavily into her side. Before she could scream Minoru had his hand over her mouth and was pulling her onto the bed.

"If you scream, I will kill you," Minoru told Niki. "Do you understand?"

She nodded her head. She knew Minoru had killed dozens of times in the past with no remorse. She had no reason to believe it would be different now.

"Tell me what you have done with the tainted cosmetics," Minoru demanded.

"I don't know...," Niki started to answer, but Minoru slapped her hard.

"Do not lie to me, Niki. Tell me what you have done with the cosmetics," Minoru repeated quickly.

Niki knew if she did not tell Minoru, he would kill her. "I had them destroyed."

"Tell me how," Minoru pushed for more information.

"I hired two of the boys in the warehouse to drive them to the dump and destroy them," she continued. "I paid them $500 to do it today."

It began to make sense to Minoru. That was why the truck was missing. They had taken the cosmetics to the dump. Maybe he could still salvage some of them. Just then there was a loud knock at the door.

"Open the door. We saw you force your way in. Ms. Matsuura, are you alright?" Two security guards had witnessed Minoru leave his room and force Niki's door open. They had been monitoring the video feeds back in the control room on the other side of the hotel. At first, they thought it was her husband, Taka, but decided they had better check just to make sure. That was why it took them so long to respond.

Niki saw this as her chance to survive and let out a piercing scream. Minoru pulled his gun and shot Niki in the torso as the two guards opened the door. Minoru rolled on the floor into the legs of the first guard causing him to fall and drop his weapon, while at the same time aiming a shot at the head of the second guard. The back of the second guard's head splattered on the open door. Minoru jumped to his feet and fired a second shot into the side of the head of the first guard who was still lying on the floor. Minoru hurried out the door. As soon as he entered the hallway, he slowed down and hid the gun in his pocket. He walked straight to the valet desk and told the valet he was a doctor and had an emergency. He would get his own car to save time. The valet didn't question Minoru. They were trained never to question the guests. Minoru got into his car and carefully drove out of the hotel trying not to raise any suspicions. Several paparazzi once again snapped his picture as he drove out the front gate.

The bullet Minoru had shot into Niki did not immediately kill her. She lay on the floor dying as a pool of blood continued to grow under her body. When she had originally opened the hotel room door to receive what she thought were flowers from room service, she had been carrying her lipstick. When Minoru knocked into her with the door, the lipstick fell from her hand and onto the wooden floor next to the carpet. She was now able to grab the lipstick and with her last dying effort wrote 'TAKA' in single quotations.

That was how Jotty, Jim, and Haruko found her less than an hour later. The police had cordoned off the area and had already printed up pictures of the triple murder suspect from the closed-circuit video camera. Jotty, Jim, and Haruko were not surprised to see the suspect was Minoru. Actually, when they arrived at the hotel and found all the police and press, they already knew Minoru had been there. What confused them was, as Niki lay dying, she wrote the name 'Taka' in her lipstick. That made absolutely no sense to any of the three. The video plainly showed Minoru forcing his way into Niki's room. As the security guards entered, the tape showed the back of the second guard's head splatter against the open door as the bullet exited the skull. A few seconds later, Minoru could be seen hiding a gun under his jacket as he exited the room. Why would Niki write 'Taka'? The police had checked and discovered Taka had just arrived back in Japan. They had not yet notified him of his wife's death.

When the National Police did inform Taka that his wife had been murdered, Taka broke down in tears as he pleaded to the cameras for his wife's killer to be found. The people of Japan could not believe how such a wonderful human being as Taka could be so unfortunate as to have someone he trusted so fully, turn out to be a violent terrorist who not only killed his beautiful and loving wife, but tried to ruin his businesses. Taka thanked the people of Japan for their prayers.

Chapter Thirty-eight

Minoru calmly drove east on Sunset Boulevard away from the Beverly Hills Hotel. He figured he had at least thirty minutes until they checked the valet lot video and discovered his license plate number. By that time, he would be on the freeway almost back to the warehouse in Cudahy. He continued down Sunset till he reached the 101 Freeway. From there he went south through downtown Los Angeles and connected to the 5 Freeway south and then the 710 south to the Florence Avenue exit. It had been approximately fifty minutes since the shootings at the hotel. Had he been back at the hotel, he would have been pleased to know he had been correct in his estimate.

When Minoru entered the warehouse, he saw the truck had returned and with it the two boys, Ignacio and Leonel. One of the ninjas met Minoru as he exited his car. He told Minoru the two young men had been very uncooperative and refused to tell them anything. At first, they both put up a bit of a fight, but that did not last long. Each had been searched and the contents of their pockets were laid on the desk in the warehouse office. The ninja told Minoru both men had over $1200 dollars in their pockets when they came back to the warehouse. The truck was empty except for one small package of lipstick. The batch number on the tubes matched the number of the missing cases Minoru and his men had been searching for.

Both Ignacio and Leonel were sitting in chairs facing each other in the warehouse office. Minoru could tell they had tried to put up a fight, for both of them had been struck several times in the face and were bleeding slightly from the mouth. Leonel was still mouthing off to one of the ninjas when Minoru walked into the office. Minoru reached into his pocket and removed one of the barbed spikes similar to the ones he had used on the security guards at the two burglaries. Both young men watched as Minoru strode into the room and headed directly to Leonel who continued to smart off. Minoru plunged the spike into Leonel's left eye, twisted it and yanked out about a fifth of Leonel's brains and dropped the spike and the brains in Ignacio's lap. Ignacio vomited and passed out falling to the floor into a mixture of Leonel's bloody brain tissue and his own vomit.

When Ignacio came to, he was sitting in the chair with his hands bound together and his mouth gagged. Minoru was standing in front of him smiling.

"I placed the gag on you to keep you from talking too much," Minoru explained to Ignacio. "You see, in the past when I have tried to question two men who did not want to cooperate and I performed my little brain removal trick with one of them, I couldn't seem to shut the other one up." Minoru smiled at Ignacio. "Now when I remove the gag, I only want you to answer my questions. I want you to say nothing more than the answer I require. Do you understand?" Ignacio nodded his head.

"Good," said Minoru, "then let's begin."

"Oh, and by the way," continued Minoru, "every time you speak out of turn or say something, I feel is not true, I will break one of your fingers like this." Very deliberately Minoru took Ignacio's hand and snapped Ignacio's middle finger just below the first knuckle. Minoru decided to let Ignacio finish screaming before he removed the gag.

Chapter Thirty-nine

Jotty, Jim, and Haruko were stumped. Why had Niki written the name 'TAKA' in her lipstick as she lay dying?

"Well, so much for your idea about Niki being the mastermind," Jim said to Jotty. "Looks like I was right when I pegged Minoru as the leader of the Red Summit," Jim said a cocky manner.

"Not so fast there, Jimbo," Haruko responded. Jotty laughed and Jim turned to glare at him. "Just because Minoru killed Niki doesn't mean he is the mastermind. Remember Niki wrote the name 'TAKA' as she was dying. That would lead me to believe she was trying to tell us Taka was behind the Red Summit."

"Don't call me Jimbo," Jim said to Haruko.

They were standing in front of the hotel looking down the street when Haruko had another of her epiphanies.

"She wasn't trying to tell us who murdered her," said Haruko. "She was trying to warn us."

"Warn us about what?" Jotty replied.

Haruko pointed to a giant billboard about a half a mile away on Sunset Boulevard. "She was trying to warn us about that."

Written on the billboard in the same way she had written it on the floor as she lay dying was the word 'TAKA'. It was in quotations just as she had written it in quotations.

"Niki was trying to warn us about the tainted lipstick," Haruko insisted.

"And I bet that is where we will find Minoru," Jim said excitedly.

Jotty was already on the phone calling his office to see if they had the address for the 'Niki Matsuura' cosmetic factory yet. They did and gave him an address in Cudahy.

"Where in tarnation is Cudahy?" Jim asked.

"It's only about forty minutes from here if we drive fast," Jotty replied.

"Then what are we waiting for," Haruko piped in. The three of them ran to the car and sped out of the driveway.

Fortunately, they were in an FBI unmarked car with a siren and flashing lights. They were able to get to the address in less than thirty minutes. They parked across the street from the factory and got out to scout the area. It was a Saturday, so the factory was closed. Cudahy is a primarily Hispanic area and the three of them stuck out like sore thumbs. As did their unmarked Mercury Marquis. When they pulled up, several young men on the street seemed to quickly disappear in the opposite direction. Jotty saw the rental car with the same license plate as the car in the hotel video, parked towards the rear of the factory. There was a large fence around the perimeter of the property and a sturdy triple-locked gate to keep people out. It would not be impossible for them to scale the tall fence with the razor wire at the top, but it was something none of them really wanted to do. Nor did they have the tools to cut the locks or to cut the fence.

"Do you want in there?" A weak high-pitched voice asked. The three of them turned around.

"What did you say?" Jotty asked.

"I know how you can get in there," the small boy repeated.

"And just how is that?" asked Jim.

"Give me five bucks and I will tell you," the boy told them.

"We will give you twenty bucks if you show us," Jim quickly replied.

"Let me have the money first," said the boy. Jim reached in his pocket and grabbed a twenty from his wallet. He was about to hand it to the boy when he quickly pulled it back.

"Show us where to get in and then I guarantee I will give you the money," Jim told the child.

The boy looked at Jim trying to decide if he could be trusted. He finally waved at the three agents to follow him. They walked about a half a block down the street past the manufacturing plant and into a deserted building adjacent to the property. Haruko was hesitant to enter, but followed as Jotty and Jim followed the small boy. When they got inside it was becoming difficult to see as the sun was beginning to set. Jotty had grabbed a flashlight from the sedan and turned it on. The boy pointed to an opening in the floor with a ladder leading to the bottom.

"There is a tunnel that leads from this building over to that empty building next to the fence. My dad told me they used to keep the live pigs in this building. They would kill the pigs in that building and use this tunnel to move the pigs over here to be killed. I don't know if my dad really knows," the little boy said.

Jim handed him the twenty bucks as Jotty shined his flashlight into the opening.

"It does look like a tunnel," Jotty said.

"Let's find out," Jim replied as he headed down the ladder.

Chapter Forty

It didn't take long for Minoru to get the information he was looking for from Ignacio. Leonel and Ignacio had loaded up all the tainted lipstick just as Niki had paid them to do. What they didn't do was take it to the dump as instructed. They did go to the dump just to get a receipt to show to Niki, but they didn't dump the lipstick there. Now Minoru had learned where the tainted lipstick was and it only took two more broken fingers to get that information. Ignacio was crying in pain and begging to be let go. Minoru thanked him for his help and promised his death would be quick for having told Minoru the information he needed. Minoru reached for his pistol to shoot Ignacio and realized he had left it in his jacket in the car. He smiled and slowly walked behind Ignacio. In a swift movement, taking less than three seconds, Minoru snapped Ignacio's neck. Ignacio's lifeless body fell to the floor as if in slow motion and lay in a pool of blood that had drained from the vacant eye socket in Leonel's head.

Minoru smiled as he looked at the dead body shells that moments ago were two young men. Suddenly, one of his ninjas outside the office signaled that intruders were approaching. Jotty and Haruko had climbed out of the opening in the floor of the vacant building next to the warehouse and were heading across the property towards the shipping warehouse. The two other ninjas reported no other intruders were seen approaching the warehouse. The ninjas all took defensive cover positions, while Minoru waited in the office with the lights on pretending to not know that the agents were approaching. Jotty and Haruko saw the silhouette of Minoru behind the lowered blinds of the warehouse office and quietly began to approach. They were still twenty feet from the office entrance when the three ninjas told them to drop their guns and not move. Jotty and Haruko had no choice but to do as told. As the ninjas moved towards the two agents, they failed to see the six-foot five-inch frame of Jim slowly climb out of an opening in the floor to the left a little behind them. When one of the ninjas did hear a noise and turned to investigate, it was too late. Jim was standing with both his six-shooters in his hand looking like a gunfighter out of the old west. In the dim light of the warehouse, he could have been mistaken for Clint Eastwood. Jotty swore that the ninja who first glimpsed Jim yelled the word 'Unforgiven' to his ninja companions just as Jim opened fire. Jim was not trying to kill the ninjas, only disarm them. He shot the gun out of the hand of the ninja closest to him who had first turned and saw him. He also shot the pistol from the hand of the ninja closet to Jotty. Haruko kicked the gun from the hand of the ninja closet to her. The warehouse erupted into a chaotic fight making it not safe for Jim to fire any more shots. Besides, he loved a good fight.

Jotty pulled his gun and ran to the warehouse office where Minoru was still inside. He pushed open the door and was met by Minoru's foot to his stomach causing him to double over and drop his gun. Very deliberately, Minoru kicked Jotty's gun out the office door and locked it from the inside.

He then opened the blinds to the office as Jotty struggled to get his breath back. Jim re-holstered his guns and the ninja closest to him came running towards him in a martial art attacking position. Jim shifted his weight moving ever so slightly to his left and using the attacking ninja's own momentum flung him flying helplessly past. What Jim had forgotten was the opening in the floor directly behind him. It was this opening that Jim had surprised the guards from. It, too, had a connecting tunnel to the other building located by the outer fence. He heard the crunching of several bones, including the spine, as the ninja smashed against the floor. It was a twelve-foot drop into the pit.

Meanwhile, Haruko was in a pitched battle with the other two ninjas. Jim moseyed over to keep an eye on her progress. Haruko was having little trouble defending herself against the attacks of the two ninjas, but was not able to do much in the way of going on the attack. When one of the ninjas was knocked away by Haruko and landed near one of the pistols that had been knocked or shot out of the hand of the ninjas earlier, he started to reach for it. Jim pulled his own pistol and fired a shot inches from the ninja's outstretched hand. When the ninja looked up in the direction of the shot, Jim was wagging his finger back and forth as if scolding the ninja and telling him to play fair.

At the same moment, Jim was distracted by the sound of Minoru raising the blinds in the office area. The ninja used the distraction to his advantage and grabbed the gun on the floor, only to be knocked five feet backwards into the air as Jim fired a bullet from each of his 45 caliber Colt pistols.

"I warned you to play fair," Jim said to the ninja that lay crumpled and dead against the wall of the warehouse. Jim once again re-holstered his pistols.

Haruko was doing fine against the two ninjas. Now that only one remained it would not be a fair fight. The ninja would lose and he seemed to sense it. He turned to watch as Jim shot the other ninja who had gone for the gun on the floor. Haruko as well was distracted by Jim's cowboy antics. The remaining ninja pulled a razor-sharp star from someplace on his body and prepared to throw it at Jim, who was holstering his pistols. Haruko saw the ninja throwing the star, but was too late to stop him. She did manage to crush the ninja's larynx killing him, but she was a second to late, for he had already released the star.

Jim wished that Haruko hadn't killed the last ninja so quickly. He would have liked the ninja to witness Jim's remarkable speed as a quick draw specialist. Before the ninja star had covered half of the twenty feet from the ninja's hand to Jim's body, he had pulled one of his revolvers and blown the star out of the air.

"Pretty impressive, huh," Jim said to Haruko as he twirled his six-shooter on his finger. Jim looked at the ninja who Haruko had just fatally injured by crushing his larynx. "Do you always kill people that way or has it only been since we met?"

Haruko just smiled and turned away.

Now that the three ninjas were dead, Jim and Haruko walked over to the office, where a smiling Minoru stared back at them. Minoru had again kicked Jotty who was sitting on the floor leaning against the inside of the office door. Jim tried the door, but it was locked. He tried to break the glass on the door but was unable to.

Minoru smiled as he spoke. "The previous tenant had this office specially built. It seems this warehouse was once used as an armored car satellite facility. This room was constructed to count and house large sums of money. The windows, door and walls are all bullet proof. You cannot get in unless I let you in."

"And you cannot get out," Jim replied.

"Oh, I don't wish to go out quite yet," Minoru replied. "At least not until you watch me kill your friend here."

This enraged Jim as he desperately tried to break into the office with no success.

"You will eventually be able to get in, with the right tools and equipment," Minoru acknowledged. "But it will be too late."

"You know I will kill you the moment you leave that office if you hurt my friend," Jim told Minoru.

"I would expect nothing less," Minoru responded. "The fact is, I will kill your friend for causing me so much trouble and all you can do is watch."

"Are you the leader of the Red Summit?" Haruko asked.

Minoru just smiled.

"When I kill you," Jim said, "It will be the end of the Red Summit."

"You may kill me, but you will never stop the Red Summit, or the ideals that will make the Red Summit and groups like it victorious."

"What about the anthrax," Jim asked. "Where is the weapon grade anthrax. We know you have it. We found traces of it at the Paleaka Ranch laboratory.

"I have no more time for your silly questions," answered Minoru as he turned to face Jotty who was slowly picking himself up off the floor.

Jim and Haruko encouraged Jotty in his fight with Minoru, but he was overmatched by Minoru's superior martial arts skills. For the next ten minutes as the two looked on helplessly, Minoru pummeled Jotty, knocking him down several times and beat his face until his eyes were almost swollen shut. Jim's fury grew and Haruko cried as they watched Minoru slowly and methodically beating Jotty to death. Jotty was again knocked to the floor and lay next to the bodies of Ignacio and Leonel. He seemed too weak to stand up to take Minoru's punishment any longer. Minoru turned once again to talk to Haruko and Jim.

"I believe it is time for you to say your final goodbyes to your friend here. It is time for me to kill him. Then I will unlock the door and give you the opportunity to kill me. Which I am sure you will take. I do not fear death, I will be looked upon as a martyr who died in the fight against the American devils," Minoru smiled as he turned to finish off Jotty.

Jim was pounding on the glass of the office and Haruko was screaming.

Jotty knew he was about to die. He had never been so badly beaten and was barely able to move. He was too weak to stand and could only continue to lie in a pool of blood and brain tissue between the bodies of the two dead warehouse workers as he desperately tried to catch his breath. As he moved his hand to try to stand, he felt a long narrow object. Jotty had felt this object before and knew what it was. He grabbed it in his hand as he felt Minoru grab the back of his blood-soaked shirt, lifting him off the floor for the final deathblow. As Minoru lifted Jotty, Minoru turned to smile at the screaming Jim and Haruko, watching at the window. Minoru failed to see that Jotty had found the ten-inch barbed spike that Minoru had used to remove Leonel's brain. Jim and Haruko did see it in Jotty's hand and stopped their screaming. As if in slow motion, Minoru looked down at Jotty perplexed as to what had caused Haruko and Jim to stop screaming and stare at their soon-to-be dead friend. As he looked down, Jotty mustered all of his remaining strength and plunged the spike deep into Minoru's chest and heart, turning it as he finally collapsed in exhaustion. Minoru gasped as Jotty twisted the spike causing the barb to severe the aortas attached to Minoru's heart. Blood gushed from Minoru's mouth and from around the embedded spike as Minoru collapsed dead on top of Jotty.

Chapter Forty-one

It took the fire department almost twenty minutes to break into the office. They had to use the 'jaws of life' to slowly cut away at the door. The entire time the firemen struggled to cut their way into the room, Jotty lay in the old armored car office too weak to move Minoru's body off of his own. When the firemen finally were able to break into the office, it was Jim who ran in first and threw Minoru's body off of Jotty.

"Thanks Jimbo," a weak but alive Jotty said.

"Don't call me Jimbo," Jim smiled as Jotty tried to laugh.

"Haruko had come into the room and was holding Jotty's hand as the paramedics prepared Jotty for transport.

"I'll take good care of Haruko, while you are recovering," Jim said grinning at Jotty. "You better get well soon, if you are going to have a shot at her."

It was Haruko's turn to slug Jim in the arm.

Agents from the Los Angeles FBI office descended on the property and confiscated all the cases of cosmetics prepared for shipment. Tests would later show none of the lipstick or facial makeup in the entire warehouse contained any of the Prion tainted byproducts. Only six tubes of lipstick found lying in the warehouse office next to the dead bodies of Leonel, Ignacio, and Minoru showed a high concentration of contamination. The level of affected Prions in each tube was sufficient to affect anyone who used the lipstick with the human form of mad cow disease. When a girl or woman placed the lipstick on her lips, she could not help but ingest a slight amount of the lipstick. Jim determined even such a minute amount could lead to Prion affection in the female's brain. It may and probably would take several years, but whoever wore the lipstick would most certainly catch the disease and suffer the debilitating and painful consequences of this incurable 'Nightmare'.

In the pocket of Leonel, the FBI did find a receipt for the county landfill dated that morning. The FBI deduced Leonel and Ignacio must have been paid by Niki to destroy the tainted lipstick, and had taken it to the county landfill to do so. Unfortunately, they did not act on this deduction for at least a week. By the time the FBI sent a team of agents to the landfill, they searched for four days and were unable to find any trace of the lipstick. They sorted through literally hundreds of tons of debris with no success. They finally concluded the tainted lipstick must be there someplace, but if they were unable to find it, no one else would find it either and ended their search. Fortunately, Leonel and Ignacio only kept out six tubes of lipstick that appeared to be unused or unopened. Or so everyone assumed.

In Japan, the country shared the pain of loss felt by one of their own. Takaishi Matsuura mourned the tragic murder of his wife along with thousands of Japanese residents who paid their respects at a public ceremony. Taka was overcome with grief as he continually thanked those who came to support him in his time of need. Haruko was NOT one of the multitudes who made the pilgrimage in support of Taka.

Taka's financial empire took a hit with the closing of the ranch facilities, but when the media and tabloids reported his losses, the people of Japan once again rallied behind him and business tripled at his chain of 'Aioka' Steakhouse restaurants. As did the menu prices seem to triple. Taka was able to keep his contract to supply meat to the Sizzle Burger fast food restaurants in Hawaii. He had it shipped from one of his new Japan facilities. He had plans to eventually reopen the Paleaka Ranch facilities once the lawsuits against David Paleaka were resolved. This time he promised to employ local residents to work the ranch as well as the paniolos who once worked for the Paleaka family.

Although a little delayed due to a hold put on his cosmetics business by the FBI investigation, 'TAKA' lipstick and makeup, by the late Niki Matsuura, was an unprecedented success in the United States and in Japan. The tragedy of Niki's murder was key to that success. Nowhere was 'TAKA' lipstick more successful than in East Los Angeles. In numerous swap meets throughout the East Los Angeles area, a savvy South Korean businessman owned several booths. He seemed to get a jump on the big retail stores and somehow acquired an ample supply of the new 'TAKA' lipstick which had been so heavily advertised but was yet to be found in the stores. The young Latina girls fell in love with the colors and the smoothness of the lipstick as they applied it to their lips. They could not buy enough of it.

For the next two weeks, while Jotty lay in the hospital recovering, Jim spent his time running tests on the cosmetics found at the plant and the containers the ingredients arrived in. Using the information from the researchers doing the same tests on the laboratory back in Hawaii, Jim was able to deduce with certainty that the tainted residue at the cosmetic factory found in shipping containers had indeed originated at the Paleaka Ranch facility. He was also able to determine the tainted meat in Atlanta contained the same high amount of Prion concentration as did the cosmetic byproducts and the meat samples found at the Paleaka

Ranch. With Jim's research information report and the report from Haruko showing it was Minoru in all of the videos at the Hilton, the bonded warehouse in San Pedro, and the British Health Laboratory in Weybridge, the FBI concluded Minoru Sakura was the leader of the Red Summit. Therefore, he was behind all of the terrorist acts and murders recently attributed to the Red Summit. Minoru's gun which was found in the rental car proved to be the gun that killed Spencer, Niki, the two security guards at The Beverly Hills Hotel, and the two researchers at the Paleaka Ranch. Despite Haruko's insistence, there was not enough proof to connect Takaishi Matsuura to any of the terrorist acts or murders. The FBI, as well as the Japanese National Police Agency, refused to investigate Taka any further.

Jotty was in a hospital in West Los Angeles recovering from the tremendous beating Minoru had given him. Haruko came to visit Jotty everyday as did Jim. Haruko was beginning to fall in love with Jotty. She spent much time sitting and talking about her suspicions and theories on the Red Summit. Jotty enjoyed listening to her talk, although he never paid much attention to what she was saying. Jim and Haruko kept Jotty informed of their progress on connecting Minoru to all the terrorist acts. Haruko continued to insist Minoru was nothing more than an errand boy for Taka and it was Taka who they really needed to go after now. Eventually, Jotty had to break the news to Haruko that Taka was no longer a suspect. Any investigation was to cease and desist immediately. Haruko was devastated. She told Jotty she would stop her obsession of trying to prove Taka's guilt, but Jotty and Jim both knew she didn't mean it. This news also changed the feelings Haruko had been feeling for Jotty. Suddenly she was all business, just like the old Haruko. She started talking about returning to Japan to continue in her previous position as Special Investigator for the National Police Agency. In fact, with the FBI claiming the demise of the Red Summit, it meant the demise of Jotty's task force. In other words, Haruko was no longer needed by the FBI and had no choice but to return to her old job. Her only consolation was that her old supervisor had been demoted to a position outside of Tokyo. It seems he was blamed for allowing his computer system to be compromised by members of a terrorist cell in Tokyo. His mistake had possibly cost the lives of several citizens and officers. He agreed to the demotion to save himself the embarrassment of facing the officers in his department. The position of supervisor had not been filled and Haruko was being considered as a prime candidate for the position. Haruko thought she just might want to take that job.

Jim was not anxious to leave the FBI just yet. He always enjoyed a good fight and seemed to have been in a lot of them since teaming up with Jotty and Haruko. He also was not convinced they had seen the last of the Red Summit. He was sure there was another laboratory somewhere near the Paleaka Ranch in Hawaii. This laboratory troubled him more than the Paleaka Ranch laboratory. Somewhere on that island, someone was making weapon grade anthrax or at the very least storing weapon grade anthrax. The military was very concerned with the anthrax powder found on the clothes of the dead researcher, as well as the cultured anthrax found on the floor amid the broken glass dish. They spent several weeks searching the ranch and the area around the ranch for clues as to where the anthrax had originated, but found nothing. They were now searching the entire island, but still with no success. Jim knew it had to be there. Why else would Spencer have been on the island? Spencer wanted out of what he was involved in and Jim knew it. He owed it to Spencer to find that laboratory. That was why when the FBI agreed to release him back to the USDA, Jim was able to finagle a position as the Farm Service Agent for the big island. This gave Jim the chance to explore the ranches on the island and talk to the residents as much as he wanted. The FBI also kept him on their payroll to continue to look for the anthrax laboratory, which they too believed was still there. Jim hated to leave Texas, but he and Dusty had become pretty good friends and Jim would get to spend a lot more time riding horses and playing cowboy with the paniolos than he ever did in Texas.

Jotty was able to leave the hospital before Haruko went back to her new assignment as acting supervisor for the Counter-terrorism Division of the National Police Agency. He was still moving a little stiffly, but his physical therapy was going well and he was actually starting to tone his muscles and lose some weight. Jotty was determined to get back into shape and reacquire the martial arts skills he once excelled in. Funny how a near death beating tends to change the way one thinks about one's health and physical condition. His face was almost looking normal again, with most of the swelling having gone down.

Haruko took Jotty and Jim to a Vegan restaurant on La Cienega in West Hollywood. Every since they discovered several tons of Prion affected meat had made it to restaurants and retail stores in Hawaii, Jotty had joined Haruko and Jim in avoiding eating red meat. Haruko obviously ate no animal products being a Vegan, but Jotty and Jim only gave up red meat. Both Jotty and Jim had a little trouble eating the tofu at the restaurant that was in the soup and this made Haruko smile for the first time since she was told to stop investigating Taka. When the main course arrived, the tofu was grilled and covered in bar-b-cue sauce.

"Now this is more like it," Jim exclaimed. "Just the way a Texan likes his bean curd," Jim said grinning.

Jotty laughed and continued to pick at his lunch. It was obvious he wanted to say something, but didn't know how to say it. Finally, it was Haruko who spoke up to Jotty.

"I want to thank you for saving my career," Haruko started. "I actually want to thank you for being my friend."

That was not what Jotty had hoped to hear. Jim excused himself, with a lame excuse to go use the restroom and, in doing so, created an awkward situation for Jotty. Before Jotty could speak, Haruko continued.

"I know you want to be more than friends, and I have often thought I would enjoy becoming more than just a friend to you as well." Haruko paused and grabbed Jotty's hand. "Now is not the time for such a relationship. I could not give myself to you or to anyone right now. I am obsessed with bringing Taka to justice for what I know he has done. I know even if you did believe he was part of the Red Summit, as I truly believe, your government would not allow you to investigate him. My government does not wish for that investigation either, but I must continue to search for what I know in my heart is the truth. I hope as acting supervisor I will have the freedom to do as I see fit. If not, I will do what I must to continue my quest for justice. Maybe soon we can be together as more than just friends, but for now all I can offer you is my friendship." Tears began to well up in her eyes.

Jotty put his arm around Haruko and held her close. It was a hard pill for Jotty to swallow.

"I will always be your friend," Jotty assured Haruko, "and I will wait for the day when we can be lovers."

Just then Jim came back from the restroom. "Whoa," Jim said as he saw them embracing. "Should I use the bathroom again?"

Haruko pulled away from Jotty and responded, "No, no, everything is fine, we were just saying goodbye."

"Oh good, then I am not interrupting," Jim responded as he sat back down. Jotty mouthed an expletive to Jim as Haruko turned her back.

Haruko told the two men about her appointment as acting supervisor for counter-terrorism. Jotty and Jim both assured her the word 'acting' would soon be removed. Haruko was leaving that night to return to Japan. Jotty reminded her that, if necessary, she was still on-call to return to the FBI's international counter-terrorism unit if it became necessary. She responded by saying she would be honored to work with the two of them again. Jotty also assured Haruko he would be visiting Japan very soon to share and gather information on other possible terrorist groups operating in her part of the world. Haruko guaranteed Jotty full access to her department's files and promised to help him regain his martial arts abilities by working out with her at her dojo whenever he visited Japan.

Jim told Haruko of his plans to return to Hawaii to work for the USDA in his old job as a Farm Service Agent. Jim was not sure about leaving his beloved Texas, but knew someday he would return home to Haskell. Jotty reminded Jim, and informed Haruko, that Jim would also still be on the FBI payroll, snooping around Taka's now closed Paleaka Ranch looking for the source of the anthrax. This seemed to cheer Haruko up a little bit knowing Jim would still be investigating Taka even if it were in somewhat of a roundabout way.

Jim and Haruko already knew the FBI had promoted Jotty to Director of Counter-Terrorism for the Far East and Southeast Asia region. It wasn't much of a surprise when Jotty told them. Although they did try their best to act surprised. Jotty had been guaranteed it was not a desk job. It would be a hands-on job that would allow him to participate in operations as actively as he felt inclined and physically able to do. For Jotty, the best part of the job would be the regular trips to Japan to visit Haruko to confer with his Japanese counterpart. He would also be able to stop by Hawaii on his way to Japan to see Jim as often as he liked. Which he promised would be very often. It seems that he, like Jim, had acquired a taste for sipping a drink while watching the sunset from the pool bar at the Marriott Hotel in Waikoloa. He also wanted to try his hand at that Cowboy Action Shooting Jim was always talking about. Jim was already talking to Dusty about organizing a SASS Chapter on the big island for when he moved there. Jotty was thinking he just might have to buy himself a pair of six-shooters although he knew he could never be in the same league as Jim when it came to accuracy and quickness.

The three friends laughed and chatted through the rest of their Vegan meal. Haruko loved the food, and Jim and Jotty seemed to enjoy it. Or at least they made a good effort at tolerating and faking their enjoyment of the numerable tofu creations. They eventually said their goodbyes and headed their separate ways. Though it seemed like the end of their journey together, they all knew that fate, or Taka, would someday bring them back together.

Chapter Forty-two

"Who has seen this report?" the Secretary inquired.

"Only myself, my deputy director, the head of our Counter-Terrorism department, and the agents who wrote the report," the FBI Director responded.

"What about this Japanese Police woman? She was part of the operation that uncovered some of this information. Will she keep her mouth shut?" the Secretary asked.

"Jotty Joplin, our new head of Far East Counter-terrorism assures me she will keep quiet," the Director affirmed.

"Has he seen the entire report?" the Secretary questioned.

"Only the parts he and his team members wrote concerning the three shipments of tainted meat consumed on the Hawaiian Islands. They are unaware of the tens of thousands of tubes of affected lipstick that were sold at the swap meets in Los Angeles. They believe all the Prion affected cosmetics were destroyed," the Director clarified.

"And we are sure all of these women who wore the lipstick, and all the people who ate the meat, will come down with this mad cow disease?" The Secretary pressed the Director for a response.

"According to our experts...," he paused momentarily, "there is no doubt about it. In five to ten years, tens of thousands of people are going to start showing the symptoms of the human form of the disease. It will be devastating. We have yet to find a cure."

Up until then the National Security Advisor had remained silent.

"Well, the experts on the President's Science Commission are not so sure that with that level and method of contamination, all those people will be affected," the Security Advisor stated sternly.

"I do not doubt their opinion," the director responded, "but that commission is not made up of scientists who have studied samples of the affected lipstick and meat consumed, nor are those commission members experts in Prion and bovine contagious disease research as our experts are."

"That is irrelevant as far as I am concerned and as far as this office is concerned," the National Security Advisor responded with finality. "I do not feel this report needs to be presented to the President, nor to Congress. I think it best that it just fade away," the National Security advisor demanded. "Do you understand what I mean, Mr. Director? We do not need this country in another panic like the one caused by that Atlanta incident. That was too costly to many friends of the President. If this new information should get out, billions of dollars could be lost by some large companies because of public fear of their products and possible lawsuits of those affected. Our President does not need such a crisis at this time. I think it best we leave that problem to the next Administration."

"What if the information somehow is leaked?" asked the Secretary.

"That is simple," the National Security Advisor replied. "Plausible deniability! The President was never briefed or aware of the report. He will be safe, but at least one of us will lose our job. Think of it as doing your duty for our country and our President."

"Just make sure that report disappears," the Secretary told the FBI Director as they walked out of the White House into another beautiful Washington D.C. morning.

KONA SNOW

When a group of missionaries are found slaughtered in Perm, Russia and the Russian's top genetic scientist turns up missing, a single potato arrives in Hawaii starting agent Jim Rikey on a quest to find out how this potato is linked to his Uncle's murder in Perm. Viktor, a top Russian operative as well as Taka Matsuura, a wealthy Japanese businessman, are prepared to use all of their resources to retrieve and control the genetic secrets this potato holds, before Jim can discover the truth.

Haruko, Jotty, and Jim are reunited, and Eddie Popp, a CIA operative, joins Jotty's NCTC team on their mission to prove that Taka is the leader of the terrorist group, the Red Summit, and put an end to its reign of terror. They must stop Taka from using the secrets the genetically modified potato conceals before millions suffer the consequences of the Kona Snow. If that indeed is Taka's plan, for weaponized anthrax has been found on a dive boat off the coast of the Big Island and if the team cannot discover the source, millions may die.

Kona Snow is the second in the bio-terror series and features many of the same characters in his first novel *Taka*. *Kona Snow* adds several other interesting characters in a much more complex web of intrigue and action that takes place on several of the Hawaiian Islands, primarily the Big Island, Kauai, and Oahu, as well as Russia, Thailand, Japan, and Southern California. *Kona Snow* continues the saga of the terrorist cell the Red Summit, led by Taka, as he now plans a two-prong attack on America.

Terry Fritts is an author, musician, and actor who resides with his wife Pauline in Riverview, FL. They often visit Hawaii and travel the world to research his novels. You can contact Terry at: tfritts01@aol.com